四川外国语大学2019年特色教材项目

文学名篇：

读·译·赏

主编 钟毅

参编 陈宇翔 邓琴 禹文凤

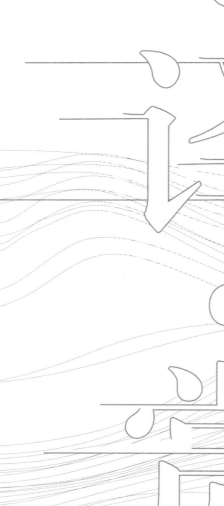

四川大学出版社
SICHUAN UNIVERSITY PRESS

图书在版编目（CIP）数据

文学名篇：读．译．赏／钟毅主编．— 成都：四
川大学出版社，2023.10
ISBN 978-7-5690-5928-1

Ⅰ．①文… Ⅱ．①钟… Ⅲ．①英语－翻译－高等学校
－教材②世界文学－文学欣赏 Ⅳ．① H315.9

中国国家版本馆 CIP 数据核字（2023）第 015610 号

书　　　名：文学名篇：读·译·赏
　　　　　　Wenxue Mingpian: Du·Yi·Shang
主　　　编：钟　毅

选题策划：余　芳
责任编辑：余　芳
责任校对：周　洁
装帧设计：墨创文化
责任印制：王　炜

出版发行：四川大学出版社有限责任公司
　　　　　地址：成都市一环路南一段 24 号（610065）
　　　　　电话：（028）85408311（发行部）、85400276（总编室）
　　　　　电子邮箱：scupress@vip.163.com
　　　　　网址：https://press.scu.edu.cn
印前制作：成都墨之创文化传播有限公司
印刷装订：四川五洲彩印有限责任公司

成品尺寸：170 mm×240 mm
印　　张：17
字　　数：264 千字

版　　次：2023 年 10 月　第 1 版
印　　次：2023 年 10 月　第 1 次印刷
定　　价：79.00 元

扫码获取数字资源

四川大学出版社
微信公众号

前　言
Preface

　　文学是人学，是文科学生学习的重要内容，外语专业学生的人文素养是非常重要的，因此，从人才培养的角度来看，学生学会欣赏文学翻译名篇，学会就翻译中发现的问题做相应的思考和探究，这一点十分必要。

　　目前，国内翻译教材的数量已相当可观，文学翻译赏析与批评类的教材不胜枚举。在教学资源如此丰富的情况下，本书仍有编写的必要，主要原因有以下四点：第一，本教程基于四川外国语大学翻译学院的"文学翻译赏析与批评"课程的讲义改编，该讲义在教学过程中得到了学生的广泛好评。本教程不仅将赏析材料进行了归纳，而且整理了教学思路供教师参考。第二，本教程内容涵盖较为全面，除讨论小说、散文、诗歌、戏剧四大传统文学样式的翻译，还涉及歌曲、影视以及目前较为流行的网络文学作品的翻译。内容的选择除了经典性，还考虑到时效性，比如选择了国产剧《甄嬛传》的翻译、网络小说的翻译和儿童绘本的翻译。第三，本教程通过提问的方式引导读者首先思考如何译，进而思考为什么这样译等更深层次的问题，学会通过阅读译本去发现翻译研究中的问题。第四，本教程特别设置了课前"翻译热身"栏目，帮助读者通过翻译实践发现其中的难点，再结合赏析寻找解决问题的方法，将实践与理论结合了起来。

教程共分八章，旨在通过对相同作品的不同译本进行比较，让学生了解不同的翻译评判标准和依据，也让学生认识到，一方面翻译需要忠实于原著，译者因此受到的限制不言而喻，但另一方面，译者也绝不是毫无施展空间的"透明的眼睛"，透过无数优秀的译作，可以看到译者的身影及其所折射出的时代背景、文化差异和个人偏好。

教程注重培养读者的翻译能力、文学素养，以及翻译问题的发现与研究能力，因此适用于翻译专业、英语专业本科高年级学生的文学翻译赏析类课程教学，也可用于 MTI 学生及翻译理论方向研究生的辅助阅读，还可以供英语水平较高的翻译爱好者阅读和自学使用。

教程的编写得到四川外国语大学教务处及翻译学院的大力支持，也得到了诸多同行老师的关心和指教，编者在此向他们一并表达最诚挚的谢意。由于编者的水平有限，教程中难免有疏漏之处，敬请读者批评指正，不胜感激。

目 录
CONTENTS

第一章

文学名篇的阅读与翻译赏析

　　文学作品以现实生活为基础，构建不同的人生和多样的生活，通过跌宕的情节从广度或深度两方面阐释人性，从多元性和复杂性两方面反映社会、历史、政治。阅读文学作品，特别是优秀的文学名篇，读者不仅能增加见闻、阅历，也能获得对人和事物更深层次的理解。阅读文学名篇还是一种学习的方式，正所谓"熟读唐诗三百首，不会吟诗也会吟"，读者可以学习到不同的语言风格和写作风格，学习不同的修辞方法，为今后的写作提供帮助和借鉴。英国著名诗人拜伦（George G. Byron）曾说："一滴墨水，可以引发无数人的思考。"（A drop of ink may make a million think.）阅读文学作品还可以激发读者的思考和想象，使思想变得深刻。对于英语学习者而言，阅读英语文学名篇，不仅能提高语言水平，还能增加文化知识。那么，如何阅读英语文学名篇？一种有效的方法就是将原文与优秀译文进行对照阅读，读者可以通过阅读译文加深对原文的理解，同时也可以对照原文，对译文形成自己的看法，最终在提高语言水平的同时，得到翻译实践和批评方面的启示。本章深入探讨了文学名篇阅读的意义和方法，以及如何进行翻译赏析，以帮助英语学习者和翻译学习者从本书的阅读中取得最大的收获。

第一节

文学名篇阅读的意义与方法

　　古往今来，多少中外大家论述过阅读的重要性。这个话题让人首先想到的也许是元朝的翁森在《四时读书乐》中写到的"蹉跎莫遣韶光老，人生唯有读书好"，告诫人们不要蹉跎岁月，应该把宝贵的时光用在读书上，因为人生中只有读书是最好的事。英国散文家培根（Francis Bacon）写的"Of Study"（《论读书》），后经王佐良先生的翻译，其中关于学习和读书的句子已成为人们传诵的经典："读书足以怡情，足以博彩，足以长才。……读书使人充实，讨论使人机智，笔记使人准确。" 英国著名戏剧家莎士比亚（William Shakespeare）也有名言："Books are the nutrient of the whole world. A life without books is like a life without sunlight; wisdom without books is like a wingless bird."（书籍是全世界的营养品。生活里没有书籍，就像大地失了阳光；智慧里没有书籍，就像鸟儿缺了翅膀。）阅读的重要性和益处毋庸赘述，但阅读的内容却值得进一步探讨。

文学作品滋养着人类的灵魂。阅读文学作品可以让人"知人"和"知世"，从而真正实现"自知"。

"知人"是因为文学作品不仅展现了人的行为、经历，还能展示人内心的所思所感。苏联作家高尔基认为文学即人学。每个人的经历是有限的，阅读文学作品中不同人的经历，可以丰富读者的认识和阅历。作品中写出不同人对待不同事情的行为，可以展示人性的各个方面。比如我国的四大名著，其中的人物和内容已成为我们的文化记忆。而通过书中个性鲜明的人物，如孙悟空、唐僧、贾宝玉、林黛玉、诸葛亮、武松、林冲，读者在感受跌宕起伏的情节的同时，也了解了当时的政治、文化、历史，了解了人际关系。可以说书中的人物、内容、思想已经成为我们这个民族的文化记忆，书中描写的个人的爱情、荣辱，家族的兴衰，朝代的更迭，让人唏嘘的同时也让人对人情、人心和人性有了更深刻的了解。又比如中国读者熟悉的俄国作家托尔斯泰（Lev Tolstoy）的《战争与和平》，该书以四个家族的经历为主线，描写了 19 世纪俄国的历史风貌，反映了当时俄国各个阶层人的生活，写出了人性的各个方面。美国戏剧家奥尼尔（Eugene O'Neill）创作的悲剧均是基于人性，读后让读者对人性中的阴暗面有了更多的认识。

所谓"知世"，就是对世事的了解。《红楼梦》第五回中的名句："世事洞明皆学问，人情练达即文章。"意即对世事洞悉明了也是一门学问，对人情熟悉通达不亚于作文章。这句话强调了洞悉世事和练达人情的重要性。洞悉世事与练达人情的方式之一就是阅读。比如《红楼梦》就被称为世情小说、人情小说，录尽了人情世故。阅读此类文学作品，可以间接体验不同的生活，间接获得经验和教训，帮助自己在生活中少走弯路。外国文学名篇是异域语言和文化的集大成者，外国文学作品自译入我国起，开阔了国人的文化视野，丰富了国人的精神世界。开阔的文化视野能帮助国人通过认识"他者"，更清楚地认识自我。

事实上，"认识自我"也许是阅读的终极意义。"自知"是一种境界，这里包含的不仅是认识和了解自我，还包括对自我总是处于变化和发展状态的认知。苏格拉底的名言"认识你自己"（Know yourself）有深刻的哲学意义，也从一方面反映了人认识自我的重要性。这里的"自己"可以是小我，也就是个体，个体通过阅读，在认同中发现自己的价值观，也在冲突中发现新的可能性，最终走出偏狭的自我。这里的自我还可以是整个人类，文学作品的功能之一就是反省人类自身。比如歌德（John W. Goethe）的名作《浮士德》（*Faust*）中的经典句子："……只要赋予整个人类的一切，我都要在我内心中体味参详，我的精神抓着至高和至深的东西不放，将全人类的苦乐堆积在我心上，于是小我便扩展成全人类的大我，最后我也和全人类一起消亡。"正如罗素（Bertrand Russell）在《论老之将至》（How to Grow Old）一文中写到的，个体生命如同一条一条的溪流，最终汇入人类历史的大海之中。优秀的文学作品往往会启发读者对个体生老病死、对全人类命运与未来进行反思。读者的思想境界也在这个过程中得到了升华。

除了上述几点，回到文学本身上来，阅读文学名篇还有帮助读者提高审美意识和审美水平的作用。文学最根本的属性是文学性，它给人以审美体验，呼唤人的感情。在文学作品尤其是名篇中，美可以体现于文字本身，如语言的格调、意蕴、修辞、音韵，也可以体现在文字塑造的形象、声音和意境中。文学名篇具有很高的审美价值，给读者以美的感受。

总之，开卷有益，《曾国藩家书》载："予定刚日读经、柔日读史之法。"（曾国藩，2016：23）阅读名家名作也许可以成为一种养生方式。

下面谈谈外语文学名篇的阅读方法。

每个人都有自己的阅读方法，没有哪一种方法适合所有人。有人喜欢默读，有人喜欢朗诵。事实上，阅读的确是一种非常个人的行为，每个人都有自己的习惯，每个人都带着自己独特的生活经历去理解读到的内容。所以有人说："没有一种活动叫作'阅读'，要么做得很差，要么做得很好。"（There is not just one activity called "reading", done either poorly or well.）有的人读完一本书，似乎没有什么收获，书中的内容给他留下的印象不深刻；有的人读完一本书之后整个意识状态仿佛都发生了变化，这本书对他的影响非常大。对于大多数人来说，要从外语文学名篇的阅读中有所收获，可以参考以下步骤：

首先，了解阅读的对象。《孟子·万章下》中说道："颂其诗，读其书，不知其人可乎？是以论其世也！"知人论世是孟子所提出来的文学批评原则和方法。我们阅读外国文学作品，同样要了解作者的生平和写作背景。现在我们看书要了解作者的生平和时代背景就是对"知人论世"的继承和沿袭，人物生平和时代背景就是我们了解图书的语境，就好像要读懂鲁迅的《狂人日记》，就要知道鲁迅的人生经历和当时的时代背景，要读懂爱伦·坡的《乌鸦》，就要知道那团影子代表他对亡妻的伤痛，要读懂太宰治的《人间失格》，那么你得了解他的五次自杀，而需读懂菲茨杰拉德的《了不起的盖茨比》，就得了解当时的历史背景为第一次世界大战后，否则很有可能产生理解的偏差。

文学形式本身就包含意义。阅读外国文学作品前，我们也需要弄清楚作品的文体、流派等。比如《乌鸦》（The Raven），它是一首抒情诗，在这类作品中，作者直抒胸臆，表达他对现实生活的感受及其感情，并透过作品反映现实、感染读者。所以我们一般不要期望这类作品有完整的情节，它们篇幅往往比较短小，一般文体为抒情诗或抒情散文等，且属于浪漫主义流派。当然如果你了解爱伦·坡，那么其作品还有哥特文学的特点，这些就给我们指明了一个阅读方向。

在阅读外国文学翻译作品前，建议阅读译者的序或者前言，因为外国文学翻译是再一次的创造性叛逆，译者的解读非常重要，大部分译者序中都会谈到翻译的目的、翻译的准则、译者对作品的理解、面对的赞助者群体，以及对作品价值的探讨。

其次，明确阅读的目的。阅读目的分为三个层次：读懂语言、思考内容、分析作者的创作艺术。

高尔基（Maxim Gorky）说："语言是文学的第一要素。"语言是思想表达的载体，虽然外国文学不需要像我们的古文古诗那样，"吟安一个字，捻断数茎须"，但是由于它陌生化的情节处理与结构形态、陌生的叙事技巧与叙述语言、陌生的场景与时代背景，我们首先要读懂语言所表达的字面意思。在文学作品创作中，由于作者受时代背景和个人生活环境的影响，其语言运用具有明显的个人色彩。在作品中，作者应用这些具有个人色彩的语言，并把语言进行精美的包装与加工，使语言更具有艺术性。比如奥斯汀诙谐幽默，她的作品也充满了诙谐幽默的讽刺，通过令人回味无穷的反讽手法使故事在轻松的喜剧风格中达到一定的艺术深度。

再次，适当做笔记或写感悟。在阅读时，适当做笔记或写感悟可以开阔自己的思维，在归纳总结中形成自己的思想。

最后，与人交流或讨论自己获得的感悟。一千个人眼中有一千个哈姆雷特。由于人的不同经历和背景，阅读相同的作品也会有不同的感受和想法。阅读之后与不同的人交流，可以得到不同的启发，从而加深对一部作品的理解。交流可以是与人面谈，也可以通过阅读其他人写的读后感或者发表论文实现。事实上，读书也是促进人与人交流的手段，阅读丰富人的知识和语言表达，使人在与人交流的过程中对一些信息可以信手拈来。

总之，读书不能只是被动地接受，要学会运用自己的理解和想象力，使其成为提高自己能力、构建自己思想体系的材料。

文学翻译批评与赏析

    文学翻译批评是深入赏析文学名篇翻译的一种方法和途径。本节主要从提高文学翻译能力的角度出发，重点介绍文学翻译的标准与原则、文学翻译批评的基本概念与主要模式。

文学翻译的标准与原则

    要谈文学翻译的标准与原则，就不得不从对翻译的认识说起。翻译是一项古老的人类活动，是人类文化和文明不可分割的重要组成部分。欧洲著名学者斯坦纳说："翻译存在是因为人们说不同的语言。"（Translation exists because men speak different languages.）（Steiner, 2001：51）这句话道出了翻译的本质特征——语言转换。围绕这一本质特征，古今中外诸多学者对翻译进行了定义，如《周礼义疏》载"译即易，谓换易言语，使相解也"。著名美国翻译理论家奈达认为："翻译就是在接受语中再现与源语言信息最接近的自然对等，首先是在意义上，其次是在风格上。"（Translating consists in reproducing in the receptor language the closest natural equivalence of the source-language message, first in terms of meaning and secondly in terms of style.）（Nida, 2001：286）对翻译持类似观点的还有西方的理论家泰特勒（Alexander Tytler）、卡特福德（John Catford），我国著名翻译家鲁迅、傅雷等。这些学者几乎都认定语言转换的本质属性，而发生文化转向之前的翻译标准也因此以原文为中心，强调"忠实"和"信"。"传统翻译界定有两个核心的思想，一是语言再现或模仿，二是忠实或等值。"（廖七一，2020：77）

20 世纪 70 年代，翻译研究出现了文化转向。文化学派把译文产生的文化因素纳入研究范畴，研究对象从文本本身延伸到文本外，研究的重点也从原文转移到了译文。文化学派的观点和研究似对翻译的本质属性有了新的理解，翻译的标准也随之出现了变化。"20 世纪 60 年代之后，传统翻译的界定已悄然改变。目的论、社会行为论、文化论、后殖民和女性批评、解构主义等学者都提出了与传统翻译观截然不同的翻译界定，极大地扩展了翻译研究的疆界，丰富了翻译研究的视角。"（廖七一，2020：78）勒菲弗尔（André Lefevere）提出改写理论，认为翻译是对原文的改写；赫曼斯（Theo Hermans）的操纵理论认为，翻译是译者出于某种特定目的对原文文本进行的不同程度的操控；图里（Gideon Toury）提出"假定翻译"（assumed translation），认为在目的语文化中被接受为翻译的就是翻译；诺德（Christiane Nord）提出"目的决定手段"（The end justifies the means），认为目标文本的目的决定翻译的策略。这些观点强调了翻译活动是有意图的行为，突出了目的语语境对翻译的影响。从德里达（Jacques Derrida）的"文本之外别无他物"（There is nothing outside the text）到埃斯卡皮（Robert Escarpit）提出、我国学者谢天振借用于译介学研究的"创造性叛逆"（creative treason），翻译的定义和标准似乎都受到这些观点的影响，有的甚至变得模糊与随意。

事实上，如何认识翻译和翻译标准与如何解读翻译的本质有很大的关系。文化学派从文化的角度去观察和解释翻译现象，他们的很多研究都是描写性的（descriptive），和前期从语言学视角研究翻译一样，文化学派的观点进一步丰富了翻译研究的视角，扩大了翻译研究的视野。笔者认为，文化学派的观点并没有否定翻译语言转换的本质属性。近年来，我国学者对翻译标准的研究和讨论更加详细和具体，比如将文章分为文学与非文学，再分别讨论文学作品中的小说、诗歌、戏剧、散文等的翻译标准，将非文学根据功能分类，进一步从法律、军事、科技、商务、外宣、公示语等不同类别进一步探讨它们的翻译标准。对于文学翻译，其标准，甚至是否有标准，一直是仁者见仁、智者见智。比如我国著名翻译家傅雷提出的"神似"，钱钟书提出的"化境"，都是对文学翻译标准的看法。

文学翻译批评的基本概念和主要模式

文学翻译的标准没有定论，对于文学翻译批评的标准，不同的学者也从不同的角度进行了讨论。下文将对文学翻译中的基本概念和接受度较高的批评模式进行介绍。

何谓翻译批评？许钧认为，"翻译批评是对翻译活动的理性反思与评价……也包括对翻译本质、过程、技巧、手段、作用、影响的总体评析"（许钧，2006：403）。这个定义详细说明了翻译批评的考察对象，即翻译批评的客体，但并没有说明谁来做出反思与评价，即翻译批评的主体。一般说来，翻译批评的主体有懂源语和译入语的学者、译者，以及只懂译入语的读者。这三类人群往往带着不同的目的进行翻译批评。学者主要对翻译作品进行学术层面的研究，译者主要是探讨翻译技术层面的问题以提高翻译能力或翻译质量，读者主要是对翻译作品的内容进行探讨。本书主要针对学习翻译和文学翻译批评的读者，因此将批评主体设定为译者和学者，从技术层面的探讨开始，引导读者往学术研究方面思考。

对于翻译批评的定义，大部分学者认为有广义和狭义之分。"我们认为，广义的翻译批评包括四个部分：翻译鉴赏、狭义的翻译批评、翻译评论和翻译（质量）评估。对应的四个英文术语分别是 translation appreciation、translation criticism、translation review 和 translation quality assessment。"（肖维青，2010：68）翻译批评是一种理性的活动，"'鉴别'是一种价值判断，主要靠学识；'欣赏'是一种审美心理活动，主要靠感觉和情绪"（肖维青，2010：69）。翻译批评与赏析的结合，就是理性与感性活动的结合，理性方面需要具体的标准、模式来加以规范，而感性方面则应该找到切入点，即找到审美的角度。

明确了文学翻译批评的概念，文学翻译批评的主体、客体和目的，接下来应该探讨的话题是翻译批评的标准。所谓标准，就是某个群体在做某件事时共同遵守的准则和依据。文学翻译批评的标准，就是对文学翻译作品进行批评时所遵守的准则和依据。我国翻译批评的传统标准就是严复提出的"信、达、雅"，事实上，时至今日，它在我国的译者和翻译批评学者中仍然有影响力。"作为 21 世纪的学者，我们今天仍接受"信达雅"为译者的自律准则和评判译作质量的标准……"（曹明伦，2006：18）随着翻译研究的发展，国内有更多的学者从不同的角度提出了对文学翻译批评的标准或模式的见解，下面介绍几个有代表性的观点。

王宏印在《文学翻译批评论稿》（2010）的"参考标准模式"这个部分中探讨了信达雅的三维模式，神似、形似的二维模式以及化境的一维模式，此三者都是在我国文学翻译批评中影响较大的模式，且通过不同学者的阐释，拥有了不同的内涵。作者在"设定工作标准"部分给出了六条标准，即语言要素、思想倾向、文化张力、文体对应、风格类型和审美趣味。这六条标准较为全面地概括了文学翻译批评中，双语读者或学者应该观察与思考的方面，为这些读者或者文学翻译批评的学者指明了思考的方向。文学翻译批评学者可以在这六条标准的基础上选择符合自己考察目标的方面，重点探讨，最终形成自己的翻译评价。对于翻译批评的基本方法，该书列出了十种——细读法、取样法、比较法、逻辑法、量化法、阐释法、互文法、历史法、模型法、评价法。书中还谈到了翻译批评应该遵循的程序——研读原作、研读译作、对比研究、效果评价、价值判断、评论角度。总之，遵循这个基本程序，使用全部或部分基本方法，文学翻译批评的初学者可以找到最基本的思路，循序渐进，最终可以提高翻译的实践能力和研究水平。

肖维青的《翻译批评模式研究》（2010）指出了翻译批评标准的两种错误倾向——无标准的批评和唯有一种标准的批评。"实际上，否认标准，主张'无标准批评'，是将翻译欣赏与批评中允许的个人偏爱、见仁见智与可以不要标准混为一谈了，这种观点早已被翻译批评的实践所驳斥。一切翻译批评家都持有一定的批评标准。"（肖维青，2010：134）同样，翻译批评没有一种标准的诠释（肖维青，2010：134），因此也不可能只有一种标准。肖维青认为，翻译批评的标准具有抽象性和具体性。"古今中外，抽象的翻译批评标准有不少，是表述不同而已，例如，忠实、信达雅、等值等。"（肖维青，2010：137）而抽象性的标准需要具体标准的补充，所谓具体，可以具体到文体，比如科技文本、医学文本，也可以具体到文本的翻译类型，比如节译和改译等。该书还详细论述了翻译批评标准的三个层面：社会道德标准、行业规范和学术尺度，并比较和分析了三个层面的差异和联系，认为翻译批评标准是开放式的多元动态体系。该书还介绍了在中西方翻译界有较大影响力的几种翻译批评模式：赖斯模式（目的论范式），根据不同的文本类型提出不同的翻译标准；纽马克模式（系统实用的翻译批评步骤），具体列出了分析原文、分析译文、原文和译文的对比分析、译文质量评价、译文在译语文化中的价值；休斯模式（文本分析与功能对应），该模式是第一个较为系统、全面的翻译质量评估模式。

杨晓荣的《翻译批评导论》（2018）将翻译批评大体分为表层或浅层批评和深层次批评两种类型，"前者一般指的是技巧性批评，后者是理论性批评"（杨晓荣，2018：67）。而技巧性批评又可以分为两类：一类关注的是正误，即对不对的问题；另一类关注的是好不好的问题，即在没有技术性错误的情况下，语言质量是否高。"理论性批评也可以大体分为两类：一类是基于技巧但不止于技巧，不是简单地对正误好坏一判了之，而是从理论上讲清技巧类问题的来龙去脉及其中蕴含的理论意义。另一类原本就以理论探索为目标，通过评论译作揭示具有理论意义的规律性的东西，借以深入认识和解释翻译现象或为有关的实践活动提供指导。"（杨晓荣，2018：67）该书总结了国内翻译界比较有特色的文本批评方法，以等值翻译论为基础的译本检验方法，以及以"原则-参数"为框架的译本评析方法。该书集中讨论了翻译标准的问题，概括了国内以往关于翻译标准的五种理论，除了信达雅、神似与化境这两种大家耳熟能详的，还提到了以语言学等多学科理论为基础的对等论、以跨学科流派思想为基础的功能主义等翻译标准论、以哲学观念和哲学方法为基本特征的翻译标准论。值得一提的是，该书在回顾理论的基础上，还对实际应用的翻译标准进行了回顾，关注了翻译的行业标准。

除上述学者及其著作对翻译批评的讨论，其他学者对翻译批评的各个方面也进行了论述。如文军认为："所谓翻译批评的方法论原则，系指从事翻译批评时应当遵守的规范，它们对各种具体批评方法具有指导作用。概略而论，翻译批评的方法论原则大约包括：客观性原则、综合性原则、层次性原则、归纳－演绎结合的原则。"（文军，2004：85-86）事实上，"翻译批评是我国现代翻译研究的一个重要领域"（韩子满，2019：1）。许多翻译研究的学者在这方面已经取得了丰硕的研究成果。初学者通过了解翻译批评，可学习文学翻译批评中的重要概念和思路，从对译文的赏析和鉴定中可学到翻译方法和技巧，也能通过进一步的思考形成更具有学术性的思考。

第二章

小说翻译

　　小说是以刻画人物形象为中心，通过叙述人的语言来描绘生活，通过完整的故事情节和环境描写来反映社会，以展开作品主题，表达作者思想感情的文学体裁。人物（Character）、情节（Plot）、环境（Environment）是小说的三要素。情节一般包括开端、发展、高潮、结局四部分，有的包括序幕、尾声。环境包括自然环境和社会环境。小说来源于生活，是现实生活的提炼，但"虚构性"是其本质，因此比现实生活更集中，更具有代表性。总的来说，由于涉及不同的生活内容，小说不仅语言丰富，还包括多种文学体裁；为塑造多样的人物形象，小说中也有不同的语体和语域，因此也兼具高雅性和通俗性。

　　小说翻译与其他文学作品的翻译一样，牵涉很多因素。首先，既然是翻译，译者必定要受到原作的束缚；其次，翻译是译者的一种创造性行为，因此与译者个人的理解和思想有很大的关系；再次，译者的个人理解和思想实际上受到其所处时代、文化、社会、政治环境的影响。除此之外，文学翻译本质上是一种跨文化交流活动，在文学翻译过程中，译者除接触语言，也接触了语言背后的文化内涵，如何有效地将源语文化移植到目标语文化之中，是译者所要面临的挑战。王克非对翻译的定义是"翻译是译者将一种语言文字所蕴含的意思换用另一种语言文字表述出来的文化活动"（王克非，2021：69），这一定义特别凸显了译者作用和翻译活动的文化性。

　　基于小说的特点和文学翻译的特点，小说翻译的批评与赏析一般主要关注以下几个方面。第一，关注人物形象的塑造、语言个性的翻译，观察译文中不同人物的性格和身份是否能在语言中得到体现。第二，关注小说修辞的翻译。小说的文学性体现的一个方面就是修辞的使用，译文中修辞的翻译如何处理会直接影响译文的文学性，同时还会牵涉文化因素的传递，因而值得注意。第三，关注小说文体风格的翻译。文体是文本构成的规格和模式，反映了文本从内容到形式的整体特点，是在某种文化中长期积淀的产物。风格可以说是对文体的强调，是能反映出作者深刻的思想和感情的文本特征。小说的翻译批评应关注译文对原文文体风格的呈现情况。第四，关注小说的叙事视角。叙事视角是从某个角度对事情的叙述，对小说来说，通常有一个主要的叙事视角，但随着情节的发展，也可能会出现多元的叙事视角。在小说翻译的批评中应关注原文的叙事视角在译文中的体现，因为叙事视角的改变可能影响到情节的变更、人物形象的改变，甚至是小说主题的表现。

本章聚焦小说的翻译。为丰富小说翻译欣赏和批评的内容，本章特别设置了经典英文小说的汉译与中国章回小说的英译这两节内容，涉及汉译英和英译汉的小说翻译中的主要问题，为小说翻译的欣赏和批评提供了思考的角度，帮助读者从"如何译"开始思考，进而探究"为什么这么译"，提高小说翻译批评和欣赏的能力。

第一节

经典英文小说的汉译

所谓经典小说，即那些最能表现小说精髓的、经久不衰的传世之作，是小说中的典范，具有权威性和代表性。英文的经典小说不胜枚举，国内译本较多、一直受读者欢迎的有《傲慢与偏见》（*Pride and Prejudice*）、《简·爱》（*Jane Eyre*）、《双城记》（*A Tale of Two Cities*）、《杀死一只知更鸟》（*To Kill a Mocking Bird*）。这些经典小说虽然写作的年代久远，但它们的现代性是非常惊人的。这些作品要么定义了现代小说，要么在很大程度上影响了现代小说的发展。它们翻译到国内，不仅拓展了中国读者的眼界，为中国读者展示了异域文化、历史和现实中的人情世故，在某些特殊时期，它们中的一些还起到了启迪读者思想的作用，助推了中国文学的现代化转型。经典小说因其鲜明的语言特点、丰富的文化信息，给翻译带来的挑战毋庸置疑，这也是一些小说有多个译本的原因之一。

不同时代、不同背景的译者在小说中展现了各自的语言功底和对小说的不同阐释。通过不同译文的对比赏析，读者不仅可以加深对原作的了解，也能得到翻译技巧、方法等方面的启示，由"如何译"更深入地思考"为何如此译"，进而拓宽翻译研究的思路。

课前准备

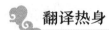 **翻译热身**

It is a truth universally acknowledged, that a single man in possession of a good fortune, must be in want of a wife.

However little known the feelings or views of such a man may be on his first entering a neighbourhood, this truth is so well fixed in the minds of the surrounding families, that he is considered as the rightful property of some one or other of their daughters.

'My dear Mr. Bennet,' said his lady to him one day, 'have you heard that Netherfield Park is let at last?'

Mr. Bennet replied that he had not.

'But it is,' returned she; 'for Mrs. Long has just been here, and she told me all about it.'

Mr. Bennet made no answer.

'Do not you want to know who has taken it?' cried his wife impatiently.

'You want to tell me, and I have no objection to hearing it.'

This was invitation enough.

（Jane Austen, *Pride and Prejudice*）

参考译文

有钱的单身汉必定需要娶个太太，这是一条举世公认的真理。

这样的单身汉刚搬到一个新地方的时候，虽然他的左邻右舍还完全不了解他的性情如何，见解如何，可是，既然这样的真理早已在他们心目中根深蒂固，他们就不免把他视为自己这个或那个女儿理应所得的一笔资产。

"我亲爱的贝纳特先生，"有一天，贝纳特太太对她的丈夫说，"内瑟菲尔德庄园终于租出去了，你听说了没有？"

贝纳特先生回答道，他没有听说过。

"的确租出去了，"她说，"朗太太刚刚上这儿来过，她把这件事原原本本都告诉了我。"

贝纳特先生没有搭话。

"你难道不想知道是谁租去的吗？"太太不耐烦地拉高嗓门。

"如果你想告诉我的话，我也不介意听。"

这句话足够鼓励她讲下去了。

（简·奥斯丁，《傲慢与偏见》，王科一译）

翻译难点聚焦

1. 对话如何体现人物的不同性格？

2. 译文如何再现原文中的幽默？

3. 原文中的长句如何用地道、流畅的译文表达？

名译赏析

原作简介

《理智与情感》是英国女作家简·奥斯丁（Jane Austen）创作的第一部长篇小说。故事以埃莉诺与玛丽安两姐妹曲折的婚恋过程为主线，通过"理智与情感"的幽默对比，提出了道德与行为的规范问题。小说的情节构思巧妙，奥斯丁采用现实主义的创作手法，描写普通人的生活方式，生动地再现了当时西方社会文化的面貌。奥斯丁在作品中不是通过细致的外貌描写与内心刻画，而是借助生动的对话和有趣的情节塑造了鲜活的人物形象。当然，作品也展现了奥斯丁幽默的语言，以及对人性深刻的洞察和辛辣的嘲讽。

原文

This circumstance was a growing attachment between her eldest girl and the brother of Mrs. John Dashwood, a gentleman-like and pleasing young man, who was introduced to their acquaintance soon after his sister's establishment at Norland, and who had since spent the greatest part of his time there.

Some mothers might have encouraged the intimacy from motives of interest, for Edward Ferrars was the eldest son of a man who had died very rich; and some might have repressed it from motives of prudence, for, except a trifling sum, the whole of his fortune depended on the will of his mother. But Mrs. Dashwood was alike uninfluenced by either consideration. It was enough for her that he appeared to be amiable, that he loved her daughter, and that Elinor returned the partiality. It was contrary to every doctrine of hers that difference of fortune should keep any couple asunder who were attracted by resemblance of disposition; and that Elinor's merit should not be acknowledged by everyone who knew her, was to her comprehension impossible.

Edward Ferrars was not recommended to their good opinion by any peculiar graces of person or address. He was not handsome, his manners required intimacy to make them pleasing. He was too diffident to do justice to himself; but when his natural shyness was overcome, his behavior gave every indication of an open, affectionate heart. His understanding was good, and his education had given it solid improvement. But he was neither fitted by abilities nor disposition to answer the wishes of his mother and sister, who longed to see him distinguished—as—they hardly knew what. They wanted him to make a fine figure in the world in some manner or other. His mother wished to interest him in political concerns, to get him into parliament, or to see him connected with some of the great men of the day. Mrs. John Dashwood wished it likewise; but in the meanwhile, till one of these superior blessings could be attained, it would have quieted her ambition to see him driving a barouche. But Edward had no turn for great men or barouches. All his wishes centered in domestic comfort and the quiet of private life. Fortunately, he had a younger brother who was more promising.

Edward had been staying several weeks in the house before he engaged much of Mrs. Dashwood's attention; for she was, at that time, in such affliction as rendered her careless of surrounding objects. She saw only that he was quiet and unobtrusive, and she liked him for it. He did not disturb the wretchedness of her mind by ill-timed conversation. She was first called to observe and approve him farther, by a reflection which Elinor chanced one day to make on the difference between him and his sister. It was a contrast which recommended him most forcibly to her mother.

"It is enough," said she; "to say that he is unlike Fanny is enough. It implies everything amiable. I love him already."

"I think you will like him," said Elinor, "when you know more of him."

"Like him!" replied her mother with a smile. "I feel no sentiment of approbation inferior to love."

"You may esteem him."

"I have never yet known what it was to separate esteem and love."

Mrs. Dashwood now took pains to get acquainted with him. Her manners were attaching, and soon banished his reserve. She speedily comprehended all his merits; the persuasion of his regard for Elinor perhaps assisted her penetration; but she really felt assured of his worth: and even that quietness of manner, which militated against all her established ideas of what a young man's address ought to be, was no longer uninteresting when she knew his heart to be warm and his temper affectionate.

No sooner did she perceive any symptom of love in his behavior to Elinor, than she considered their serious attachment as certain, and looked forward to their marriage as rapidly approaching.

（Jane Austen, *Sense and Sensibility*）

 译文

译文一

这桩事就出在她大女儿和约翰·达什伍德夫人的弟弟之间，两人渐渐萌发了爱慕之情。那位弟弟是个很有绅士派头的逗人喜爱的年轻人，他姐姐住进诺兰庄园不久，就介绍他与她们母女结识了。从那以后，他将大部分时间都消磨在那里。

有些做母亲的从利害关系出发，或许会进一步撮合这种密切的感情，因为爱德华·费拉斯乃是一位已故财主的长子；不过，有些做母亲的为了慎重起见，也许还会遏制这种感情，因为爱德华除了一笔微不足道的资产之外，他的整个家产将取决于母亲的遗嘱。可是达什伍德太太对这两种情况都不予考虑。对她来说，只要爱德华看上去和蔼可亲，对她女儿一片钟情，而埃丽诺反过来又钟情于他，那就足够了。因为财产不等而拆散一对志趣相投的恋人，这与她的伦理观念是格格不入的。埃丽诺的优点竟然不被所有认识她的人所公认，简直叫她不可思议。

她们之所以赏识爱德华·费拉斯，倒不是因为他人品出众，风度翩翩，他并不漂亮，那副仪态嘛，只有和他熟悉了才觉得逗人喜爱。他过于腼腆，这就使他越发不能显现本色了。不过，一旦消除了这种天生的羞怯，他的一举一动都表明他胸怀坦率，待人亲切。他头脑机灵，受教育后就更加聪明。但是，无论从才智还是从意向上看，他都不能使他母亲和姐姐称心如意，她们期望看到他出人头地——比如当个——她们也说不上当个啥。她们想让他在世界上出出这样或那样的风头。他母亲希望他对政治发生兴趣，以便能跻身于议会，或者结攀一些当今的大人物。约翰·达什伍德夫人抱有同样的愿望，不过，在这崇高理想实现之前，能先看到弟弟驾着一辆四轮马车，她也就会心满意足了。谁想，爱德华偏偏不稀罕大人物和四轮马车，他一心追求的是家庭的乐趣和生活的安逸。幸运的是，他有个弟弟比他有出息。

爱德华在姐姐家盘桓了几个星期，才引起达什伍德太太的注意；因为她当初太悲痛，对周围的事情也就不注意了。她只是看他不声不响，小心翼翼，为此对他发生了好感。他从来不用不合时宜的谈话，去扰乱她痛苦的心灵。她对他的进一步观察和赞许，最早是由埃丽诺偶然说出的一句话引起来的。那天，埃丽诺说他和他姐姐大不一样。这个对比很有说服力，帮他博得了她母亲的欢心。

"只要说他不像范妮，这就足够了，"她说，"这就是说他为人厚道，处处可亲。我已经喜爱上他了。"

"我想，"埃丽诺说，"你要是对他了解多了，准会喜欢他的。"

"喜欢他！"母亲笑吟吟地答道。"我心里一满意，少不了要喜爱他。"

"你会器重他的。"

"我还不知道怎么好把器重和喜爱分离开呢。"

随后，达什伍德太太便想方设法去接近爱德华。她态度和蔼，立即使他不再拘谨，很快便摸清了他的全部优点。她深信爱德华有意于埃丽诺，也许正是因此，她才有这么敏锐的眼力。不过，她确信他品德高尚。就连他那文静的举止，本是同她对青年人的既定的看法相抵触的，可是一旦了解到他待人热诚，性情温柔，也不再觉得令人厌烦了。

她一察觉爱德华对埃丽诺有点爱慕的表示，便认准他们是在真心相爱，巴望着他们很快就会结婚。

（简·奥斯丁，《理智与情感》，孙致礼译）

译文二

当时的情况是，她的大女儿和约翰·达什伍德太太的弟弟逐渐相好起来了；这位年轻人举止正派，讨人欢喜，他姐姐来到诺兰庄园住下不久，就介绍他跟她们认识了，以后他绝大部分时间都住在那里。

有些做母亲的出自利害考虑，也许会鼓励这种亲密关系，因为爱德华·费勒斯是一位已故财主的长子；有些做母亲的由于慎重，也许会加以约束，因为他本人的钱很少，他的财富全得靠他母亲的遗嘱决定。但是达什伍德太太却哪一桩都不放在心上。在她看，只要他看起来可爱，爱她的女儿，埃莉诺也有意爱他，这就够了。贫富悬殊就得拆散一对情意相投的情侣，她压根儿就反对；而且，她认为，凡是认识埃莉诺的人，决不可能不承认她的美德。

她们对爱德华·费勒斯抱有好感，并非由于他的仪表和谈吐有什么特殊的魅力。他不漂亮，态度呢，必得相处熟了，才能让人喜爱。他脸皮太薄，露不出他的真面目；但是等到他克服了天生的羞怯以后，他的一举一动却都显得心胸开朗，富于感情。他理解力强，教育又扎实地增进了他的见识。但是无论他的才能或者性格都无法满足他母亲和他姐姐的愿望，她们渴望他成名——成什么样的名，她们也没有准主意。她们要他不管怎样总要能崭露头角才行。他母亲想劝他搞政治，让他进议会，或者看到他交上几位当代名人朋友。约翰·达什伍德太太也是这样盼望的；不过，在他获得这一类鸿运之前，如果能看到他坐上一辆四轮大马车，倒也能安抚一下她的野心。可是爱德华无论是对名人或者对大马车都根本没有兴趣。他一心想的只是家庭舒适和安宁的生活。幸好他有个弟弟，比他有出息。

爱德华在这座府邸里住了好几个礼拜，才多少引起了达什伍德太太的注意；因为那时她心情悲恸，对周围事物全不关心。她只看到他文静，不冒失，因而喜欢他。她伤心时，他没有不知趣地找她说话，打搅她。有一天埃莉诺偶尔谈起他的为人跟他姐姐不同，这才引起她对他的注意，觉得他不错。这样的对比，对她母亲来说，正好是为他做了最强有力的推荐。

"这就够了，"她说，"说他跟范妮为人不同，这就足够了。这等于说，他一切都可爱。我已经爱上他了。"

"我想，"埃莉诺说，"等你对他多了解些的时候，你会喜欢他的。"

"喜欢他！"她母亲微笑着说，"我不光是喜欢，是爱。"

"你会敬重他的。"

"我从来还不懂敬和爱怎么能是两回事。"

达什伍德太太现在竭力跟他亲近。她态度亲切，很快就消除了他的拘谨。不消多少时候，她便了解到他的一切优点；她认为他对埃莉诺是有意思的，也许就是这个信念帮了她的忙，使她能洞察一切吧；不过她也真是相信他人好；当她看出他为人热心，脾气可爱的时候，甚至他那沉默的态度也不再是不足取的了，虽然那是她根本反对的，她原认为那不是年轻人应有的风度。

她刚一看出他对埃莉诺的态度有点爱慕的苗头，就认为他们一定是真心相爱了，并且盼望他们很快就会结婚。

（简·奥斯丁，《理智与情感》，武崇汉译）

赏析思路点拨

小说的创作离不开人物的塑造，原著中人物的性格在两篇译文中也得到了不同程度的展现。达什伍德太太感情丰富，性格容易冲动，说话做事不谨慎。在原文中，她对爱德华的赞美之情溢于言表，这在内敛的英国人看来是异乎寻常的表现。原文中她使用了"love""like""approbation""esteem"等词来表达她对爱德华的赞赏，在英语中，这些词表达喜爱的程度不同，在翻译过程中，两位译者也用了不同方式试图传达出这些词的差异。孙致礼的译文中使用了"喜爱""喜欢""器重"三个词语，但汉语中"喜爱"和"喜欢"的区别不大，没有英语中"like"和"love"分得那么清楚。"器重"一般表示上级对下级的重视，一定程度上体现了达什伍德太太和爱德华之间的长辈与晚辈的关系。武崇汉的译文在这几个词的翻译上体现了译者的巧思，不仅用"喜欢"与"爱"两个词体现出原文"like"和"love"的区别，还用了"敬重"一词来还原原文中的"esteem"，最后用"敬"和"爱"贴切地表达了达什伍德太太对爱德华的感情，这两个字合在一起是汉语中的"敬爱"一词，也是"尊敬与热爱"的意思。

上述几个词出现在达什伍德太太与女儿埃莉诺的对话当中，这段对话充分体现了母女不同的性格。达什伍德太太在对爱德华并不十分熟悉的情况下使用了"love"一词，这在性格谨慎、内敛的埃莉诺看来是不恰当的，因此她刻意纠正母亲的用词，用了"like""approbation""esteem"等词来避免提及"love"。两篇译文也通过对上述词语的翻译充分还原了原著中人物的性格。

原文还部分体现了奥斯丁式的幽默，比如第二段中，爱德华的母亲和姐姐对他的前途抱有期望。孙致礼的译文："她们期望看到他出人头地——比如当个——她们也说不上当个啥。"武崇汉的译文："她们渴望他成名——成什么样的名，她们也没有准主意。"从再现原文幽默这一方面来看，孙译更胜一筹，武译稍显严肃。

除了上面几点，对译文的赏析还可以关注以下两个较为突出的方面：一是长句翻译的流畅度；二是用词是否准确且符合中文表达习惯，如孙译本中使用的"撮合""遏制""盘桓"。

课后思考

1. 小说翻译如何重现原文的修辞特点？

2. 小说翻译如何实现语篇的流畅？

3. 两篇译文的不同之处主要表现在哪些方面？

原文

She was small and slight in person; pale, sandy-haired, and with eyes habitually cast down: when they looked up they were very large, odd, and attractive; so attractive that the Reverend Mr. Crisp, fresh from Oxford, and curate to the Vicar of Chiswick, the Reverend Mr. Flowerdew, fell in love with Miss Sharp; being shot dead by a glance of her eyes which was fired all the way across Chiswick Church from the school-pew to the reading-desk. This infatuated young man used sometimes to take tea with Miss Pinkerton, to whom he had been presented by his mamma, and actually proposed something like marriage in an intercepted note, which the one-eyed apple-woman was charged to deliver. Mrs. Crisp was summoned from Buxton, and abruptly carried off her darling boy; but the idea, even, of such an eagle in the Chiswick dovecot caused a great flutter in the breast of Miss Pinkerton, who would have sent away Miss Sharp but that she was bound to her under a forfeit, and who never could thoroughly believe the young lady's protestations that she had never exchanged a single word with Mr. Crisp, except under her own eyes on the two occasions when she had met him at tea.

By the side of many tall and bouncing young ladies in the establishment, Rebecca Sharp looked like a child. But she had the dismal precocity of poverty. Many a dun had she talked to, and turned away from her father's door; many a tradesman had she coaxed and wheedled into good-humor, and into the granting of one meal more. She sat commonly with her father, who was very proud of her wit, and heard the talk of many of his wild companions—often but ill-suited for a girl to hear. But she never had been a girl, she said; she had been a woman since she was eight years old. Oh, why did Miss Pinkerton let such a dangerous bird into her cage?

(William Makepeace Thackeray, *Vanity Fair*)

译文

　　她身量瘦小，脸色苍白，头发是淡黄色的。她惯常低眉垂目，抬起眼来看人的时候，眼睛显得很特别，不但大，而且动人。契息克的弗拉活丢牧师手下有一个副牧师，名叫克里斯泼，刚从牛津大学毕业，竟因此爱上了她。夏泼小姐的眼风穿过契息克教堂，从学校的包座直射到牧师的讲台上，一下子就把克里斯泼牧师结果了。这昏了头的小伙子曾经由他妈妈介绍给平克顿小姐，偶然也到她学校喝茶。他托那个独眼的卖苹果女人给她传递情书，被人发现，信里面的话简直等于向夏泼小姐求婚。克里斯泼太太得到消息，连忙从勃克思登赶来，立刻把她的宝贝儿子带走。平克顿小姐想到自己的鸽笼里藏了一只老鹰，不由得心慌意乱，若不是有约在先，真想把她赶走。那女孩竭力辩白，说她只在平克顿小姐监视之下和克里斯泼先生在茶会上见过两面，从来没有跟他说过话。她虽然这么说，平克顿小姐仍旧将信将疑。

　　利蓓加·夏泼在学校里许多又高又大、跳跳蹦蹦的同学旁边，好像还没有长大成人。其实贫穷的生活已经使她养成阴沉沉的脾气，比同年的孩子懂事得多。她常常和逼债的人打交道，想法子打发他们回去。她有本领甜言蜜语的哄得那些做买卖的回心转意，再让她赊一顿饭吃。她爸爸见她机灵，十分得意，时常让她和自己一起坐着听他那些粗野的朋友聊天，可惜他们说的多半是姑娘们不该听的野话。她说自己从来没有做过孩子，从八岁起就是成年妇人了。唉！平克顿小姐为什么让这么凶恶的鸟儿住在她的笼子里呢？

　　　　　　　　　　　　（威廉·梅克比斯·萨克雷，《名利场》，杨必译）

原文

　　When Caroline Meeber boarded the afternoon train for Chicago, her total outfit consisted of a small trunk, a cheap imitation alligator-skin satchel, a small lunch in a paper box, and a yellow leather snap purse, containing her ticket, a scrap of paper with her sister's address in Van Buren Street, and four dollars in money. It was in August, 1889. She was eighteen years of age, bright, timid, and full of the illusions of ignorance and youth. Whatever touch of regret at parting characterized her thoughts, it was certainly not for advantages now being given up. A gush of tears at her mother's farewell kiss, a touch in her throat when the cars clacked by the flour mill where her father worked by the day, a pathetic sigh as the familiar green environs of the village passed in review, and the threads which bound her so lightly to girlhood and home were irretrievably broken.

To be sure there was always the next station, where one might descend and return. There was the great city, bound more closely by these very trains which came up daily. Columbia City was not so very far away, even once she was in Chicago. What, pray, is a few hours—a few hundred miles? She looked at the little slip bearing her sister's address and wondered. She gazed at the green landscape, now passing in swift review, until her swifter thoughts replaced its impression with vague conjectures of what Chicago might be.

When a girl leaves her home at eighteen, she does one of two things. Either she falls into saving hands and becomes better, or she rapidly assumes the cosmopolitan standard of virtue and becomes worse. Of an intermediate balance, under the circumstances, there is no possibility. The city has its cunning wiles, no less than the infinitely smaller and more human tempter. There are large forces which allure with all the soulfulness of expression possible in the most cultured human. The gleam of a thousand lights is often as effective as the persuasive light in a wooing and fascinating eye. Half the undoing of the unsophisticated and natural mind is accomplished by forces wholly superhuman. A blare of sound, a roar of life, a vast array of human hives, appeal to the astonished senses in equivocal terms. Without a counsellor at hand to whisper cautious interpretations, what falsehoods may not these things breathe into the unguarded ear! Unrecognized for what they are, their beauty, like music, too often relaxes, then weakens, then perverts the simpler human perceptions.

（Theodore Dreiser, *Sister Carrie*）

译文

嘉罗琳·米蓓登上午后开往芝加哥的那趟列车时，她的全部家当，总共只有一只已交行李车托运的小箱子，一只廉价的仿鳄鱼皮手提包，内装一些梳妆用的零星物品、一纸盒小点心和一只带有摁扣的黄皮钱包，里面装着她的车票、记着她姐姐在范伯伦街住址的纸条和四块美元。那是在一八八九年八月间。当时她十八岁，聪明、羞怯，由于无知和年轻而充满了幻想。不管她跟亲人惜别时心里有什么惆怅之情，当然绝不是因为抛弃了家里的舒适环境。她跟母亲吻别时热泪有如泉涌；列车轰隆隆地驶过她父亲白天在那里打工的面粉厂，她嗓子眼顿时哽塞了；多么熟悉的村子，周围的绿色田野在眼前一掠而过。她禁不住伤心地叹了一口气。缕缕柔丝，过去曾把她若即若离地跟少女时代和故乡拴在一起，如今却无法补救地给扯断了。

这一切的一切，当时她肯定没有意识到。不论有多大的变化，都可以设法补救的。反正总是有下一站可以下车回去。大城市就在前头，每天来来往往的列车使它跟全国各地更密切地联结在一起。一旦她到了芝加哥，哥伦比亚城也离得并不太远。请问——一百英里，几个钟头的路算得上什么呢？她尽管可以回去嘛。况且她的姐姐还在那儿。她两眼直瞅着那张记下她姐姐住址的小纸条暗自纳闷。她凝视着眼前匆匆闪过的绿野风光，万千思绪掠过心头，已无心揣摩旅行观感，却猛地一转念，胡猜乱想芝加哥这个城市是什么样儿的。从孩提时期起她老是听到它的鼎鼎大名。过去她的家曾打算迁到那里去。这一回她要是寻摸到了好的事情，他们一家子就都可以来了。不管怎么说，芝加哥可大啦。五光十色，市声嘈杂，到处是一片喧腾。人们都很富。大的火车站不止一个。这趟朝前猛冲的列车，就是正在飞也似的驶往那里。

一个女孩子十八岁离家出门，结局只有两种之一。要么遇好人搭救而越变越好，要么很快接受了大都市道德标准而越变越坏。在这样的环境里，要保持中间状态是不可能的。这个大都市里到处有狡诈的花招，同样还有不少比它小得多、颇有人情味的诱人的东西。那里有种种巨大的力量，会通过优雅文化的魅力来引诱人。成千上万闪耀的灯光，实际上有时跟恋人频送秋波一样有力。天真的普通人之所以堕落，一半是由某些完全超人的力量造成的。喧嚣的市声，沸腾的生活，还有数不清的蜂窝式大楼——这一切使人们受惊，越发感到迷惑不安。如果说身旁没有人低声耳语，给予谆谆忠告，真不知道该有多少虚妄谎言灌入缺乏警惕者的耳里！这些光怪陆离的景象不是那么容易让人识破，它们表面上的美有如靡靡之音一般，往往使头脑简单的人先是思想松懈，继而意志薄弱，最后便堕落下去了。

（西奥多·德莱塞，《嘉莉妹妹》，潘庆舲译）

第二节

中国章回小说的英译

我国古代的小说经历了较长的发展阶段，首先萌芽于先秦时期，在两汉魏晋南北朝获得了较大的发展，当时分为志人小说和志怪小说。中国古代小说发展成熟的时期是唐朝，当时被称作传奇，到了宋金时期又开始流行话本。发展的高峰期是元末与明清时期，这时候出现了长篇白话小说。明清时期的章回体小说可以称为我国古代小说的巅峰，如四大名著，还有《儒林外史》《聊斋志异》等不朽的作品。自明末清初以来，西方传教士首先对中国的文学作品进行了翻译，客观上促进了中华文化的传播。新中国成立后用了近 20 年，创造了第一个文学对外翻译的高峰。外译作品既有四大名著以及李白、杜甫诗歌等古典文学经典，也有《林海雪原》《青春之歌》等红色经典，还有《狂人日记》《子夜》等中国现代文学名家作品。

　　本节选择的赏析文段是四大名著中《西游记》的第二十七回"尸魔三戏唐三藏　圣僧恨逐美猴王"，译文分别来自美籍华人余国藩（Anthony C. Yu）和汉学家詹纳尔（William John Francis Jenner）。《西游记》的最早英译本大约出现于 1913 年，上海基督教文学会出版了著名英国传教士李提摩太的译本 *A Mission to Heaven*；1930 年，海伦·海斯的译本 *The Buddhist Pilgrim's Progress* 在伦敦和纽约出版。这两个版本只选择了部分章节进行翻译，是节译本。最早引起广泛关注的《西游记》译本是 1942 年面世的英国翻译家卫利（Arthur David Waley）的译本，译名为 *Monkey: Folk Novel of China*。事实上，这个版本也只选取了原书的三十回，也是一个节译本。20 世纪 80 年代前后，在中国和美国，有两个全译本几乎同时面世，一个是英国人詹纳尔翻译的 *Journey to the West*，在 1977 年到 1986 年间由北京外文出版社付印；另一个是余国藩翻译的 *The Journey to the West*，在 1977 年到 1983 年间由芝加哥大学出版社刊行。这两个译本也是迄今仅见的两个《西游记》全译本。

课前准备

翻译热身

　　这猴王整衣端肃，随童子径入洞天深处观看：一层层深阁琼楼，一进进珠宫贝阙，说不尽那静室幽居，直至瑶台之下。见那菩提祖师端坐在台上，两边有三十个小仙侍立台下，果然是：大觉金仙没垢姿，西方妙相祖菩提。不生不灭三三行，全气全神万万慈。空寂自然随变化，真如本性任为之。与天同寿庄严体，历劫明心大法师。美猴王一见，倒身下拜，磕头不计其数，口中只道："师父！
师父！我弟子志心朝礼！志心朝礼！"

（吴承恩，《西游记》）

参考译文

　　The Monkey King straightened his clothes and followed the boy deep into the depths of the cave. He saw majestic pavilions and towers of red jade, pearl palaces and gateways of cowry, and countless rooms of silence and secluded cells leading all the way to a jasper dais. He saw the Patriarch Subhuti sitting on the dais and thirty-six minor Immortals standing below it.

　　A golden Immortal of great enlightenment, free from filth,

　　Subhuti, the marvel of the Western World.

　　Neither dying nor born, he practices the triple meditation,

　　His spirit and soul entirely benevolent.

　　In empty detachment he follows the changes;

　　Having found his true nature he lets it run free.

　　As eternal as Heaven, and majestic in body,

　　The great teacher of the Law is enlightened through aeons.

　　As soon as the Handsome Monkey King saw him he bowed low and knocked his head on the ground before him many times, saying, "Master, master, your disciple pays his deepest respects."

（Wu Cheng-en, *The Journey to the West*, translated by Anthony C. Yu）

翻译难点聚焦

1. 翻译中如何传达原著的语言风格？
2. 译文如何再现原文中的修辞？
3. 宗教词汇如何翻译？

名译赏析

原作简介

《西游记》具有独特的艺术魅力。总的说来，除了巧妙的故事情节，《西游记》中人物的塑造极具个性，这些个性通过人物的外形、语言、行为、心理活动等方面表现了出来，并在一个个斗争、冲突的故事中得以发展和完善。该书的语言通俗易懂，描写生动准确，文中幽默、讽刺的手法处处可见。《西游记》中还包含了深奥的宗教文化，全书贯穿了两种宗教，以佛家文化为主、道家文化为辅。此外，书中还有儒家文化的印记，下文将要欣赏到的章节中唐僧说"父母在，不远游"，而这句话正是儒家经典《论语·里仁》中的语句。《西游记》的博大精深决定了其翻译的难度，余国藩和詹纳尔都以自己的方式用另一种语言讲述了其中的故事。

原文

第二十七回　尸魔三戏唐三藏　圣僧恨逐美猴王

却说常言有云：山高必有怪，岭峻却生精。

果然这山上有一个妖精，孙大圣去时，惊动那怪。他在云端里，踏着阴风，看见长老坐在地下，就不胜欢喜道："造化！造化！几年家人都讲东土的唐和尚取大乘，他本是金蝉子化身，十世修行的原体。有人吃他一块肉，长寿长生。真个今日到了。"那妖精上前就要拿他，只见长老左右手下有两员大将护持，不敢拢身。他说两员大将是谁？说是八戒、沙僧。八戒、沙僧虽没甚么大本事，然八戒是天蓬元帅，沙僧是卷帘大将，他的威气尚不曾泄，故不敢拢身。妖精说："等我且戏他戏，看怎么说。"

好妖精，停下阴风，在那山凹里，摇身一变，变做个月貌花容的女儿，说不尽那眉清目秀，齿白唇红，左手提着一个青砂罐儿，右手提着一个绿磁瓶儿，从西向东，径奔唐僧。圣僧歇马在山岩，忽见裙钗女近前。翠袖轻摇笼玉笋，湘裙斜拽显金莲。汗流粉面花含露，尘拂峨眉柳带烟。仔细定睛观看处，看看行至到身边。三藏见了，叫："八戒，沙僧，悟空才说这里旷野无人，你看那里不走出一个人来了？"八戒道："师父，你与沙僧坐着，等老猪去看看来。"那呆子放下钉钯，整整直裰，摆摆摇摇，充作个斯文气象，一直的觌面相迎。真个是远看未实，近看分明，那女子生得：冰肌藏玉骨，衫领露酥胸。柳眉积翠黛，杏眼闪银星。月样容仪俏，天然性格清。体似燕藏柳，声如莺啭林。半放海棠笼晓日，才开芍药弄春晴。那八戒见他生得俊俏，呆子就动了凡心，忍不住胡言乱语，叫道："女菩萨，往那里去？手里提着是甚么东西？"分明是个妖怪，他却不能认得。那女子连声答应道："长老，我这青罐里是香米饭，绿瓶里是炒面筋，特来此处无他故，因还誓愿要斋僧。"八戒闻言，满心欢喜，急抽身，就跑了个猪颠风，报与三藏道："师父！吉人自有天报！师父饿了，教师兄去化斋，那猴子不知那里摘桃儿耍子去了。桃子吃多了，也有些嘈人，又有些下坠。你看那不是个斋僧的来了？"唐僧不信道："你这个夯货胡缠！我们走了这向，好人也不曾遇着一个，斋僧的从何而来！"八戒道："师父，这不到了？"

三藏一见，连忙跳起身来，合掌当胸道："女菩萨，你府上在何处住？是甚人家？有甚愿心，来此斋僧？"分明是个妖精，那长老也不认得。那妖精见唐僧问他来历，他立地就起个虚情，花言巧语来赚哄道："师父，此山叫做蛇回兽怕的白虎岭，正西下面是我家。我父母在堂，看经好善，广斋方上远近僧人，只因无子，求福作福，生了奴奴，欲扳门第，配嫁他人，又恐老来无倚，只得将奴招了一个女婿，养老送终。"三藏闻言道："女菩萨，你语言差了。圣经云：父母在，不远游，游必有方。你既有父母在堂，又与你招了女婿，有愿心，教你男子还，便也罢，怎么自家在山行走？又没个侍儿随从。这个是不遵妇道了。"那女子笑吟吟，忙陪俏语道："师父，我丈夫在山北凹里，带几个客子锄田。这是奴奴煮的午饭，送与那些人吃的。只为五黄六月，无人使唤，父母又年老，所以亲身来送。忽遇三位远来，却思父母好善，故将此饭斋僧，如不弃嫌，愿表芹献。"三藏道："善哉！善哉！我有徒弟摘果子去了，就来，我不敢吃。假如我和尚吃了你饭，你丈夫晓得，骂你，却不罪坐贫僧也？"那女子见唐僧不肯吃，却又满面春生道："师父啊，我父母斋僧，还是小可；我丈夫更是个善人，一生好的是修桥补路，爱老怜贫。但听见说这饭送与师父吃了，他与我夫妻情上，比寻常更是不同。"三藏也只是不吃，旁边却恼坏了八戒。那呆子努着嘴，口里埋怨道："天下和尚也无数，不曾象我这个老和尚罢软！现成的饭三分儿倒不吃，只等那猴子来，做四分才吃！"他不容分说，一嘴把个罐子拱倒，就要动口。

只见那行者自南山顶上，摘了几个桃子，托着钵盂，一筋斗，点将回来，睁火眼金睛观看，认得那女子是个妖精，放下钵盂，掣铁棒，当头就打。唬得个长老用手扯住道："悟空！你走将来打谁？"行者道："师父，你面前这个女子，莫当做个好人。他是个妖精，要来骗你哩。"三藏道："你这猴头，当时倒也有些眼力，今日如何乱道！这女菩萨有此善心，将这饭要斋我等，你怎么说他是个妖精？"行者笑道："师父，你那里认得！老孙在水帘洞里做妖魔时，若想人肉吃，便是这等：或变金银，或变庄台，或变醉人，或变女色。有那等痴心的，爱上我，我就迷他到洞里，尽意随心，或蒸或煮受用；吃不了，还要晒干了防天阴哩！师父，我若来迟，你定入他套子，遭他毒手！"那唐僧那里肯信，只说是个好人。行者道："师父，我知道你了，你见他那等容貌，必然动了凡心。若果有此意，叫八戒伐几棵树来，沙僧寻些草来，我做木匠，就在这里搭个窝铺，你与他圆房成事，我们大家散了，却不是件事业？何必又跋涉，取甚经去！"那长老原是个软善的人，那里吃得他这句言语，羞得个光头彻耳通红。三藏正在此羞惭，行者又发起性来，掣铁棒，望妖精劈脸一下。那怪物有些手段，使个解尸法，见行者棍子来时，他却抖擞精神，预先走了，把一个假尸首打死在地下。唬得个长老战战兢兢，口中作念道："这猴着然无礼！屡劝不从，无故伤人性命！"行者道："师父莫怪，你且来看看这罐子里是甚东西。"沙僧搀着长老，近前看时，那里是甚香米饭，却是一罐子拖尾巴的长蛆，也不是面筋，却是几个青蛙、癞虾蟆，满地乱跳。长老才有三分儿信了，怎禁猪八戒气不忿，在旁漏八分儿唆嘴道："师父，说起这个女子，他是此间农妇，因为送饭下田，路遇我等，却怎么栽他是个妖怪？哥哥的棍重，走将来试手打他一下，不期就打杀了；怕你念甚么《紧箍儿咒》，故意的使个障眼法儿，变做这等样东西，演幌你眼，使不念咒哩。"

三藏自此一言，就是晦气到了：果然信那呆子撺唆，手中捻诀，口里念咒，行者就叫："头疼！头疼！莫念！莫念！有话便说。"

（吴承恩，《西游记》）

译文

译文一

Chapter 27
The Corpse Fiend Thrice Tricks Tang Sanzang
The Holy Monk Angrily Dismisses the Handsome Monkey King

There is a saying that goes, "If the mountain is high it's bound to have fiends; if the ridge is steep spirits will live there."

This mountain did indeed have an evil spirit who was startled by Monkey's appearance. It strode through the clouds on a negative wind, and on seeing the venerable Sanzang on the ground below thought happily, "What luck, what luck. At home they've been talking for years about a Tang Monk from the East who's going to fetch the 'Great Vehicle'; he's a reincarnation of Golden Cicada, and has an Original Body that has been purified through ten lives. Anyone who eats a piece of his flesh will live for ever. And today, at last, he's here." The evil spirit went forward to seize him, but the sight of the two great generals to Sanzang's left and right made it frightened to close in on him. Who, it wondered, were they? They were in fact Pig and Friar Sand, and for all that their powers were nothing extraordinary, Pig was really Marshal Tian Peng while Friar Sand was the Great Curtain-lifting General. It was because their former awe-inspiring qualities had not yet been dissipated that the fiend did not close in. "I'll try a trick on them and see what happens," the spirit said to itself.

The splendid evil spirit stopped its negative wind in a hollow and changed itself into a girl with a face as round as the moon and as pretty as a flower. Her brow was clear and her eyes beautiful; her teeth were white and her lips red. In her left hand she held a blue earthenware pot and in her right a green porcelain jar. She headed East towards the Tang Priest.

> The holy monk rested his horse on the mountain,
> And suddenly noticed a pretty girl approaching.
> The green sleeves over her jade fingers lightly billowed;
> Golden lotus feet peeped under her trailing skirt.
> The beads of sweat on her powdered face were dew on a flower,
> Her dusty brow was a willow in a mist.
> Carefully and closely he watched her
> As she came right up to him.

"Pig, Friar Sand," said Sanzang when he saw her, "don't you see somebody coming although Monkey said that this was a desolate and uninhabited place?" "You and Friar Sand stay sitting here while I go and take a look." The blockhead laid down his rake, straightened his tunic, put on the airs of a gentleman, and stared at the girl as he greeted her. Although he had not been sure from a distance, he could now see clearly that the girl had

> Bones of jade under skin as pure as ice,
>
> A creamy bosom revealed by her neckline.
>
> Her willow eyebrows were black and glossy,
>
> And silver stars shone from her almond eyes.
>
> She was as graceful as the moon,
>
> As pure as the heavens.
>
> Her body was like a swallow in a willow-tree,
>
> Her voice like an oriole singing in the wood.
>
> She was wild apple-blossom enmeshing the sun,
>
> An opening peony full of the spring.

When the idiot Pig saw how beautiful she was his earthly desires were aroused, and he could not hold back the reckless words that came to his lips. "Where are you going, Bodhisattva," he said, "and what's that you're holding?" Although she was obviously an evil fiend he could not realize it. "Venerable sir," the girl replied at once, "this blue pot is full of tasty rice, and the green jar contains fried wheat-balls. I've come here specially to fulfil a vow to feed monks." Pig was thoroughly delighted to hear this. He came tumbling back at breakneck speed and said to Sanzang, "Master, 'Heaven rewards the good'. When you sent my elder brother off begging because you felt hungry, that ape went fooling around somewhere picking peaches. Besides, too many peaches turn your stomach and give you the runs. Don't you see that this girl is coming to feed us monks?" "You stupid idiot," replied Sanzang, who was not convinced, "we haven't met a single decent person in this direction, so where could anyone come from to feed monks?" "What's she then, master?" said Pig.

When Sanzang saw her he sprang to his feet, put his hands together in front of his chest, and said, "Bodhisattva, where is your home? Who are you? What vow brings you here to feed monks?" Although she was obviously an evil spirit, the venerable Sanzang could not see it either. On being asked about her background by Sanzang, the evil spirit immediately produced a fine-sounding story with which to fool him. "This mountain, which snakes and wild animals won't go near, is called White Tiger Ridge," she said. "Our home lies due West from here at the foot of it. My mother and father live there, and they are devout people who read the scriptures and feed monks from far and near. As they had no son, they asked Heaven to bless them. When I was born they wanted to marry me off to a good family, but then they decided to find me a husband who would live in our home to look after them in their old age and see them properly buried." "Bodhisattva, what you say can't be right," replied Sanzang. "The Analects say, 'When father and mother are alive, do not go on long journeys; if you have to go out, have a definite aim.' As your parents are at home and have found you a husband, you should let him fulfil your vow for you. Why ever are you walking in the mountains all by yourself, without even a servant? This is no way for a lady to behave." The girl smiled and produced a smooth reply at once: "My husband is hoeing with some of our retainers in a hollow in the North of the mountain, reverend sir, and I am taking them this food I've cooked. As it's July and all the crops are ripening nobody can be spared to run errands, and my parents are old, so I'm taking it there myself. Now that I have met you three monks from so far away, I would like to give you this food as my parents are so pious. I hope you won't refuse our paltry offering." "It's very good of you," said

Sanzang, "but one of my disciples has gone to pick some fruit and will be back soon, so we couldn't eat any of your food. Besides, if we ate your food your husband might be angry with you when he found out, and we would get into trouble too." As the Tang Priest was refusing to eat the food, the girl put on her most charming expression and said, "My parents' charity to monks is nothing compared to my husband's, master. He is a religious man whose lifelong pleasure has been repairing bridges, mending roads, looking after the aged, and helping the poor. When he hears that I have given you this food, he'll love me more warmly than ever." Sanzang still declined to eat it. Pig was beside himself. Twisting his lips into a pout, he muttered indignantly, "Of all the monks on earth there can't be another as soft in the head as our master. He won't eat ready-cooked food when there are only three of us to share it between. He's waiting for that ape to come back, and then we'll have to split it four ways." Without allowing any more discussion he tipped the pot towards his mouth and was just about to eat.

At just this moment Brother Monkey was somersaulting back with his bowl full of the peaches he had picked on the Southern mountain. When he saw with the golden pupils in his fiery eyes that the girl was an evil spirit, he put the bowl down, lifted his cudgel, and was going to hit her on the head when the horrified Sanzang held him back and said, "Who do you think you're going to hit?" "That girl in front of you is no good," he replied. "She's an evil spirit trying to make a fool of you." "In the old days you had a very sharp eye, you ape," Sanzang said, "but this is nonsense. This veritable Bodhisattva is feeding us with the best of motives, so how can you call her an evil spirit?" "You wouldn't be able to tell, master," said Monkey with a grin. "When I was an evil monster in the Water Curtain Cave I used to do that if I wanted a meal of human flesh. I would turn myself into gold and silver, or a country mansion, or liquor, or a pretty girl. Whoever was fool enough to be besotted with one of these would fall in love with me, and I would lure them into the cave, where I did what I wanted with them. Sometimes I ate them steamed and sometimes boiled, and what I couldn't finish I used to dry in the sun against a rainy day. If I'd been slower getting here, master, you'd have fallen into her snare and she'd have finished you off." The Tang Priest refused to believe him and maintained that she was a good person. "I know you, master," said Monkey. "Her pretty face must have made you feel randy. If that's the way you feel, tell Pig to fell a few trees and send Friar Sand look off to for some grass. I'll be the carpenter, and we'll build you a hut here that you and the girl can use as your bridal chamber. We can all go our own ways. Wouldn't marriage be a worthwhile way of living? Why bother plodding on to fetch some scriptures or other?" Sanzang, who had always been such a soft and virtuous man, was unable to take this. He was so embarrassed that he blushed from his shaven pate to his ears.

While Sanzang was feeling so embarrassed, Monkey flared up again and struck at the evil spirit's face. The fiend, who knew a trick or two, used a magic way of abandoning its body: when it saw Monkey's cudgel coming it braced itself and fled, leaving a false corpse lying dead on the ground. Sanzang shook with terror and said to himself, "That monkey is utterly outrageous. Despite all my good advice he will kill people for no reason at all." "Don't be angry, master," said Monkey. "Come and see what's in her pot." Friar Sand helped Sanzang over to look, and he saw that far from containing tasty rice it was full of centipedes with long tails. The jar had held not wheat-balls but frogs and toads, which were now jumping around on the ground. Sanzang was now beginning to believe Monkey. This was not enough, however, to prevent a furious Pig from deliberately making trouble by saying, "Master, that girl was a local countrywoman who happened to meet us while she was taking some food to the fields. There's no reason to think that she was an evil spirit. My elder brother was trying his club out on her, and he killed her by mistake. He's deliberately trying to trick us by magicking the food into those things because he's afraid you'll recite the Bandtightening spell. He's fooled you into not saying it."

This brought the blindness back on Sanzang, who believed these trouble-making remarks and made the magic with his hand as he recited the spell. "My head's aching, my head's aching," Monkey said. "Stop, please stop. Tell me off if you like."

(Wu Cheng-en, Journey to the West, translated by W. J. F. Jenner)

译文二

The cadaver demon three times mocks Tripitaka Tang;
The holy monk in spite banishes Handsome Monkey King.

Now, the proverb says: A tall mountain will always have monsters; A rugged peak will always produce fiends.

In this mountain there was indeed a monster-spirit, who was disturbed by the Great Sage Sun's departure. Treading dark wind, she came through the clouds and found the elder sitting on the ground. "What luck! What luck!" she said, unable to contain her delight. "For several years my relatives have been talking about a Tang Monk from the Land of the East going to fetch the Great Vehicle. He is actually the incarnation of the Gold Cicada, and he has the original body that has gone through the process of self-cultivation during ten previous existences. If a man eats a piece of his flesh, his age will be immeasurably lengthened. So, this monk has at last arrived today!" The monster was about to go down to seize Tripitaka when she saw two great warriors standing guard on either side of the elder, and that stopped her from drawing near. Now, who could these warriors be, you ask? They were, of course, Eight Rules and Sha Monk. Eight Rules and Sha Monk, you see, might not have great abilities, but after all, Eight Rules was the Marshal of Heavenly Reeds and Sha Monk was the Great Curtain-Raising Captain. Their authority had not been completely eroded, and that was why the monster dared not approach them. Instead, the monster said to herself, "Let me make fun of them a bit, and see what happens."

Dear monster! She lowered her dark wind into the field of the mountain, and, with one shake of her body, she changed into a girl with a face like the moon and features like flowers. One cannot begin to describe the bright eyes and the elegant brows, the white teeth and the red lips. Holding in her left hand a blue sandstone pot and in her right a green porcelain vase, she walked from west to east, heading straight for the Tang Monk.

The sage monk resting his horse on the cliff

Saw all at once a young girl drawing near:

Slender hands hugged by gently swaying green sleeves;

Tiny feet exposed beneath a skirt of Hunan silk.

Perspiring her face seemed flower bedewed;

Dust grazed her moth-brows like willows held by mist.

And as he stared intently with his eyes,

She seemed to be walking right up to his side.

When Tripitaka saw her, he called out, "Eight Rules, Sha Monk, just now Wukong said that this is an uninhabited region. But isn't that a human being who is walking over there?"

"Master," said Eight Rules, "you sit here with Sha Monk. Let old Hog go take a look." Putting down his muckrake and pulling down his shirt, our Idiot tried to affect the airs of a gentleman and went to meet her face to face. Well, it was as the proverb says: You can't determine the truth from afar. You can see clearly when you go near. The girl's appearance was something to behold!

Ice-white skin hides jadelike bones;

Her collar reveals a milk-white bosom.

Willow brows gather dark green hues;

Almond eyes shine like silver stars.

Her features like the moon are coy;

Her natural disposition is pure.

Her body's like the willow-nested swallow;

Her voice's like the woods' singing oriole.

A half-opened haitang caressed by the morning sun.

A newly bloomed peony displaying her charm.

When Idiot saw how pretty she was, his worldly mind was aroused and he could not refrain from babbling. "Lady Bodhisattva!" he cried. "Where are you going? What's that you are holding in your hands?" This was clearly a fiend, but he could not recognize her! The girl immediately answered him, saying, "Elder, what I have in the blue pot is fragrant rice made from wine cakes, and there's fried wheat gluten in the green vase. I came here for no other reason than to redeem my vow of feeding monks." When Eight Rules heard these words, he was very pleased. Spinning around, he ran like a hog maddened by plague to report to Tripitaka, crying, "Master! 'The good man will have Heaven's reward!' Because you are hungry, you ask Elder Brother to go beg for some vegetarian food. But we really don't know where that ape has gone to pick his peaches and have his fun! If you eat too many peaches, you are liable to feel a bit stuffed and gaseous anyway! Take a look instead. Isn't that someone coming to feed the monks?"

"Coolie, you're just clowning!" said an unbelieving Tang Monk. "We've been traveling all this time and we haven't even run into a healthy person! Where is this person who's coming to feed the monks?"

"Master," said Eight Rules, "isn't this the one?"

When Tripitaka saw the girl, he jumped up and folded his hands. "Lady Bodhisattva," he said, "where is your home? What sort of family is yours? What kind of vow have you made that you have to come here to feed the monks?" This was clearly a fiend, but our elder could not recognize her either! When that monster heard the Tang Monk asking after her background, she at once resorted to falsehood.

With clever, specious words, she tried to deceive her interrogator, saying, "Master, this mountain, which turns back serpents and frightens wild beasts, bears the name of White Tiger. My home is located due west of here. My parents, still living, are frequent readers of sūtras and keen on doing good works. They have fed liberally the monks who come to us from near and far. Because my parents had no son, they prayed to the gods, and I was born. They would have liked to marry me off to a noble family, but, wary of helplessness in their old age, they took in a son-in-law instead, so that they would be cared for in life and death." Hearing this, Tripitaka said, "Lady Bodhisattva, your speech is rather improper! The sage classic says, 'While father and mother are alive, one does not travel abroad; or if one does, goes only to a proper destination.' If your parents are still living, and if they have taken in a husband for you, then your man should have been the one sent to redeem your vow. Why do you walk about the mountain all by yourself? You don't even have an attendant to accompany you. That's not very becoming of a woman!"

Smiling broadly, the girl quickly tried to placate him with more clever words. "Master," she said, "my husband is at the northern fold of this mountain, leading a few workers to plow the fields. This happens to be the lunch I prepared for them to eat. Since now is the busy season of farm work, we have no servants; and as my parents are getting old, I have to run the errand myself. Meeting you three distant travelers is quite by accident, but when I think of my parents' inclination to do good deeds, I would like very much to use this rice as food for monks. If you don't regard this as unworthy of you, please accept this modest offering."

"My goodness! My goodness!" said Tripitaka. "I have a disciple who has gone to pick some fruits, and he's due back any moment. I dare not eat. For if I, a monk, were to eat your rice, your husband would scold you when he learns of it. Will it then not be the fault of this poor monk?"

When that girl saw the Tang Monk refuse to take the food, she smiled even more seductively and said, "O Master! My parents, who love to feed the monks, are not even as zealous as my husband. For his entire life is devoted to the construction of bridges and the repairing of roads, in reverence for the aged and pity for the poor. If he heard that the rice was given to feed Master, his affection for me, his wife, would increase manyfold." Tripitaka, however, simply refused to eat, and Eight Rules on one side became utterly exasperated. Pouting, our Idiot grumbled to himself, "There are countless priests in the world, but none is more wishy-washy than this old priest of ours! Here's ready-made rice, and three portions to boot! But he will not eat it. He has to wait for that monkey's return and the rice divided into four portions before he'll eat." Without permitting further discussion, he pushed over the pot with one shove of his snout and was about to begin.

Look at our Pilgrim! Having picked several peaches from the mountain peak in the south, he came hurtling back with a single somersault, holding the alms bowl in his hand. When he opened wide his fiery eyes and diamond pupils to take a look, he recognized that the girl was a monster. He put down the bowl, pulled out his iron rod, and was about to bring it down hard on the monster's head. The elder was so aghast that he pulled his disciple back with his hands. "Wukong," he cried, "whom have you come back to hit?"

"Master," said Pilgrim, "don't regard this girl in front of you as a good person. She's a monster, and she has come to deceive you." "Monkey," said Tripitaka, "you used to possess a measure of true discernment. How is it that you are talking nonsense today? This Lady Bodhisattva is so kind that she wants to feed me with her rice. Why do you say that she's a monster?" "Master," said Pilgrim with a laugh, "how could you know about this? When I was a monster back at the Water-Curtain Cave, I would act like this if I wanted to eat human flesh. I would change myself into gold or silver, a lonely building, a harmless drunk, or a beautiful woman. Anyone feeble-minded enough to be attracted by me I would lure back to the cave. There I would enjoy him as I pleased, by steaming or boiling. If I couldn't finish him off in one meal, I would dry the leftovers in the sun to keep for rainy days. Master, if I had returned a little later, you would have fallen into her trap and been harmed by her." That Tang Monk, however, simply refused to believe these words; he kept saying instead that the woman was a good person.

"Master," said Pilgrim, "I think I know what's happening. Your worldly mind must have been aroused by the sight of this woman's beauty. If you do have the desire, why not ask Eight Rules to cut some timber and Sha Monk to find us some grass. I'll be the carpenter and build you a little hut right here where you can consummate the affair with her. We can each go our own way then. Wouldn't that be the thing to do? Why bother to undertake such a long journey to fetch the scriptures?" The elder, you see, was a rather tame and gentle person. He was so embarrassed by these few words that his whole bald head turned red from ear to ear.

As Tripitaka was struck dumb by his shame, Pilgrim's temper flared again. Wielding his iron rod, he aimed it at the monster's face and delivered a terrific blow. The fiend, however, had a few tricks of her own. She knew the magic of Releasing the Corpse. When she saw Pilgrim's rod coming at her, she roused her spirit and left, leaving behind the corpse of her body struck dead on the ground. Shaking with horror, the elder mumbled, "This ape is so unruly, so obdurate! Despite my repeated pleadings, he still takes human life without cause." "Don't be offended, Master," said Pilgrim, "just come see for yourself what kind of things are in the pot." Sha Monk led the elder near to take a look. The fragrant rice made from wine cakes was nowhere to be found; there was instead a potful of large maggots with long tails. There was no fried wheat gluten either, but a few frogs and ugly toads were hopping all over the place. The elder was about to think that there might be thirty percent truthfulness in Pilgrim's words, but Eight Rules would not let his own resentment subside. He began to cast aspersions on his companion, saying, "Master, this woman, come to think of it, happens to be a farm girl of this area. Because she had to take some lunch to the fields, she met us on the way. How could she be deemed a monster? That rod of Elder Brother is quite heavy, you know. He came back and wanted to try his hand on her, not anticipating that one blow would kill her. He's afraid that you might recite that so-called Tight-Fillet Spell, and that's why he's using some sort of magic to hoodwink you. It's he who has caused these things to appear, just to befuddle you so that you won't recite the spell."

This single speech of Eight Rules, alas, spelled disaster for Tripitaka! Believing the slanderous suasion of our Idiot, he made the magic sign with his hand and recited the spell. At once Pilgrim began to scream, "My head! My head! Stop reciting! Stop reciting! If you've got something to say, say it."

（Wu Cheng-en, The Journey to the West, translated by Anthony C. Yu）

赏析思路点拨

《西游记》中有诸多宗教词汇，从本节的选段可见一斑。比如选段原文的第二段："……唐和尚取大乘，他本是金蝉子化身，十世修行的原体。"这句话中就有"大乘""金蝉子""修行""原体"等佛教词汇，詹纳尔和余国藩对前面三个词语的翻译相同，即"Great Vehicle""Golden Cicada""Original Body"，但对于"修行"一词，两位译者有不同的理解，詹纳尔的译文为"purified"，而余国藩的译文则是"go through the process of self-cultivation"。"修行"一词的内涵非常丰富，不仅在不同的时代有不同的含义，在不同的领域也有不同的解读。总的说来，修行可以笼统理解为人在思维活动、心理活动、行为活动、社会活动等方面实现更高修养的行为或过程。从这个层面上讲，余国藩的译文较为准确，而詹纳尔将之译为"purify"，认为修行实则是人得以净化的过程。再如原文第三段第一句话中的"阴风"，余译为"dark wind"，而詹译为"negative wind"。"dark"既有阴郁、邪恶（sinister，evil）的意思，也可以表示颜色上的阴沉、黑暗，因此可以说余译是一词双关。而阴风在中国文化中表示的是寒冷且邪恶的风，"negative"也可以表示阴郁（gloomy）之意，因此"negative"也传达出了原词的含义。两个译本中宗教词汇翻译的不同，可以从两位译者的不同文化背景和不同的学识背景两个方面找到原因。

除了宗教词汇，选段的原文中对女性的描述细致而精妙，相关的表达如"月貌花容""冰肌玉骨""金莲"，两位译者的翻译也有较大的差异。"月貌花容"，詹纳尔翻译为"with a face as round as the moon and as pretty as a flower"，余国藩翻译为"with a face like the moon and features like flowers"。余译只说这张脸像月亮且有花的特征，意思较为笼统，但留给人美好的想象空间。而詹纳尔的译文明确指出了月亮很圆（round）、花很美（pretty）的特征，但"月貌花容"中的"月"并非要突出其形状为圆形，而是借用荧光般的月华表达相貌的美好，因此，该译文对原文中人物外貌的描写有一定程度的偏离。除此之外，仔细比较两个译文，会发现两位译者在文化相关性高的描写上有诸多差异。

原文选段中还有一些粗俗语，主要体现在人物的语言当中，如唐僧责骂猪八戒为"夯货""呆子"，责骂孙悟空为"猴头"，两位译者的处理方式也值得读者进一步思考。《西游记》中人物性格鲜明，具体表现在他们的外貌、行为和语言中，两个译本是否还原了人物形象，是否对人物形象进行了重塑与改写，也是比较两个译本时值得观察的方面。

课后思考

1. 两个译本中宗教词汇的翻译有无特别之处？

2. 余国藩与詹纳尔的译本风格有很大的差异，这与两位译者的身份和翻译理念有什么关系？

3. 对文中文化词汇的翻译，两位译者主要采用了哪些翻译方法和技巧？

延伸阅读

原文

康熙见韦小宝与众小太监拾夺不下鳌拜，势道不对，绕到鳌拜背后，拔出匕首，一刀插入了他背心。

鳌拜猛觉背心上微痛，立即背肌一收，康熙这一刀便刺得偏了，未中要害。鳌拜顺手掷开韦小宝，犹如旋风般转过身来，眼前一个少年，正是皇帝。

鳌拜一呆，康熙跃开两步。鳌拜大叫一声，终于明白皇帝要取自己性命，挥拳便向康熙打来。康熙侧身避过。鳌拜抓住两名小太监，将他们脑袋对脑袋的一撞，二人登时头骨破裂。他跟着左手一拳，直打进一名小监的胸膛，右脚连踢，将四名小监踢得撞上墙壁，一个个筋折骨断，哼也没哼一声，便已死去，接着左足踹在一名抱住他右腿的小监肚上，那小监立时肚破肠裂。他霎时之间连杀八人，余下四名小监都吓得呆了，不知如何是好。

韦小宝手挺匕首，向他扑去。鳌拜左拳直击而出。韦小宝只感一股劲风扑面而至，气也喘不过来，挥匕首向他手臂插落。鳌拜手臂微斜，避过匕首，随即挥拳击出，打中韦小宝左肩。韦小宝身子飞出，掠过书桌，一交摔在香炉上，登时炉灰飞扬。

康熙始终十分沉着，使开"八卦游龙掌"和鳌拜游斗，但康熙在这路掌法上的造诣颇为有限，更遇到了鳌拜这等天生神勇的猛将，实在并无多大用处。鳌拜被他打中两掌，毫不在乎，左脚踢出，正中康熙右腿。康熙站立不定，向前伏倒。鳌拜吼声如雷，大呼："大伙儿一起死了罢！"双拳往他头顶擂落。康熙和韦小宝扭打日久，斗室中应变的身法甚是熟练迅捷，眼见鳌拜拳到，当即一个打滚，滚到了书桌底下。

鳌拜左腿飞起，踢开书桌，右腿连环，又待往康熙身上踢去，突然间尘灰飞扬，双眼中都是细灰。鳌拜哇哇大叫，双手往眼中乱揉，右腿在身前飞快踢出，生恐敌人乘机来攻。

原来韦小宝见事势紧急，从香炉中抓起两把炉灰，向鳌拜撒去。香灰甚细，一落入鳌拜双眼，立时散开。鳌拜蓦地里左臂上一痛，却是韦小宝投掷匕首，刺不中他胸口要害，却插入了他手臂。这时书房中桌翻凳倒，乱成一团，韦小宝见鳌拜背后有张椅子，正是皇帝平时所坐的龙椅，当即奋力端起青铜香炉，跳上龙椅，对准了鳌拜后脑，奋力砸落。

这香炉是唐代之物，少说也有三十来斤重，鳌拜目不见物，难以闪避，砰的一声响，正中头顶。鳌拜身子一晃，摔倒在地，晕了过去。香炉破裂，鳌拜居然头骨不碎。

康熙大喜，叫道："小桂子，真有你的。"他早已备下牛筋和绳索，忙在倒翻了的书桌抽屉中取将出来，和韦小宝两人合力，把鳌拜手足都绑住了。韦小宝已吓得全身都是冷汗，手足发抖，抽绳索也使不出力气，和康熙两人你瞧瞧我，我瞧瞧你，都是喜悦不胜。

鳌拜不多时便即醒转，大叫："我是忠臣，我无罪！这般阴谋害我，我死也不服。"

韦小宝喝道："你造反！带了刀子来到上书房，罪该万死。"

鳌拜叫道："我没带刀子！"

韦小宝喝道："你身上明明不是带着两把刀子？背上一把，手臂上一把，还敢说没带刀？"韦小宝强词夺理，鳌拜怎辩得他过？何况鳌拜头顶给铜香炉重重一砸，背上和臂上分别插一刀，虽非致命，却也受伤不轻，情急之下，只是气急败坏地大叫大嚷。

康熙见十二名小太监中死剩四人，说道："你们都亲眼瞧见了，鳌拜这厮犯上作乱，竟想杀我。"四个小太监惊魂未定，脸如土色。有一人连称："是，是！"其余三人却一句话也说不出来。

康熙道："你们出去，宣我旨意，召康亲王杰书和索额图二人进来。刚才的事，一句话也不许提起，若有泄露风声，小心你们的脑袋。"四名小太监答应了出去。

鳌拜兀自大叫："冤枉，冤枉！皇上亲手杀我顾命大臣，先帝得知，必不饶你！"

康熙脸色沉了下来，道："想个法儿，叫他不能胡说！"

韦小宝应道："是！"走过去伸出左手，捏住了鳌拜的鼻子。鳌拜张口透气，韦小宝右手拔下他臂上的匕首，往他口中乱刺数下，在地下抓起两把香灰，硬塞在他嘴里。鳌拜喉头荷荷几声，几乎呼吸停闭，那里还说得出话来？韦小宝又拔下他背上的匕首，将一双匕首并排插在书桌上，自己守在鳌拜身旁，倘若见他稍有异动，立即便拔匕首戳他几刀。

（金庸，《鹿鼎记（壹）》）

译文

Kang Xi could see that Trinket and the eunuchs were in serious trouble. He crept round behind Oboi, pulled out his own knife, and stabbed him in the back.

The instant Oboi felt the steel against his skin he flinched and drew in his back. This sent the dagger slightly off course, and it failed to do any serious harm. He threw Trinket down and whirled round, only to see that his new assailant was none other than the Emperor.

Oboi stared at Kang Xi, and Kang Xi leapt back a couple of steps. Oboi let out a great cry, as he finally realized the truth, that the Emperor was plotting to take his life.

Flailing his fists in the air, he leapt into the attack. Kang Xi retreated. Oboi seized two of the eunuchs and knocked their heads together, smashing both of their skulls. At the same time he dealt another of the eunuchs a sharp punch in the chest, and kicked out with his right foot, sending four others tumbling back towards the wall, their sinews torn, their bones broken. Without so much as uttering a cry, they fell dead to the ground. Another eunuch still clung to Oboi's right leg, and Oboi began stamping on him. The eunuch's stomach burst open and his innards spilt on to the floor. In a matter of seconds, Oboi had sent eight opponents to their deaths. The remaining four eunuchs just stood there staring in helpless terror.

Trinket now came at him again, dagger in hand. Oboi struck at him with his left fist. Trinket sensed that the blow coming at him had the force of a thunderbolt. He did not even have time to take a breath. He lunged at Oboi's arm with the dagger. Oboi dodged, and brought his fist down heavily on Trinket's left shoulder, sending him catapulting over the desk. He landed on the brazier that stood on the floor beyond the table, and the ashes went flying up into the air.

Kang Xi had been watching all of this in silence. Now he decided to try his Roving Dragon technique against Oboi. But Kang Xi was a novice in this style, whereas Oboi was a veteran and a ferocious fighter. Kang Xi managed to get home a couple of blows, but they seemed to have no effect. Oboi kicked out with his left foot and struck Kang Xi on the right leg, bringing him crashing down to the floor.

'Die one, die all!' bellowed Oboi, and as he did so he brought down both of his fists with a great thundering smash towards Kang Xi's head. Luckily, in this instance Kang Xi's months of sparring with Trinket paid off. He dodged skilfully, escaped the oncoming blow, and rolled under the desk.

Oboi came after him, kicking the desk away with his left leg. He circled his right leg and was about to land a direct kick on Kang Xi's body, when a great cloud of ash exploded into the air and blew directly into his eyes. Oboi began howling and rubbing his eyes wildly with both hands. He continued to kick out frantically with his right foot, afraid that his enemy would use this occasion to counter-attack.

Trinket had watched the situation deteriorate rapidly. It was he who had grasped two handfuls of ash from the brazier and thrown them into Oboi's face.

The fine particles of ash worked their way quickly into Oboi's eyes. The next thing Oboi felt was a sharp pain in his left arm. Trinket had flung his dagger at the man's chest, but had missed his target. By now the Upper Library was in complete chaos, with chairs and tables lying higgledy-piggledy all over the floor. Trinket spotted one chair right behind Oboi—it was in fact Kang Xi's Dragon chair, and it was upright! He grabbed the brazier, leapt up on to the chair, took aim, and brought the full weight of the brazier smashing down on the back of Oboi's head.

This brazier was almost a thousand years old. It was an antique of the Tang dynasty, and weighed at least thirty catties. Blinded by the ash, Oboi was unable to see it coming, and it landed on his head with an almighty crash. He tottered and fell to the ground unconscious. The brazier lay shattered. Oboi's great head remained intact.

Kang Xi was ecstatic.

'Laurie!' he cried. 'You've saved us all!'

He fumbled about in the drawers of his desk and pulled out some lengths of leather and rope, which he had put there in advance. Then he and Trinket between them bound Oboi's hands and feet. Trinket was now in a cold sweat and trembling too violently to get a proper grip on the rope. He and Kang Xi looked at each other, speechless with joy and excitement.

Oboi soon came round and began shouting:

'I'm a loyal subject! I've done no wrong! This is a wicked plot against me! I'll never give in! I'll fight to the death!'

'Traitor!' cried Trinket in return. 'Coming into the Emperor's Upper Library with a knife! You deserve to die a thousand times over!'

'I never brought a knife!' protested Oboi.

'No!' crowed Trinket. 'Not one, but two—the one in your back, and the one in your arm! Try denying that!'

Oboi was really in no state to argue with Trinket. What with the brazier, and the two knife wounds, he was in no state to do anything more than huff and puff and cry out in protest.

Kang Xi turned to the four eunuchs who were still alive, and said to them: 'You all saw it with your own eyes, didn't you? This traitor Oboi tried to take my life!'

The four eunuchs stood there ashen-faced, still greatly shaken by their recent brush with death. One of them managed to pipe:

'Yes! Yes!'

But the other three stood there in silence.

'You can go now,' ordered Kang Xi. 'I want you to send for Prince Kang and Songgotu. Tell them both to report to me immediately. Not a word of what has just taken place in this room! If any one of you breathes a word of it, I'll have his head off!'

The eunuchs retreated in obedience.

Oboi continued to cry out:

'Justice! Justice! The Emperor himself has tried to take the life of his loyal subject! The Lord above will be my witness! The Lord will not spare you!'

Kang Xi frowned.

'Laurie, find a way of stopping up this man's mouth!' he cried.

'Yes, I will,' said Trinket. He stepped forward and took hold of Oboi's nose with his left hand, pinching it between his fingers. Oboi immediately opened his mouth to take a breath, whereupon Trinket with his right hand drew the dagger from Oboi's arm and rammed the handle of it down his throat several times. Then he took a couple of handfuls of ash from the brazier and stuffed them down Oboi's throat. Oboi began choking noisily, and was only able to breathe with the greatest of difficulty. Then Trinket drew the other dagger from his shoulder and stuck both daggers into the top of Kang Xi's desk. He himself stood beside Oboi, watching over him, ready to plunge both daggers into him again at the slightest sign of any movement.

(Louis Cha, *The Deer and The Cauldron*, translated by John Minford)

第三章

戏剧翻译

戏剧是文学类型的一种，由演员扮演角色，当众表演故事情节以反映社会生活，是以表演为中心的文学、音乐、舞蹈、美术等艺术的综合形式。戏剧分戏曲、话剧、歌剧、舞剧等；按作品类型可分为悲剧、喜剧、正剧等；按体裁又可分为历史剧、现代剧、童话剧等。在现代中国，"戏剧"一词有两种含义：狭义专指以古希腊悲剧和喜剧为开端，在欧洲各国发展起来继而在全世界广泛流行的演出形式，英文为"drama"，中国又称之为话剧；广义还包括东方一些国家、民族的传统舞台演出形式，诸如中国的戏曲、日本的歌舞伎、印度的古典戏剧、朝鲜的唱剧等。戏剧有四个要素：演员、故事、舞台和观众。其中，演员是最重要的元素。不过，作为文学的戏剧，戏剧文本则是最基本的要素，是一台戏的先决条件。在戏剧四要素中，剧本具有一定的独立性。在不演出的状态下，剧本可以作为单独的文学样式进行欣赏。

戏剧翻译具有一定的复杂性和特殊性，戏剧翻译除了要涉及书面文本由源语向目的语转换的语际翻译，还需要考虑语言之外的所有因素（Bassnett, 1985：87）。换句话说，戏剧翻译并非仅仅止步于文字的转换，还需要考虑译文语言的舞台性、视听性、口语性、观众的接受性、语言的动作性等因素。从更加具体的层面看，戏剧翻译涉及如下转换：从一种语言转换成另一种语言（难点在习语、俚语、语气、称呼、反语、俏皮话或双关语）；从一种文化转换成另一种文化（习俗、假象、态度）；从一个时代转换成另一个时代；从一种戏剧风格转换成另一种戏剧风格；从一种类型转换成另一种类型（悲剧转换成喜剧或滑稽剧）；从一种媒体转换成另一种媒体（舞台剧转换成广播剧、电视剧或电影）；从纯戏剧文本转换成音乐剧／摇滚剧、歌剧／舞剧；从书面文本转换成舞台文本；从情感／概念转换成事件；从语言表演转换成非语言表演；从一个演出团体转换成另一个演出团体（受专业训练的专业团体转换成学生或儿童的业余团体）；从一类观众转换成另一类观众（为学校表演的戏剧转换成为聋哑人表演的戏剧）。（孟伟根，2012：6-7）

基于戏剧的特点和戏剧翻译的特殊性，戏剧翻译的批评和赏析主要针对戏剧文本，即剧本。所关注的问题主要涉及：第一，戏剧翻译文本的特点。要明了该剧本是要在舞台上表演还是要在案头阅读，对其翻译文本的语言特色、形式特征等方面的批评和赏析才有根据。第二，戏剧翻译的文化转换。在批评和欣赏戏剧翻译文本的时候，了解戏剧文本的文化特征和交集目的尤为重要。只有在此情况下，才能对译者所采用的翻译策略进行合理的批评和赏析。同时，源语文本的文化背景和目的语受众的文化背景也是批评和欣赏的重要基础。第三，关注戏剧翻译中语言的节奏、韵律的转换。不同的文学系统具有各自独特的诗学特征。中国戏曲中无论是念白还是唱词多以韵文的形式出现，而其翻译作品中则将其处理为素体或者西方诗学中的格律。关注格律的消解或重新创造，一定程度上能够让批评者或赏析者更加深入地了解译者行为、翻译策略甚至翻译政策等细微层面。

本章内容关注戏剧翻译，为了丰富戏剧翻译的欣赏和批评内容，特别设置了英国戏剧汉译和中国戏剧英译两节的内容。同时，为了将翻译拓展到比较文学的视域，本章在选材时注意了材料之间的相关性。英国戏剧选择了莎士比亚的经典作品《罗密欧与朱丽叶》，中国戏剧选择了汤显祖的经典之作《牡丹亭》，涉及戏剧翻译中的主要问题，帮助读者思考和探究"如何译""为何译"等问题，更鼓励批评者和欣赏者从比较文学的范畴深入探究两个经典文本，提高戏剧翻译批评和鉴赏能力。

第一节

莎士比亚经典戏剧的汉译

莎士比亚戏剧涉及当时的重大社会问题，集中表现了人文主义思想，代表了文艺复兴戏剧的最高成就。"他非一代骚人，实属万古千秋。"这是英国作家本·琼森（Ben Jonson）在第一部《莎士比亚全集》扉页上的题诗。这足以证明莎士比亚及其戏剧已经成为世界性的文化符号。莎士比亚的作品内容具有惊人的多样性和极高的娱乐性。此外，时代也进一步成就了莎士比亚。而《莎士比亚全集》的出版则奠定了莎士比亚崇拜这一传统。这些因素使得翻译莎士比亚作品业已成为一种文化现象。由于莎士比亚作品基本都是以诗体写成，还原本真的莎士比亚作品给翻译带来了极大的挑战。莎士比亚作品语言具有时代特点，文化意涵非常丰富，中西的文化差异和道德取向也存在一定的差异，这就给翻译带来了另一方面的巨大挑战。莎士比亚作品的汉译者众多，分布于不同的时代。批评和赏析不同时代译者处理翻译挑战的不同做法，不仅有益于读者在语言层面了解基本翻译方法和技巧，更能够使读者从这些巧妙的省译、改写中去探索翻译的本体性问题，拓展对翻译这一概念的理解。

课前准备

 翻译热身

Act I Scene 4

Romeo If I profane with my unworthiest hand

This holy shrine, the gentle sin is this:

My lips, two blushing pilgrims, ready stand

To smooth that rough touch with a tender kiss.

Juliet Good pilgrim, you do wrong your hand too much,

Which mannerly devotion shows in this,

For saint shave hands that pilgrims' hands do touch,

And palm to palm is holy palmers' kiss.

Romeo Have not saints lips, and holy palmers too?

Juliet Ay, pilgrim, lips that they must use in prayer.

Romeo O, then, dear saint, let lips do what hands do:

They pray, grant thou, lest faith turn to despair.

Juliet Saints do not move, though grant for prayers' sake.

Romeo Then move not, while my prayer's effect I take.

Thus from my lips, by thine, my sin is purged.

Juliet Then have my lips the sin that they have took.

Romeo Sin from my lips?

O trespass sweetly urged!

Give me my sin again.

Juliet You kiss by th'book.

（William Shakespeare, *The Tragedy of Romeo and Juliet*）

参考译文

第一幕　第四场

罗密欧 倘如我这卑贱无比的手掌亵渎了

你神圣的殿堂，我尚有赎罪良方：

我且用这双唇，这对赧颜的香客，

奉上轻吻，安抚那粗鲁的轻狂。

朱丽叶 好信徒，莫过分怪罪你的手掌，

它这样表示虔诚，理所应当；

圣徒的手儿本容许信徒磕碰，

掌心相合与信徒的亲吻同芳。

罗密欧 圣徒与信徒岂不空长了双唇？

朱丽叶 啊，信徒，那本是用来祈祷上苍。

罗密欧 啊，圣徒，那就让这双唇求您开恩，

以唇代手，免使得希望变成绝望。

朱丽叶 圣徒有求必应，但不会屈尊就香。

罗密欧 那您就请勿动玉体，请容我领受恩祥，

借您的朱唇，把我唇间的罪孽洗荡。

朱丽叶 但你唇间的罪过便到我的唇上隐藏。

罗密欧 我唇间的罪过？啊，您这怨愤真棒！

那就让这罪过回到老地方。

朱丽叶 你接吻的理由还真是堂皇。

（威廉·莎士比亚，《罗密欧与朱丽叶》，辜正坤译）

翻译难点聚焦

1. 译文如何传递文化负载词中的信息，例如 "pilgrim" " palmer" "book" 等？

2. 译者是如何保留原文的韵律感的？

3. 译文的可读性如何？译文的表演性如何？

名译赏析

 原作简介

《罗密欧与朱丽叶》（*Romeo and Juliet*）是威廉·莎士比亚著名悲剧作品之一。戏剧讲述了两位青年男女相恋，却因家族仇恨而遭不幸，最终两家和好的故事。该剧在莎士比亚所处的年代颇为流行，与《哈姆雷特》一道成为最常上演的戏剧。莎士比亚使用了富有诗意的戏剧结构，特别是在喜剧和悲剧之间来回切换，增添了紧张气氛。他强化了配角的作用，并使用次要剧情来润泽故事。戏剧因不同的角色而体现出不同的风格，有时因角色的成长而随之改变。例如，随着剧情的发展，罗密欧的话语越来越多地采用了十四行诗的形式。《罗密欧与朱丽叶》被多次改编，在剧场、银幕、音乐剧中上演。

 原文

THE PROLOGUE

[Enter Chorus]

Chorus Two households, both alike in dignity,

In fair Verona, where we lay our scene,

From ancient grudge break to new mutiny,

Where civil blood makes civil hands unclean.

From forth the fatal loins of these two foes

A pair of star-cross'd lovers take their life,

Whose misadventur'd piteous overthrows;

Doth with their death bury their parents' strife.

The fearful passage of their death-mark'd love,

And the continuance of their parents' rage,

Which, but their children's end, nought could remove,

Is now the two hours' traffic of our stage;

The which if you with patient ears attend,

What here shall miss, our toil shall strive to mend.

……

[Enter Romeo]

……

Benvolio Good morrow, cousin.

Romeo Is the day so young?

Benvolio But new struck nine.

Romeo Ay me, sad hours seem long.

Was that my father that went hence so fast?

Benvolio It was. What sadness lengthens Romeo's hours?

Romeo Not having that, which, having, makes them short.

Benvolio In love?

Romeo Out,—

Benvolio Of love?

Romeo Out of her favour where I am in love.

Benvolio Alas, that love, so gentle in his view,

Should be so tyrannous and rough in proof!

Romeo Alas that love, whose view is muffled still,

Should, without eyes, see pathways to his will!

Where shall we dine? O me! What fray was here?

Yet tell me not, for I have heard it all.

Here's much to do with hate, but more with love:

Why, then, O brawling love, O loving hate,

O anything of nothing first create!

O heavy lightness, serious vanity, Misshapen chaos of well-seeming forms,

Feather of lead, bright smoke, cold fire, sick health,

Still-waking sleep that is not what it is!

This love feel I, that feel no love in this.

Dost thou not laugh?

Benvolio No, coz, I rather weep.

Romeo Good heart, at what?

Benvolio At thy good heart's oppression.

Romeo Why, such is love's transgression.

Griefs of mine own lie heavy in my breast,

Which thou wilt propagate, to have it pressed

With more of thine: this love that thou hast shown

Doth add more grief to too much of mine own.

Love is a smoke made with the fume of sighs,

Being purged, a fire sparkling in lovers' eyes,

Being vexed, a sea nourished with loving tears.

What is it else? A madness most discreet,

A choking gall and a preserving sweet.

Farewell, my coz.

（William Shakespeare, *The Tragedy of Romeo and Juliet*）

译文

译文一

开场诗

[致辞者上]

致辞者 话说名都维罗纳，曾有两家

巨族豪门，论声望不分乙甲，

却是宿愿冤家，今日又厮杀，

可怜双双公民手，平添血疤。

运命作耍，两家世仇偏生下

苦命鸳鸯，英年自尽在墓阆。

凄惨惨去也，一曲殉情悲歌，

终换来，交恶双亲和解佳话。

叹双方父母多少年来雷霆斗，

只可惜斗不掉重重恨锁仇枷，

到头来却只灭掉了自家亲娃。

这段伤情遂演成今日台上戏。

看客宽心，大意如今已说罢，

因由细节，还请静听慢品察。

…………

[罗密欧上]

…………

班伏里奥 早安，老兄。

罗密欧 现在还算早吗？

班伏里奥 时钟才敲九点嘛。

罗密欧 唉！心有愁思日月长啊。

刚才匆忙而去的是我父亲吧？

班伏里奥 正是。何种愁思拉长了罗密欧的日月？

罗密欧 愁不能获得可使光阴变短的东西。

班伏里奥 跌进情网了吗？

罗密欧 跌出来了——

班伏里奥 出了情网？

罗密欧 出了她的芳心——我对她徒怀痴念啊！

班伏里奥 唉！没想到爱神表面文质彬彬，

实际上却如此残暴无情！

罗密欧 唉！想不到爱神虽然总是蒙着眼睛，

不用双目，却会把大小道路看个分明！

我们在哪里用餐？哟！这里有过纷争？

不过，别告诉我，其实我早就知道内情。

打斗多出于恨，但更多却出于爱。

爱，爱得天翻地覆；恨，恨得骨肉情深！

啊，一切事物原本是无中生有！

啊，沉重的轻浮，正经的愚蠢，

表面的齐整，混乱的变形，

铅羽，明雾，冷的火焰，病的康宁，

名为睡眠，实则是永远的清醒！

我感觉这是爱，可里面却没有情。

你不会笑我吗？

班伏里奥 不，兄弟，我真想热泪涕零。

罗密欧 好人啊，哭什么呢？

班伏里奥 哭你善心受到如此的欺凌。

罗密欧 唉！这就是爱情误入迷津，

愁肠百结重压在我心庭，

蒙你感同身受，你的悲情

在我太多的忧愁之上再加上

一重愁怨，只令我愁绪倍增。

爱情是声声叹息卷起的烟雾，

烟雾一散，情人眼里便只剩下火星；

恋情受阻，便只见滔滔泪海波横。

还有何辞可喻？最疯狂却又最审慎，

苦，苦到喉哽；甜，甜到钻心。

啊，再见，老兄。

（威廉·莎士比亚，《罗密欧与朱丽叶》，辜正坤译）

译文二

开场诗

[致辞者上]

致辞者 故事发生在维罗纳名城，

有两家门第相当的巨族，

累世的宿怨激起了新争，

鲜血把市民的白手污渎。

是命运注定这两家仇敌，

生下了一双不幸的恋人，

他们的悲惨凄凉的陨灭，

和解了他们交恶的尊亲。

这一段生生死死的恋爱，

还有那两家父母的嫌隙，

把一对多情的儿女杀害，

演成了今天这一本戏剧。

交代过这几句挈领提纲，

请诸位耐着心细听端详。

·············

[罗密欧上]

·············

班伏里奥 早安，兄弟。

罗密欧 天还是这样早吗？

班伏里奥 刚敲过九点钟。

罗密欧 唉！在悲哀里度过的时间似乎是格外长的。急忙忙地走过去的那个人，不就是我的父亲吗？

班伏里奥 正是。什么悲哀使罗密欧的时间过得这样长？

　　罗密欧 因为我缺少了可以使时间变得短促的东西。

　　班伏里奥 你跌进恋爱的网里了吗？

　　罗密欧 我还在门外徘徊——

　　班伏里奥 在恋爱的门外？

　　罗密欧 我不能得到我的意中人的欢心。

　　班伏里奥 唉！想不到爱神的外表这样温柔，实际上却是如此残暴！

　　罗密欧 唉！想不到爱神蒙着眼睛，却会一直闯入人们的心灵！

　　我们在什么地方吃饭？

　　哎哟！又是谁在这儿打过架了？可是不必告诉我，我早就知道了。

　　这些都是怨恨造成的后果，可是爱情的力量比它要大过许多。

　　啊，吵吵闹闹的相爱，亲亲热热的怨恨！

　　啊，无中生有的一切！啊，沉重的轻浮，严肃的狂妄，整齐的混乱，铅铸的羽毛，光明的烟雾，寒冷的火焰，憔悴的健康，永远觉醒的睡眠，否定的存在！我感觉到的爱情正是这么一种东西，可是我并不喜欢这一种爱情。你不会笑我吗？

　　班伏里奥 不，兄弟，我倒真有点儿想哭。

　　罗密欧 好人，为什么呢？

　　班伏里奥 因为瞧着你善良的心受到这样的痛苦。

　　罗密欧 唉！这就是爱情的错误，我自己已经有太多的忧愁重压在我的心头，你对我表示的同情，徒然使我在太多的忧愁之上再加一重忧愁。爱情是叹息吹起的一阵烟，恋人的眼中有它净化了的火星，恋人的眼泪是它激起的波涛。它又是最智慧的疯狂，哽喉的苦味，吃不到嘴的蜜糖。再见，兄弟。

　　　　　　　　　　（威廉·莎士比亚，《莎士比亚悲剧集》，朱生豪译）

赏析思路点拨

首先，关于开场诗。虽然开场诗的两个译本在形式和内容上很好地传递了原文的内核，但其风格存在一定的差异。

读完译文一中的开场诗，多数读者能想到曹雪芹在《红楼梦》第五回中所写的十二支红楼梦曲子。从行文节奏来看，该译文改变了原文的节奏。译文一中开场诗的韵律让中国读者读起来倍感亲切，朗朗上口。从所用意象来看，译者采用了"换例法"，将"鸳鸯""雷霆"等意象植入其中。译者如此译的目的，除了希望更多地靠近读者之外，也许还有提升中国读者自身文化意识、加强文化身份认同的考量。

译文二虽然是开场诗，但更有叙事的味道。因其缺少节奏，译文二抒情的意味有所减弱。不过莎士比亚戏剧所属的英国文学，其诗学长久以来以叙事为主导。译作恰好贴合了原作的诗学规范。

因此，我们不能对译文一和译文二进行非好即坏的评判，而是应该回到具体的历史语境、诗学语境中，品析不同译笔的精妙。

其次，关于"O brawling love, O loving hate"。译文一将其译为："爱，爱得天翻地覆；恨，恨得骨肉情深！"译文二将其译为："啊，吵吵闹闹的相爱，亲亲热热的怨恨！"二者都围绕着"爱"与"恨"两个主要元素展开。我们不妨回归原文"O brawling love，O loving hate"。原文中"love"与"hate"为名词，而"brawling"和"loving"两个现在分词赋予了两个名词动态感。这不由得让人想起弗雷德里克·威尔（Frederic Will）的一段话："I like to think of them (original texts) as participial, rather than nounlike or verblike. ... translators can make this substance clear, only by enacting it. ...literary originals, are participles. They enact the nouns they are by becoming verbs. They become verbs by enacting the nouns they are." (Will, 1993)

既然原作犹如分词，译者可以激活其名词性质，使其变为名词，显示出静态，亦可激活其动词性质，将其变为动词，显示出动态，那么，此处就不难理解译文一和译文二之间的差异了。译文一贴合原文，将"爱"与"恨"的名词形式保留，提取出分词"brawling"的动词意味，进而通过重复，提取出名词"爱"的动词意味，使得整句话荡气回肠。译文二则直接将"love"与"hate"动词化，将其译为"相爱"与"怨恨"，"brawling"和"loving"则起修饰作用，整句话的动态感大大减弱。不过，这只是在单句的层面上探讨。正如巴斯奈特（Susan Bassnett）强调的一样，译者的任务就是找到原作的"种子"，并试图将其移植到目标文化的土壤中，让其生根、发芽、开花、结果。译文一和译文二的译者不正是如此吗？因此，笔者鼓励读者将此句置于更广的文本语境、文化语境中去仔细品味，或许还能获得更多的体会与收获。

课后思考

1. 莎士比亚戏剧翻译如何呈现原文的韵律特点？

2. 戏剧翻译如何实现语言的动态力量？

3. 两个译本有哪些不同之处？这些不同之处哪些适合舞台上表演，哪些适合案头阅读？

延伸阅读

 原文

Juliet How cam'st thou hither, tell me, and wherefore?

The orchard walls are high and hard to climb,

And the place death, considering who thou art,

If any of my kinsmen find thee here.

Romeo With love's light wings did I o'er-perch these walls,

For stony limits cannot hold love out,

And what love can do that dares love attempt:

Therefore thy kinsmen are no stop to me.

Juliet If they do see thee, they will murder thee.

Romeo Alack, there lies more peril in thine eye

Than twenty of their swords: look thou but sweet,

And I am proof against their enmity.

Juliet I would not for the world they saw thee here.

Romeo I have night's cloak to hide me from their eyes,

And but thou love me, let them find me here:

My life were better ended by their hate,

Than death prorogued, wanting of thy love.

Juliet By whose direction found'st thou out this place?

Romeo By love, that first did prompt me to enquire:

He lent me counsel and I lent him eyes.

I am no pilot, yet wert thou as far

As that vast shore washed with the farthest sea,

I should adventure for such merchandise.

Juliet Thou know'st the mask of night is on my face,

Else would a maiden blush bepaint my cheek

For that which thou hast heard me speak tonight.

Fain would I dwell on form, fain, fain deny

What I have spoke: but farewell compliment!

Dost thou love me? I know thou wilt say 'Ay',

And I will take thy word. Yet if thou swear'st,

Thou mayst prove false: at lovers' perjuries

They say Jove laughs. O gentle Romeo,

If thou dost love, pronounce it faithfully:

Or if thou think'st I am too quickly won,

I'll frown and be perverse and say thee nay,

So thou wilt woo, but else, not for the world.

In truth, fair Montague, I am too fond,

And therefore thou mayst think my behaviour light:

But trust me, gentleman, I'll prove more true

Than those that have more coying to be strange.

I should have been more strange, I must confess,

But that thou overheard'st, ere I was ware,

My true love's passion: therefore pardon me,

And not impute this yielding to light love,

Which the dark night hath so discovered.

Romeo Lady, by yonder blessed moon I vow,

That tips with silver all these fruit-tree tops —

Juliet O, swear not by the moon, th'inconstant moon,

That monthly changes in her circlèd orb,

Lest that thy love prove likewise variable.

Romeo What shall I swear by?

Juliet Do not swear at all:

Or if thou wilt, swear by thy gracious self,

Which is the god of my idolatry,

And I'll believe thee.

Romeo If my heart's dear love,—

Juliet Well, do not swear. Although I joy in thee,

I have no joy of this contract to night:

It is too rash, too unadvised, too sudden,

Too like the lightning, which doth cease to be

Ere one can say 'It lightens'. Sweet, goodnight!

This bud of love, by summer's ripening breath,

May prove a beauteous flower when next we meet.

Goodnight, goodnight, as sweet repose and rest

Come to thy heart as that within my breast!

Romeo O, wilt thou leave me so unsatisfied?

Juliet What satisfaction canst thou have tonight?

Romeo Th'exchange of thy love's faithful vow for mine.

Juliet I gave thee mine before thou didst request it:

And yet I would it were to give again.

Romeo Wouldst thou withdraw it? For what purpose, love?

Juliet But to be frank and give it thee again.

And yet I wish but for the thing I have.

My bounty is as boundless as the sea,

My love as deep: the more I give to thee,

The more I have, for both are infinite.

I hear some noise within. Dear love, adieu!—[*Nurse*] *calls within*

Anon, good nurse!—Sweet Montague, be true.

Stay but a little, I will come again.

[*Exit, above*]

Romeo O blessèd, blessèd night! I am afeard,

Being in night, all this is but a dream,

Too flattering-sweet to be substantial.

[*Enter Juliet, above*]

Juliet Three words, dear Romeo, and goodnight indeed.

If that thy bent of love be honourable,

Thy purpose marriage, send me word tomorrow,

By one that I'll procure to come to thee,

Where and what time thou wilt perform the rite,

And all my fortunes at thy foot I'll lay,

And follow thee my lord throughout the world.

[*Nurse calls*] *Within* 'Madam!'

Juliet I come, anon.— But if thou mean'st not well,

I do beseech thee,—

[*Nurse calls*] *Within* 'Madam!'

By and by, I come.—

To cease thy strife, and leave me to my grief.

Tomorrow will I send.

Romeo So thrive my soul—

Juliet A thousand times goodnight!

Exit, [*above*]

Romeo A thousand times the worse, to want thy light.

Love goes toward love as schoolboys from their books,

But love from love, towards school with heavy looks.

（William Shakespeare, *The Tragedy of Romeo and Juliet*）

译文

朱丽叶 你怎么进来的，告诉我，来此何为？

园墙高峻，多么难于攀登；

想想你的身份，若我的家人

发现你的踪影，你岂能死里逃生！

罗密欧 凭借爱的轻翼我飞越高墙，

区区石垣焉能遮挡纯爱深深；

爱既敢爱，就敢为所欲为，

你的家人岂挡得住我爱的飞奔。

朱丽叶 他们若发现你，一定会取你性命。

罗密欧 唉！你眼中的雄威远胜他们

二十柄刀剑；你但能眼角传情，

我便如铁甲防身，何惧他们的仇恨？

朱丽叶 我绝不愿让他们发现你的踪影。

罗密欧 凭夜幕遮护，他们看不见我的身形。

只要你爱我，我宁肯他们知我在此；

与其得不到你的爱而苟延年命，

倒不如爽快地在仇人剑下亡生。

朱丽叶 你居然找到这儿，是谁的指引？

罗密欧 是爱神，仗着他的鼓动我才四处探询；

凭借了我的双眼，承蒙他指点迷津。

我虽然领航乏术，却也愿不避艰辛，

扬帆出海，找寻你这无价之宝，

哪怕你远在无边无际的天涯海滨。

朱丽叶 你知道，若非有黑夜作帘栊，

当此夜，你正亲聆我的心衷，

必看到我脸上飞来处女的羞红。

我真想循规蹈矩，说我刚才是言不

由衷。可是罢了，繁文缛节之风！

若真对我情深意浓？你须答："浓"；

我情愿信你的话；可你的海誓山盟，

或恐是欺诈；人道，恋人们变节不忠，

天神却笑脸相容。温柔的罗密欧啊！

你要是真爱我，就坦言，开诚布公；

你若嫌我太快地就向你委身相从，

那我就皱眉，让拒绝显摆威风，让你

再来追求；否则我绝难以"不"相送。

英俊的蒙太古啊，我真是过分痴情，

或使你觉得我的言行是轻浮的举动；

可相信我，先生，我将向你证明，

我的真诚比故作矜持者的更加郑重。

我承认，我本该加倍地假作端庄，不料

你乘我不备，偷听到我心曲流溢胸中；

请原谅我，休将我看作是轻率相从，

休把我的承诺视为投怀送抱，

怪只怪天机不慎泄漏于夜空。

罗密欧 小姐，我发誓，凭着那天际月轮皎皎，

素辉如银，正染亮果园千树林梢——

朱丽叶 啊！起誓休对月轮，月无恒轮可靠，

月巡周天，阴晴圆缺，月月知多少；

指月为誓，只怕你情意变，楚暮秦朝。

罗密欧 那我以何起誓为好？

朱丽叶 何须起誓；

你若真有此心，证物自以贵体为妙，

我对君身，敬若神道仙曹，

你的话，我必信奉在心梢。

罗密欧 若是我出自深心的大爱——

朱丽叶 别，别起誓。我虽对你心有所属，

却不喜私订终身在此宵；

这太鲁莽、轻率，如雷霆电扫，

倏然轰哮，不等人道："雷来了！"

即转眼似云灭烟消。晚安吧，好人儿！

这爱蕾初结，有夏日熏风吹撩，

他日邂逅，必绽出叶绿花娇。

晚安，晚安！愿我们两人的心儿

都变得同样恬甜美好。

罗密欧 啊！你就这样离去，不让我心满意足吗？

朱丽叶 你今夜还要如何满足呢？

罗密欧 你还没有和我交换海誓山盟。

朱丽叶 我已经不求而自献上深爱，

我但愿能重新表白这一片痴心。

罗密欧 你是想收回承诺？为什么？爱人。

朱丽叶 只为了慷慨地再献衷情。

我要的只是我现有的爱：

我的慷慨像大海浩渺无垠，

我的爱也海一样深，越给你

我越富有，两者无穷无尽。

里面有人叫我；亲爱的，再会吧！——

幕内［奶妈］呼唤

就来了，好奶妈！——温柔的蒙太古，

你要对我真心。我还会来。稍等稍等。

罗密欧啊，幸福之夜！但我又心神不宁，

只恐夜中的一切也许只是梦境，

如此称心快意，怎能梦里成真！

（威廉·莎士比亚，《罗密欧与朱丽叶》，辜正坤译）

第二节

汤显祖经典戏剧的英译

不同于肇始于古希腊时期的西方戏剧，在中国，"生活的'泛戏剧化'是戏剧美的流散，阻碍了戏剧美在艺术意义上的凝聚，造成了戏剧本身的姗姗来迟"（余秋雨，2013：12）。中国戏剧从巫术仪式到角抵小戏，从南戏到杂剧，从元剧到传奇，逐步走向成熟和顶峰。传奇时代，太仓人魏良辅，融合南北，改革声腔，创立了昆山水磨调，低回婉转，清丽悠远。这极大地促进了明清传奇的创作。从16世纪末到17世纪末可谓中国戏剧丰收的世纪（余秋雨，2013：182），其中最杰出的代表少不了《牡丹亭》。

汤显祖是晚明文坛上的重要人物，是世界级的文化名人，其作品"临川四梦"轰动全国，深刻影响了戏剧界、思想界和普通民众的精神生活。居四梦之首的《牡丹亭》"伤感而又温暖，凄绝而又粹美，上承《西厢》之娟媚，下启《红楼》之清丽，是中国文学史上卓然特立的经典"（李建军，2016：13-14）。

从1939年阿克顿（H. Acton）选译的《牡丹亭·春香闹学》开始，汤显祖的

《牡丹亭》便开启了其近八十年的漫长英译历程。众多译本中不乏经典之作。针对翻译昆曲剧本形式如曲牌、唱词、念白方面的挑战，以及内容方面如典故、俗语等的挑战，这些译者都采取了各自的方式应对。批评和赏析这些经典译者的作品，不仅能够使读者了解语际书写如何发生，更能够激发他们进一步探究此等书写为何发生。

课前准备

 **翻译热身**

第一出　标目

【蝴蝶花】（末上）忙处抛人闲处住。百计思量，没个为欢处。白日消磨肠断句，世间只有情难诉。玉茗堂前朝复暮。红烛迎人，俊得江山助。但是相思莫相负，牡丹亭上三生路。

【汉宫春】杜宝黄堂，生丽娘小姐，爱踏春阳。感梦书生折柳，竟为情伤。写真留记，葬梅花道馆凄凉。三年上，有梦梅柳子，于此赴高唐。果尔回生定配，赴临安取试，寇起淮扬。正把杜公围困，小姐惊惶。教柳郎行探，反遭疑激恼平章。风流况，施行正苦，报中状元郎。

············

第十出　惊梦

【绕地游】（旦上）梦回莺啭，乱煞年光遍。人立小庭深院。（贴）炷尽沉烟，抛残绣线，恁今春关情似去年？

【乌夜啼】（旦）晓来望断梅关，宿妆残。（贴）你侧着宜春髻子恰凭栏。（旦）剪不断，理还乱，闷无端。（贴）已分付催花莺燕借春看。（旦）春香，可曾叫人扫除花径？（贴）分付了。（旦）取镜台、衣服来。（贴取镜台衣服上）云髻罢梳还对镜，罗衣欲换更添香。镜台、衣服在此。

（汤显祖，《牡丹亭》）

 参考译文

SCENE ONE: Legend

PROLOGUE SPEAKER:

I. By busy world rejected, in my own world of retreat

I pondered a hundred schemes

Finding joy in none.

Daylong I polished verses for the bowel's torture

for the telling of "love, in all life hardest to tell."

Dawns warmed and twilights shadowed my

White Camellia Hall

till "with red candle I welcomed friends"—

and always "the hills and streams raised high my powers."

Let me only keep faith with the history of this longing, of the road

that led through three incarnations to the peony pavilion.

To the Perfect Du Bao

was born a daughter Bridal,

who longed to walk in the spring light.

Roused by dream of young scholar

who broke off branch from willow

she pined and died of love

but left her portrait memorial

in the Apricot Blossom Shrine where her cold grave lay.

Three years passed

and a scholar, named Liu for "willow,"

Mengmei for "dream of apricot,"

Found at this Gaotang his dream of love.

Then in truth she returned to life and became his bride.

But when the examinations took him to Lin'an

Bandits arose at Huaiyang,

besieged Perfect Du

and filled Bridal with fear.

Sent by her to seek news

Liu raised doubts and anger

in the mind of Du Bao, now First Minister.

A romantic tale

but a tale whose execution

almost cause the execution

of Prize Candidate Liu Mengmei,

announced in the nick of time.

......

SCENE TEN: The Interrupted Dream

BRIDAL DU:

I. From dream returning, orioles coil their song

through all the brilliant riot of the new season

to listener in tiny leaf-locked court.

SPRING FRAGRANCE:

Burnt to ashes the aloes wood

cast aside the broidering thread,

no longer able as in past years

to quiet stirrings of the spring's passions.

BRIDAL:

Like one "eyeing the apricot flower to slake her thirst"

at dawn, cheeks blurred with the last night's rouge,

I gaze at Apricot Blossom Pass.

FRAGRANCE:

The coils of your hair

dressed with silken swallows in the mode of spring

Tilt aslant as you lean

across the balustrade.

BRIDAL:

Rootless ennui,

"where are the scissors can cut

the comb can untangle this grief?"

FRAGRANCE:

I have told the oriole and the swallow

to leave their urging of the flowers

and with spring as their excuse

to come look at you.

DRIDAL：

Fragrance, have you given orders for the paths to be swept?

FRAGRANCE:

Yes.

BRIDAL:

Now bring my mirror and my gown.

FRAGRANCE:(reenters with these)

"Could coiffure set to perfection

still she questions the mirror,

Robe of gauze soon to be changed

still she adds sweetening incense."

I've brought your mirror and gown.

（Tang Xianzu, *The Peony Pavilion*, translated by Cyril Birch）

翻译难点聚焦

1. 原作的情节是通过何种手段体现的，而译者是如何在译文中凸显情节的？
2. 原作中汤显祖引用了典故，译者在译文中是如何处理的？
3. 译者是如何处理曲牌名的？

名译赏析

原作简介

《牡丹亭》，原名《还魂记》，又名《杜丽娘慕色还魂记》，是明代剧作家汤显祖的代表作，描写了大家闺秀杜丽娘和书生柳梦梅的生死之恋。与《西厢记》《窦娥冤》《长生殿》合称为中国四大古典戏剧。

故事梗概如下：南宋时期南安太守杜宝之独女杜丽娘，在学罢家庭教师陈最良的诗经《关雎》一课之后，居然动了怀春之情，于梦中邂逅一书生，醒后因思念梦中情郎，郁郁寡欢而亡。杜宝赴淮阳升任安抚使前，将杜丽娘葬后花园梅树下，并修梅花庵，嘱一道姑守之。

杜丽娘的灵魂来到地府，判官却查出她命不该绝，命定有一段姻缘，便放她返回人间。后书生柳梦梅赴京赶考，因故寓于梅花庵，并因此与杜丽娘游魂相遇相知。其后杜丽娘指使柳梦梅掘坟，开其棺木复活，两人结为夫妻。随后柳梦梅赶考并高中状元。

柳梦梅受杜丽娘之托，往淮阳见杜宝时，杜宝不相信杜丽娘复活，欲将柳梦梅除之而后快，判处就地正法。在紧急关头，知情者急告杜宝以实情，并指出柳梦梅乃新科状元，不宜杀之。杜宝却怀疑柳梦梅是妖怪，上奏皇帝。

此后该案归朝廷处理，皇帝查明真相，柳梦梅终于与杜丽娘相聚，杜宝也与女婿尽释前嫌，全剧欢喜而终。

原文与译文

没乱里春情难遣	From turbulent heart these springtime thoughts of love will not be banished	Why, this sudden torrent of emotions brought on by the season:
蓦地里怀人幽怨	— O with what suddenness Comes this secret discontent!	Are they passions, are they yearnings? — I know not the reason.
则为俺生小婵娟 拣名门一例一例神仙眷	I was a pretty child, and so of equal eminence must the family be truly immortals, no less To receive me in marriage.	Born I was into this eminent family, whose tradition Is to marry me into a family of equally high position.

甚良缘 把青春抛的远	But for what grand alliance is this springtime of my youth So cast away?	But waiting indefinitely for such a union ideal Is quietly wasting away my golden years.
俺的睡情谁见 则索因循腼腆 想幽梦谁边	What eyes may light upon my sleeping form? My only course this coy delaying but in secret dreams by whose side do I lie?	No one knows my dreams that seem to be all to real Hidden as they are as my untold fears? Only in dreams can I let my mind freely wander,
和春光暗流转 迁延 这衷怀那处言 淹煎 泼残生除问天	Shadowed against spring's glory I twist and turn. Lingering where to reveal my true desires! Suffering This wasting, Where but to Heaven shall my lament be made!	Yet dreams, with the passing of spring, only wither. Yes, wither and wither, my dreams — to whom could I tell? How in secret I grieve; only Heaven knows my hell!
（汤显祖，2016：23）	（Birch，2002：46—47）	（汪班，2009：277）

赏析思路点拨

　　上文选自《牡丹亭》中《山坡羊》这一经典段落。《山坡羊》曲牌的风格气氛低沉，多用于悲愤、凄切、伤情、怨恨等剧情场合（王守泰，1994：524）。此段唱词为杜丽娘梦醒后怅然若失发出的感叹。作为名门闺秀，杜丽娘婚姻无法自主，春情不能表露，终日只能深居闺房，不能踏入花园半步，其情感被当时的礼教长期压抑。就整出惊梦的情节而言，《山坡羊》全属心理描写，杜丽娘的悲愤、凄切、叛逆全然迸发。

白之（Birch）在处理该曲首句"没乱里春情难遣，蓦地里怀人幽怨"的时候，显得比较平铺直叙，"From turbulent heart these springtime thoughts of love will not be banished"（心绪烦乱，春情无法排遣）。其中的情感并不明显，直到"——O with what suddenness/Comes this secret discontent!"这里才通过"O"和句末的感叹号凸显了些许情感，然而这种情感并非悲愤、凄切、伤情，而是一种"突然"。

而汪班译本，开篇即以"Why"发问，"Why, this sudden torrent of emotions brought on by the season"（春天为何带来这突然纷乱的心绪），随后将问题细化，"Are they passions, are they yearnings?"（是情？是欲？），最后得出结论："——I know not the reason."设问而无解这一手段形成了强烈的冲击，体现出一种悲愤、无奈的感情。

第二处，"甚良缘，把青春抛的远"集中体现了悲愤之情。白之的处理是"But for what grand alliance/is this springtime of my youth/So cast away?"其中，"cast away"为"throw away""reject"之意，有快刀斩乱麻的效果。但这样缩短了审美体验，从而弱化了悲愤、怨恨的情感。而汪班的处理"But waiting indefinitely for such a union ideal/Is quietly wasting away my golden years"中，"waiting for"的使用，增加了时间的效果，延长了读者的审美体验，凸显了杜丽娘等待所谓门当户对的良缘这一过程的漫长。而"quietly wasting my golden years"中"wasting"是一个漫长的过程，再加上"quietly"的使用，更加凸显出等待所谓良缘这一过程无声无息地侵蚀了杜丽娘的青春年华。这种延长时间、强调滴水穿石的手法，使得悲愤、凄切甚至怨恨等感情在此处表现得淋漓尽致。与此处情感表现手法类似的还有"迁延"与"淹煎"。白之的手段比较直接，"lingering"和"suffering"虽然在情感上的表现非常强烈，但是从声音效果来看，在体现该曲牌低沉的气氛方面，则不如汪班的重复手法："Yet dreams, with the passing of spring, only wither./ Yes, wither and wither, my dreams — to whom could I tell?"通过对单个词的重复，达到情感绵长的效果。《山坡羊》属于南曲的曲牌，其风格较北曲来说更加温婉绵长。白之的"lingering"和"suffering"其实更适合北曲的风格，而汪班的"only wither./Yes, wither and wither"更符合南曲曲牌的温婉绵长之风格。

课后思考

1. 中国传统戏曲外译时，是否有必要保留原作的韵律？如果无法保留，有什么样的应对策略？

2. 如何保留戏曲曲词文化方面的异质性？

延伸阅读

原文

"莺逢日暖歌声滑，人遇风情笑口开。一径落花随水入，今朝阮肇到天台。"小生顺路儿跟着杜小姐回来，怎生不见？〔回看介〕呀，小姐，小姐！〔旦作惊起介〕〔相见介〕〔生〕小生那一处不寻访小姐来，却在这里！〔旦作斜视不语介〕〔生〕恰好花园内，折取垂柳半枝。姐姐，你既淹通书史，可作诗以赏此柳枝乎？〔旦作惊喜，欲言又止介〕〔背想〕这生素昧平生，何因到此？〔生笑介〕小姐，咱爱杀你哩！

【山桃红】则为你如花美眷，似水流年，是答儿闲寻遍。在幽闺自怜。小姐，和你那答儿讲话去。〔旦作含笑不行〕〔生作牵衣介〕〔旦低问〕那边去？〔生〕转过这芍药栏前，紧靠着湖山石边。〔旦低问〕秀才，去怎的？〔生低答〕和你把领扣松，衣带宽，袖梢儿揾着牙儿苫也，则待你忍耐温存一晌眠。〔旦作羞〕〔生前抱〕〔旦推介〕〔合〕是那处曾相见，相看俨然，早难道这好处相逢无一言？

（汤显祖，《牡丹亭》）

LIU MENGMEI: As song of oriole purls in warmth of sun,

so smiling lips open to greet romance.

Tracing my path by petals borne on stream,

I find the Peach Blossom Source of my desire.

I came along this way with Miss Du — how is it that she is not with me now? (*He looks behind him and sees her*) Ah, Miss Du!

(*She rises, startled from sleep, and*

Greets him. He continues)

So this is where you were — I was looking for you everywhere. (*She glances shyly at him, but does not speak*) I just chanced to break off this brunch from a weeping willow in the garden. You are so deeply versed in works of literature, I should like you to compose a poem to honor it.

(*She starts in surprised delight and opens her lips to speak,*

but checks herself)

BRIDAL(Aside): I have never seen this young man in my life — what is he doing here?

LIU(smiling at her): Lady, I am dying of love for you!

VIII. With the flowering of your beauty

as the river of years rolls past,

everywhere I have searched for you

pining secluded in your chamber.

Lady, come with me just over there where we can talk.

(She gives him a shy smile, but refuse to

move. He tries to draw her by the sleeve)

BRIDAL (*in a low voice*): Where do you mean?

LIU: There, just beyond this railing peony-lined

against the mound of weathered Taihu rocks.

BRIDAL (*in a low voice*): But sir, what do you mean to do?

LIU(*also in a low voice*): Open the fastening at your neck

loose the girdle at your waist,

while you

screening your eyes with your sleeve,

while teeth clenched on the fabric as if against pain,

bear with me patiently a while

then drift into gentle slumber.

(BRIDAL turns away, blushing. LIU advances

to take her in his arms, but she resists him.)

LIU, BRIDAL: Somewhere at some past time you and I met.

Now we behold each other in solemn awe

but do not say

in this lovely place we should meet and speak no word.

(LIU exits, carrying off BRIDAL by force)

（Tang Xianzu, *The Peony Pavilion*, translated by Cyril Birch）

第四章

散文翻译

　　散文注重文学性，"散文文学性的主要特征是……风格多样，意境悠远，情感丰富，题材广泛，艺术因素浓烈，尤其是注重美学上的效果；在艺术追求上，讲究模仿现实，虚构事实，高度想象和大胆创造"（赵秀明、赵张进，2010：10），给读者赏心悦目的审美体验。散文的"形散而意不散"，使其行文有着明显的特征，"散文讲究句式长短开阖，跌宕起伏，音节奇偶相间，轻重交错。这种文体特征译者不可不辨"（曹明伦，2004：90）。

　　散文翻译也要注意文学性在译文中的再现，注重再现原文的意义和语言的优美。许渊冲提出了译诗的"三美"原则，并认为应首先注重意美，然后才是音美，最后是形美（许渊冲，1987：70）。这对于散文翻译也是适用的，既然散文是"美文"，那么，首先要注意意义的传达，其次要保留散文语言的节奏美，最后还要尽可能保留原文形式。总之，散文翻译需要考虑的方面和诗歌翻译比较类似，两者都是文学性的语言表达，除了含义准确，还有更高的翻译要求。

　　基于散文的特点，其翻译对译者本身就提出了具备一定文学素养的要求，翻译时不仅要传达意义，还要传达出"美感"。具体来说，在翻译中应当注意以下几点：一，再现原文的"美"，比如意美、音美、形美。在这个过程中要有取舍，为保留形式美，在不影响大局的情况下适当省略个别词句是可以考虑的。二，语句流畅，再现原文节奏，可以适当拆分或者组合词句。三，关注修辞的翻译。排比、比喻、拟人、重复等修辞手法在散文中很常见，是否再现原文中的修辞效果是衡量译文优劣的重要标准。四，注重散文风格的再现。散文题材众多，不同的题材具有不同的行文风格，或者闲适，或者激昂，等等。在翻译时，用词一定要选择和原文风格最相近的，从而和原文风格实现统一。

　　本章的内容关注散文的翻译，为丰富散文翻译欣赏和批评，设置了两小节内容，分别选择对中国现代散文英译和英美现代散文汉译进行分析。通过对比原文和不同的译本，提高读者对散文翻译的赏"美"能力，引导读者思考提高翻译散文的能力可以从哪些方面入手，哪些方面是可以注意的，前人的翻译为我们提供了怎样的借鉴。

第一节

中国现代散文英译

　　散文这个名称是在五四新文学革命之后才确定下来的，其表达形式较为自由。现代散文和古代散文有一定的继承关系，但也有很大不同，现代散文在经历五四运动后，受到新思想的影响，在个性解放的大背景下，表现出和古代散文不同的特点（俞元桂，1988：1–3）。中国散文发展至今，经历了几个阶段，出现了鲁迅、朱自清、冰心、艾青等散文大家。翻译中国现代散文，可以让外国读者欣赏中国的文学之美，传播中国人的思想，达到文化交流的目的。本节选择了朱自清的《匆匆》《背影》以及柯灵的《巷》进行分析，重点对朱自清的两篇散文作品进行译本对比赏析，让读者从散文的特点出发，观察学习翻译大家是如何将散文原文的"美"融入译文的。朱自清的语言朴实，柯灵的《巷》频繁使用四字成语，排比等修辞手法也比较常用。在这样的情况下，译者是如何保留原文的风格的？原文、译文都能带来"美"的享受，读者可在阅读中分析遣词造句，进而思考如何提升自我的文学素养，扎实自己的文学功底。

课前准备

翻译热身

　　燕子去了，有再来的时候；杨柳枯了，有再青的时候；桃花谢了，有再开的时候。但是，聪明的，你告诉我，我们的日子为什么一去不复返呢？——是有人偷了他们罢：那是谁？又藏在何处呢？是他们自己逃走了罢——现在又到了哪里呢？

（朱自清，《匆匆》）

参考译文

译文一

If swallows go away, they will come back again. If willows wither, they will turn green again. If peaces shed their blossoms, they will flower again. But, tell me, you the wise, why should our days go by never to return? Perhaps they have been stolen by someone. But who could it be and where could he hide them? Perhaps they have just run away by themselves. But where could they be at the present moment?

（张培基译）

译文二

The swallows may go, but they will return another day; the willows may whither, but they will turn green again; the peach blossoms may fade and fall, but they will bloom again. You who are wiser than I, tell me, then: why is it that the days, once gone, never again return? Are they stolen by someone? Then, by whom? And where are they hidden? Or do they run away by themselves? Then, where are they now?

（葛浩文译）

译文三

Swallow may have gone, but there is a time of return; willow trees may have died back, but there is a time of regreening; peach blossoms may have fallen, but they will bloom again. Now, you the wise, tell me, why should our days leave us, never to return? — If they had been stolen by someone, who could it be? Where could he hide then? If they had made the escape themselves, then where could they stay at the moment?

（朱纯深译）

翻译难点聚焦

1. 如何再现排比句的韵律美?
2. 反问句应如何翻译?
3. 译文是否再现了原文的节奏?

名译赏析

 原作简介

感叹时光匆匆流逝的文学作品比比皆是,劝导大家珍惜时间的名言警句也层出不穷。朱自清的《匆匆》思考了时间的含义,时间走得匆匆还一去不复返,那么来到人世间到底有着怎样的意义呢?这篇散文写于 1922 年 3 月,正值五四运动落潮之际,朱自清对当时的现实感到失望,心情苦闷,这让他有感而发,开始思考时间和人生。

原文

在逃去如飞的日子里,在千门万户的世界里的我能做些什么呢?只有徘徊罢了,只有匆匆罢了;在八千多日的匆匆里,除徘徊外,又剩些什么呢?过去的日子如轻烟,被微风吹散了,如薄雾,被初阳蒸融了;我留着些什么痕迹呢?我何曾留着像游丝样的痕迹呢?我赤裸裸来到这世界,转眼间也将赤裸裸的回去罢?但不能平的,为什么偏要白白走这一遭啊?

你聪明的,告诉我,我们的日子为什么一去不复返呢?

(朱自清,《匆匆》)

译文

译文一

Living in this world with its fleeting days and teeming millions, what can I do but waver and wander and live a transient life? What have I been doing during the 8,000 fleeting days except wavering and wandering? The bygone days, like wisps of smoke, have been dispersed by gentle winds, and, like thin mists, have been evaporated by the rising sun. What traces have I left behind? No, nothing, not even gossamer-like traces. I have come to this world stark naked, and in the twinkling of an eye, I am to go back as stark naked as ever. However, I am taking it very much to heart: why should I be made to pass through this world for nothing at all?

O you the wise, would you tell me please: why should our days go by never to return?

（张培基译）

译文二

During these fleeting days what can I, only one among so many, accomplish? Nothing more than to pace irresolutely, nothing more than to hurry along. In these more than 8,000 days of hurrying, what have I to show but some irresolute wanderings? The days that are gone are like smoke that has been dissipated by a breeze, like thin mists that have been burned off under the onslaught of the morning sun. What mark will I leave behind? Will the trace I leave behind be so much as a gossamer thread? Naked I came into this world, and in a twinkling still naked I will leave it. But what I cannot accept this: why should I make this journey in vain?

You who are wiser than I, please tell me why it is that once gone, our days never return.

（葛浩文译）

译文三

What can I do, in this bustling world, with my days flying in their escape? Nothing but to hesitate, to rush. What have I been doing in that eight-thousand-day rush, apart from hesitating? Those bygone days have been dispersed as smoke by a light wind, or evaporated as mist by the morning sun. What traces have I left behind me? Have I ever left behind any gossamer traces at all? I have come to this world, stark-naked; am I to go back, in a blink, in the same stark-nakedness? It is not fair though: why should I have made such a trip for nothing!

You the wise, tell me, why should our days leave us, never to return?

（朱纯深译）

赏析思路点拨

在字词的理解上，三个译文表现出不同的思考，对"匆匆"的译法也各不相同：张译是"live a transient life""fleeting"；葛译是"hurry along""hurrying"；朱译是"rush"。在这三个译本中，译文都表达出了原文"匆匆"的含义，但是张译还译出了另一层含义，"live a transient life"（度过短暂的一生），点出了"匆匆"的内涵，即人生的短暂。对于"徘徊"一词，张译是"waver and wander"，葛译是"pace irresolutely"，朱译是"hesitate"。葛译"pace irresolutely"和原文本义贴近，但是在美感上不如张译的"waver and wander"。朱译将该词理解为犹豫，译为"hesitate"，这样一来，少了徘徊的画面感。总体来说，"匆匆"和"徘徊"这两个词的译法体现出张译更注重散文美的传达。

在修辞的处理上，三个译本的处理方式略有不同。"过去的日子如轻烟，被微风吹散了，如薄雾，被初阳蒸融了"，这句话运用了明喻和对仗两种修辞手法。对于这句话的翻译，三个译本中最贴近原文节奏感的就是张译。张译是"The bygone days, like wisps of smoke, have been dispersed by gentle winds, and, like thin mists, have been evaporated by the rising sun"，很好地再现了原文的节奏感。英语多长句，中文多短句，但是散文翻译更加注重语言本身的美感，翻译的形式也在表达某种含义。原文的节奏充分表达出作者心中对于时光飞逝的无奈，张译保留了这样的节奏，也再现了原文的风格。另一处比喻句是"我何曾留着像游丝样的痕迹呢"。张译为"No, nothing, not even gossamer-like traces"，这三小段步步推进，与其他两个译本相比，节奏明快，将作者想要表达的情绪凸显了出来。这句话的翻译，三个译本都再现了原文的含义，都体现出了"意美"。但是从"音美"和"形美"的角度看，张译更佳，让读者印象深刻。

课后思考

1. 散文翻译如何重现原文的修辞特点？

2. 散文翻译如何再现原文风格？

3. 不同译者译文的不同之处主要表现在哪些方面，是否都再现了散文之"美"？

延伸阅读

 原文

　　我说道："爸爸，你走吧。"他望车外看了看，说："我买几个橘子去。你就在此地，不要走动。"我看那边月台的栅栏外有几个卖东西的等着顾客。走到那边月台，须穿过铁道，须跳下去又爬上去。父亲是一个胖子，走过去自然要费事些。我本来要去的，他不肯，只好让他去。我看见他戴着黑布小帽，穿着黑布大马褂、深青布棉袍，蹒跚地走到铁道边，慢慢探身下去，尚不大难。可是他穿过铁道，要爬上那边月台，就不容易了。他用两手攀着上面，两脚再向上缩；他肥胖的身子向左微倾，显出努力的样子。这时我看见他的背影，我的泪很快地流下来了。我赶紧拭干了泪，怕他看见，也怕别人看见。我再向外看时，他已抱了朱红的橘子往回走了。过铁道时，他先将橘子散放在地上，自己慢慢爬下，再抱起橘子走。到这边时，我赶紧去搀他。他和我走到车上，将橘子一股脑儿放在我的皮大衣上。于是扑扑衣上的泥土，心里很轻松似的，过一会说，"我走了；到那边来信！"我望着他走出去。他走了几步，回过头看见我，说："进去吧，里边没人。"等他的背影混入来来往往的人里，再找不着了，我便进来坐下，我的眼泪又来了。

（朱自清，《背影》）

译文

译文一

I said, "Dad, you might leave now." But he looked out of the window and said, "I'm going to buy you some tangerines. You just stay here. Don't move around." I caught sight of several vendors waiting for customers outside the railings beyond a platform. But to reach that platform would require crossing the railway track and doing some climbing up and down. That would be a strenuous job for father, who was fat. I wanted to do all that myself, but he stopped me, so I could do nothing but let him go. I watched him hobble towards the railway track in his black skullcap, black cloth mandarin jacket and dark blue cotton-padded cloth long gown. He had little trouble climbing down the railway track, but it was a lot more difficult for him to climb up that platform after crossing the railway track. His hands held onto the upper part of the platform, his legs huddled up and his corpulent body tipped slightly towards the left, obviously making an enormous exertion. While I was watching him from behind, tears gushed from my eyes. I quickly wiped them away lest he or others should catch me crying. The next moment when I looked out of the window again, father was already on the way back, holding bright red tangerines in both hands. In crossing the railway track, he first put the tangerines on the ground, climbed down slowly and then picked them up again. When he came near the train, I hurried out to help him by the hand. After boarding the train with me, he laid all the tangerines on my overcoat, and patting the dirt off his clothes, he looked somewhat relieved and said after a while, "I must be going now. Don't forget to write me from Beijing." I gazed after his back retreating out of the carriage. After a few steps, he looked back at me and said, "Go back to your seat. Don't leave your things alone." I, however, did not go back to my seat until his figure was lost among crowds of people hurrying to and fro and no longer visible. My eyes were again wet with tears.

（张培基译）

译文二

"Don't wait, father," I said. He looked out of the window. "I'll just buy you a few tangerines," he said. "Wait here, and don't wander off." Just outside the station were some vendors. To reach them he had to cross the lines, which involved jumping down from the platform and clambering up again. As my father is a stout man this was naturally not easy for him. But when I volunteered to go instead he would not hear of it. So I watched him in his black cloth cap and jacket and dark blue cotton-padded gown, as he waddled to the tracks and climbed slowly down — not so difficult after all. But when he had crossed the lines he had trouble clambering up the other side. He clutched the platform with both hands and tried to heave his legs up, straining to the left. At the sight of his burly back tears started to my eyes, but I wiped them hastily so that neither he nor anyone else might see them. When next I looked out he was on his way back with some ruddy tangerines. He put these on the platform before climbing slowly down to cross the lines, which he did after picking the fruit up. When he reached my side I was there to help him up. We boarded the train together and he plumped the tangerines down on my coat. Then he brushed the dust from his clothes, as if that was a weight off his mind. "I'll be going now, son," he said presently. "Write to me once you get there." I watched him walk away. After a few steps he turned back to look at me. "Go on in!"

he called. "There's no one in the compartment." When his back disappeared among the bustling crowd I went in and sat down, and my eyes were wet again.

（杨宪益译）

原文

小巷的动人处就是它无比的悠闲。无论是谁，只要你到巷里去踯躅一会，你的心情就会如巷尾不波的古井，那是一种和平的静穆，而不是阴森和肃杀。它闹中取静，别有天地，仍是人间。它可能是一条现代的乌衣巷，家家有自己的一本哀乐帐，一部兴衰史，可是重门叠户，讳莫如深，夕阳影里，野花闲草，燕子低飞，寻觅归家。只是一片澄明如水的气氛，净化一切，笼罩一切，使人忘忧。

（柯灵，《巷》）

译文

The charm of the lane lies in its absolute serenity. No matter who you are, if you loiter around in the lane for a while, your mind will become as unruffled as the ancient well at the end of the lane. There you will experience a kind of peaceful calmness rather than gloomy sternness. There reigns peace and quiet in the midst of noisy bustle. It is a world of its own on earth. It may be a modern version of *Wu Yi Xiang*, a special residential area of nobility in the Jin Dynasty southeast of today's Nanjing, where each family, secluded behind closed doors, has its own covered-up story of joys and sorrows, and rise and decline. When the sun is setting, swallows will fly low over wild flowers and grass on their way to their nests. The all-pervading and all-purifying atmosphere of water-like placidness makes one forget all cares and worries.

（张培基译）

第二节

英美现代散文汉译

和中国散文"走出去"相应的，是外国优秀散文"走进来"。通过散文翻译，国外的优秀散文被介绍到中国，不同的散文作品给国内读者带来不同的感受，如"培根的简古，布朗的委婉，密尔顿的雄浑，戴登的俊逸，笛福的矫健，斯威夫特的犀利，艾狄生的温文，蒲柏的警策，约翰逊的典重，兰姆的天真……"（高健，1985：1920）。在散文翻译当中，如何再现不同散文的风格，如何将原作者表达的思想和情感用汉语传达给国内读者，是译者需要考虑的问题。英美现代散文和中国现代散文一样，注重"音美"，读者会感受到散文音乐般的节奏，而其语言和句式又构建出"形式美"，因此只翻译出意义是不够的。那么，译者在翻译过程中如何体现原文的风格和美呢？读者可在对比赏析的过程中，分析其方法及原因，关注译者对修辞的翻译和对语篇整体的把握，并且思考译者的文学素养对散文翻译的重要性。

课前准备

翻译热身

But there he was, never making much money, but with all the comforts of home around him, eating his stewed eels, sitting in his galluses out in the orchard in the cool of the evening, with a plump baby to climb up in his lap, whenever he felt like having a baby on his lap and had his old trousers on and didn't care much what happened to him. There he was, shingling his house only when it got to leaking so it put the kitchen fire out. Drinking a little ale now and then, when he came by it easy. No big hayfields to worry about. No wife that craved more than one new dress a year, and that one she generally ran up herself on her sewing machine. One best pair of trousers to his name, which the moths got into, but not so deep but what they could be healed up with a needle. Not many books to excite him and keep him awake nights, or put ideas into his head and make him uneasy. No itch ever spreading out upon him to go out and take the world by its horns. There he was, in clover!

（Robert P. Tristram Coffin, "My Average Uncle"）

参考译文

然而就是这样一个人，从未挣过大钱，却尽情享受着家的舒适温馨，吃着炖鳗鱼，穿着背带裤，凉爽的黄昏，坐在果园里。想抱孩子时，便有个胖娃娃爬到膝头上来，穿的是旧裤子，所以不怕孩子糟蹋。他就是这样一个人，屋顶漏雨，厨房里的火都快浇灭了他才去修。要是啤酒来得容易，偶尔也喝上一杯。没有大块干草场要他操心。妻子也从不吵着一年要两件新衣服，就是那一件，还是她亲自动手，用缝纫机做的。在他的名下只有一条像样的裤子，还让蛀虫蛀了，但并不严重，三针两线就可补好。没有几本书使他激动不已，彻夜难眠，或是把各种思想塞进他的脑袋里，使他坐立不安。没有难以抑制的渴望在内心泛滥，使他离开家门去闯世界。他就是这样一个人，日子过得舒舒服服，安安逸逸！

（刘庆荣译）

翻译难点聚焦

1. 译文是怎样再现原文的"形美"的？

2. 原文中"There he was, in clover!"的节奏在译文中是如何体现的？

3. 译文是否再现了原文中的修辞美？

名译赏析

原作简介

《论读书》是文艺复兴时期英国哲学家、散文家弗朗西斯·培根创作的一篇论说散文。句式多采用并列式，多用排比和比喻等修辞手法，句子富有节奏感，读来朗朗上口。这篇文章蕴含哲理，言简意赅，很有说服力，让读者意识到读书的正确方法以及重要意义，引导读者通过读书实现自我提升。

原文

Studies serve for delight, for ornament, and for ability. Their chief use for delight, is in privateness and retiring; for ornament, is in discourse; and for ability, is in the judgement and disposition of business. For expert men can execute, and perhaps judge of particulars, one by one; but the general counsels, and the plots and marshalling of affairs, come best from those that are learned. To spend too much time in studies is sloth; to use them too much for ornament, is affectation; to make judgement wholly by their rules, is the humour of a scholar. They perfect nature, and are perfected by experience: for natural abilities are like natural plants, that need pruning by study; and studies themselves do give forth directions too much at large, except they be bounded in by experience. Crafty men contemn studies, simple men admire them, and wise men use them; for they teach not their own use; but that is a wisdom without them, and above them, won by observation.

（Francis Bacon, "Of study"）

译文

译文一

读书足以怡情，足以傅彩，足以长才。其怡情也，最见于独处幽居之时；其傅彩也，最见于高谈阔论之中；其长才也，最见于处世判事之际。练达之士虽能分别处理细事或一一判别枝节，然纵观统筹，全局策划，则舍好学深思者莫属。读书费时过多易惰，文采藻饰太盛则矫，全凭条文断事乃学究故态。读书补天然之不足，经验又补读书之不足，盖天生才干犹如自然花草，读书然后知如何修剪移接；而书中所示，如不以经验范之，则又大而无当。有一技之长者鄙读书，无知者羡读书，唯明智之士用读书，然书并不以用处告人，用书之智不在书中，而在书外，全凭观察得之。

（王佐良译）

译文二

学习可以作为消遣，作为装点，也可以增进才能。其为消遣之用，主在独处、归休之时；为装点，则在高谈阔论之中；为才能，则在明辨是非、深谋远虑之间；因为专于一技者可以操持甚或判断一事一物，而唯有博学之士方能纵观全局，通权达变。过度沉溺于学习是怠惰；过度炫耀学问是华而不实；食书不化乃书生之大疾。学习可以完善天性，并通过经验得以完善自身；因为天生之才犹如天然之草木，尚需通过学习加以修整；而纸上学问未免空谈，除非由经验加以约束。聪颖者鄙视学习，愚鲁者羡慕学习，明智者利用学习；学习本身并不教人如何运用；唯有观察可以带来超越学习的智慧。

（孙有中译）

译文三

读书能给人乐趣、文雅和能力。人们独居或退隐的时候，最能体会到读书的乐趣；谈话的时候，最能表现出读书的文雅；判断和处理事务的时候，最能发挥由读书而获得的能力。那些有实际经验而没有学识的人，也许能够一一实行或判断某些事物的细微末节，但对于事业的一般指导、筹划与处理，还是真正有学问的人才能胜任。耗费过多的时间去读书便是迟滞，过分用学问自炫便是矫揉造作，而全凭学理判断一切，则是书呆子的癖好。学问能美化人性，经验又能充实学问。天生的植物需要人工修剪，人类的本性也需要学问诱导，而学问本身又必须以经验来规范，否则便太迂阔了。技巧的人轻视学问，浅薄的人惊服学问，聪明的人却能利用学问。因为学问本身并不曾把它的用途教给人，至于如何去应用它，那是在学问之外、超越学问之上、由观察而获得的一种聪明呢！

（廖运范译）

赏析思路点拨

首先，在短语的翻译上，三篇译文呈现出不同的理解。比如，"above them"，王译为"而在书外"，孙译为"超越学习"，廖译为"学问之外、超越学问之上"。从这个词组的翻译来看，王译强调"书外"，后两者强调"超越"。虽然"above"有"在……之上"之意，可表达超越的意思，但联系上下文，原作者强调的是书中学不到的，要通过观察得之，因此译为"书外"简单易懂，很好地传达了原文的含义。此外，王佐良"不在书中，而在书外"这一译文还在传达意义的基础上，将"形"美凸显了出来。

其次，原文使用了大量排比句，三个译本都保留了这样的行文方式。但是原文简洁明了，短句居多。从译文篇幅来看，王译字数最少，廖译字数偏多。从整体行文上看，王译是表达最简洁的版本，其译文所采用的是古文风格，行文流畅，善用四字词语，表达简练，更符合原文的整体风格。因此，虽然三个版本的译文都表达出了原文的"意"，都实现了"意美"，但是，从整体行文来看，王译的遣词造句更具"音美、形美"，这样的译文，读来意义深刻，朗朗上口。

课后思考

1. 散文翻译如何重现原文的修辞特点？

2. 散文翻译如何再现原文的"意美、音美、形美"？

延伸阅读

 原文

You hear it all along the river. You hear it, loud and strong, from the rowers as they urge the junk with its high stern, the mast lashed alongside, down the swift running stream. You hear it from the trackers, a more breathless chant, as they pull desperately against the current, half a dozen of them perhaps if they are taking up wupan, a couple of hundred if they are hauling a splendid junk, its square sail set, over a rapid. On the junk a man stands amidships beating a drum incessantly to guide their efforts, and they pull with all their strength, like men possessed, bent double; and sometimes in the extremity of their travail they craw on the ground, on all fours, like the beasts of the field. They strain, strain fiercely, against the pitiless might of the stream. The leader goes up and down the line and when he sees one who is not putting all his will into the task he brings down his split bamboo on the naked back. Each one must do his utmost or the labour of all is vain. And still they sing a vehement, eager chant, the chant of the turbulent waters. I do not know how words can describe what there is in it of effort. It serves to express the straining heart, the breaking muscles, and at the same time the indomitable spirit of man which overcomes the pitiless force of nature. Though the rope may part and the great junk swing back, in the end the rapid will be passed; and at the close of the weary day there is the hearty meal...

（W. S. Maugham, "The Song of the River"）

译文

　　沿河上下都可以听见那歌声。它响亮而有力，那是船夫，他们划着木船顺流向下，船尾翘得很高，桅杆系在船边。它也可能是比较急促的号子，那是纤夫，他们拉纤逆流而上。如果拉的是小木船，也许就只五六个人，如果拉的是扬着横帆的大船过急滩，那就要二百来人。船中央站着一个汉子不停地击鼓助威，引导他们加劲。于是他们使出全部力量，像着了魔似的，腰弯成两折，有时力量用到极限就全身趴在地上匍匐前进，像田里的牲口。他们使劲，拼命使劲对抗着水流无情的威力。领头的在纤绳前后跑来跑去，见到有人没有全力以赴，竹板就打在他光着的背上。每个人都必须竭尽全力，否则就要全功尽弃。就这样他们还是唱着激昂而热切的号子，那汹涌澎湃的河水号子。我不知道词语怎样能描写出其中所包含的拼搏，它表现的是绷紧的心弦，几乎要断裂的筋肉，同时也表现了人类克服无情的自然力的顽强精神。虽然绳子可能扯断，大船可能倒退，但最终险滩必将通过，在筋疲力尽的一天结束时可以痛快地吃上一顿饱饭……

（陈文伯译）

原文

　　The October leaves have fallen on the lake. On bright, calm days they lie in thousands on the now darkening water, mostly yellow flotillas of poplar, floating continuously down from great trees that themselves shake in the windless air with the sound of falling water, but on rainy days or after rain they seem to swim or be driven away, and nothing remains to break the surface except the last of the olive-yellow lily pads that in high summer covered every inch of water like plates of emerald porcelain. The lilies have gone too, the yellow small-headed kind that in bud are like swimming snakes, and the great reeds are going, woven by wind and frost into untidy basket islands under which coot and moorhen skid for cover at the sound of strangers.

（Herbert Ernest Bates, "October Lake"）

译文

译文一

十月的木叶已经簌簌落满湖上。在晴朗无风的日子里，它们成千上万地停留在此刻业已色泽转暗的水面；这无数黄色小舟般的落叶大多为白杨树叶，纷纷不停地从那些即使在无风天气也颤动不已的高树之上淅淅沥沥地飘落下来，但是遇上雨天或是雨后，它们便又被飘得无影无踪，于是，除了那在盛夏时节宛如翡翠似的盏盏瓷盘把整个湖面盖个满当而如今色作橄榄黄的睡莲残叶之外，这时湖上是一片利落。就连不少睡莲也已不在；那在蓓蕾时期有如浪里金蛇似的一种色黄头细的水草以及茂密的芦苇也都稀疏起来，它们被风霜编织成了许多凌乱的篮篓似的汀渚，这里的大鹬松鸡一听到什么陌生者的响动便溜到那底下去躲藏。

（高健译）

译文二

十月秋阳漠漠，湖面色泽渐暗，成千上万的枯叶飘落在湖上，好像布满黄色的小舰队。它们多为白杨树叶，高大的树身在无风天气也颤动不已，黄叶渐渐沥沥地往下落。但是在雨天或是雨后，这些小舰队似乎又飘然而去，湖面上只剩下残留的睡莲叶，它们在盛夏时节像翡翠盘似的把湖面盖个满当，而如今已色作橄榄黄。那在蓓蕾时期游蛇似的黄色细草，以及茂密的芦苇，也都稀疏起来，它们被风霜织成了许多凌乱的篓状小洲，水鸡一听到什么陌生的声音便溜到那底下去躲藏。

（革文译）

第五章

歌曲翻译

音乐家贝多芬曾说：“音乐是比一切智慧、一切哲学更高的启示。（Musik ist höhere Offenbarung als alle Weisheit und Philosophie.）”（转引自向云，2017：1）。音乐是人类生活中不可缺少的精神调剂品，是人类寄托思想感情的艺术品，更是人类精神文明的组成部分之一。音乐作品可以分为声乐和器乐。器乐可分成独奏曲、重奏曲和合奏曲。器乐作品是通过乐器演奏出来的，不需要翻译，观众欣赏其旋律和节奏；而声乐作品是通过人声表达的，“它是词和曲的结合，即歌词构成社会生活内容和文学形象，而曲调构成音乐形象，二者综合起来将审美信息传递给人们。歌词是歌曲的重要组成部分，赋予它明确的情感指向，是理解和接受歌曲艺术品的钥匙”（薛范，2002：42）。歌曲根据形式、风格的不同，又可分为民歌、流行歌曲、艺术歌曲、通俗歌曲、乡村歌曲、儿童歌曲等，因此也兼具雅俗共赏性。

在研究歌曲翻译之前，需要先区分几个术语，包括“歌曲翻译”“歌词翻译”“歌曲译配”和“歌词大意”。在许多期刊中出现了将此类术语混用乱用的情况。著名音乐家和翻译家薛范在《歌曲翻译探索与实践》一书中提到，歌曲创作是作曲家先选定歌词，并依据词的表现需要，在体裁、曲式等方面进行精心设计，也就是量体裁衣，为“脚”定制合适的“鞋”。“而歌曲翻译，曲调已是定型的。歌曲的旋律线、节奏类型和节拍式都已由原作者框定，我们译配歌曲时，译出的歌词必须服从于原作者已框定的旋律走向、节奏类型和节拍，努力做到译词和原曲的完美结合，也就是为‘现成的鞋’找到‘最合适的脚’。”（薛范，2002：107）。实际上他在书中已经提到了“歌曲译配”这一词了，但在撰写该书时，却没有将“歌曲翻译”和“歌曲译配”严格区分开来。胡凤华在其《“歌曲译配”与“歌曲翻译”辩》一文中提到，实际上“歌曲翻译”是一个上义词，它包括了“歌曲译配”，而“歌曲译配”又包括“歌词翻译”和“与原曲配”。不过，有时“歌曲翻译”也指“歌词翻译”。所以只有“歌曲译配”既包括译词又包括与原曲配，即翻译的作品是可以进行演唱的。而“歌词大意”隶属于“歌词翻译”，不过只是翻译歌词的大体意思而不是全译。这几个术语之间的关系参见图 5-1（胡凤华，2007：100）：

图5-1 "歌曲译配"与"歌曲翻译"的联系

注：虚线表示歌曲翻译有时实指歌词翻译，>表示上下位词义关系。

　　歌和诗具有很大的相似性，在古代中国，诗和歌本为一体，歌就是"能唱的诗"。到元明以后，诗与歌才逐渐开始分家。和诗一样，歌词也讲究格律，是作者用诗意的语言来抒发自己内心的情感，但诗歌更注重视觉艺术，主要供人阅读，品尝字词句之美；而歌曲更注重听觉艺术，主要供人倾听，享受旋律之跳动。所以歌曲翻译是集文学、翻译、音乐于一身的艺术。由于歌曲翻译的特殊性，它不仅要求译配者精通两种语言，具有一定的文学素养，还需要译配者熟谙音乐，具备诗歌格律和音韵方面的知识。在我国歌曲翻译的历史长河中，涌现出了一批十分优秀的歌曲翻译家，包括薛范、毛宇宽、尚家骧、周枫、邓映易等人，他们译配的歌曲如《莫斯科郊外的晚上》《友谊地久天长》《欢乐颂》《铃儿响叮当》《雪绒花》在我国广为流传。

　　基于歌曲翻译的特点，其批评与赏析一般主要关注以下几个方面。第一，关注歌曲情感的传递。歌曲的作者在进行歌曲创作时赋予了每一首歌情感含义，在翻译成其他语言时，需要观察译曲是否可以传递出同样的情感，译曲听众是否能和原曲听众产生同样的感受。第二，关注歌曲风格的移植。歌曲风格多样，包括民歌、布鲁斯、艺术歌曲、流行音乐、乡村音乐、摇滚乐、说唱乐等。歌曲风格不同，其语言风格也不同。例如，流行音乐多使用当前流行的语言，所以不能翻译成诗歌那样优雅的文字。翻译前应确定语言的整体基调。第三，关注歌曲文化的转换。翻译是跨语言和跨文化的交际活动，"歌曲文本反映的是一种独特的文化知识，歌词语言是其文化的载体。文化是其存在的基础"（向云，2017：153）。但有时会出现文化差异、文化空缺的情况，这时我们就需要关注译者是如何处理歌曲翻译中的文化转换的。第四，关注歌曲韵律的再现。除赏析歌词之美外，还可以赏析歌曲的节奏和音韵之美，因为要保证译曲的可唱性。而音乐对歌曲翻译的制约主要在于：（1）韵律。首先歌词需要押韵，再者单词的重音必须要落在音乐的强拍上，否则就会造成"倒字"。（2）节奏感。一个音节对应一个字，否则就会无法进行演唱。（3）声调感（或称"字调感"）。字调是汉语的独特语音现象，在英文歌曲汉译时，如果曲调和字调不般配，也会造成"倒字"现象（薛范，2002：137）。

　　本章主要关注歌曲的翻译，为丰富歌曲翻译鉴赏的内容，设置了经典英语歌曲汉译和经典汉语歌曲英译两节内容，提出了汉译英和英译汉的主要问题，为歌曲翻译的欣赏和批评提供了思考的角度，并提供了多种译本供读者讨论交流。

第一节

经典英语歌曲汉译

　　中华人民共和国成立初期，刚从战争中走出来的中国人民迫切需要能够治愈心灵创伤的精神文化产品。然而，当时国内的音乐家正处于从创作战争作品向创作和平建设时期作品转变的阶段，一时间很难创作出能够满足和平建设时期人们精神生活所需要的音乐作品。因此，音乐家们开始将注意力转移到歌曲翻译上。为了弥补当时国内音乐创作的不足，在中国音乐家协会的指导下，一本外国歌曲集——《外国名歌200首》出版了（明言，2014：62）。此书共发行80万册，产生了广泛的社会影响力和历史文化穿透力，歌曲传遍中国的大街小巷。后来薛范、邓映易等歌曲翻译家也相继出版了自己译配的作品集。他们译配的经典英文歌曲有《友谊地久天长》（"Auld Lang Syne"）、《铃儿响叮当》（"Jingle Bells"）、《雪绒花》（"Edelweiss"）、《答案在风中飘荡》（"Blowin' in the Wind"）等，这些歌曲虽年代久远，但影响深远。有些歌曲还出现在中小学音乐教材中，影响了一代又一代人，满足了中国人民的精神需求，丰富了中华曲库，让中国听众切实感受到了异域文化。后来随着互联网的快速发展，迪士尼大片《海洋奇缘》（*Moana*）、《冰雪奇缘》（*Frozen*）、《飞屋环游记》（*Up*）等迅速抢占中国电影市场，主题曲和插曲也迅速传播，这些电影能在中国的票房上取得巨大成功，不可说不得益于其高质量的汉语译配曲。经典歌曲经久不衰的原因在于其韵律节奏的优美性，艺术语言的雅俗共赏性以及其思想内涵的共通性。因此，往往同一首经典曲目会引来不同译配家的翻译。对比原词和不同版本的译词，不仅有助于读者理解原曲，也有助于读者学习翻译批评与鉴赏。

课前准备

翻译热身

Should auld acquaintance be forgot,

And never brought to mind?

Should auld acquaintance be forgot,

And auld lang syne?

We twa hae run about the braes,

And pou'd the gowans fine,

But we've wander'd monie a weary fit,

Sin'auld lang syne.

We twa hae paidl'd in the burn

Frae mornin' sun till dine,

But seas between us braid hae roar'd

Sin'auld lang syne.

And there's a hand, my trusty fiere,

And gie's a hand o' thine,

And we'll take a right guid-willie waught,

For auld lang syne.

（Robert Burns, "Auld Lang Syne"）

参考译文

怎能忘记旧日朋友

心中不常怀想

旧日朋友岂能相忘

友谊地久天长

我们同游故乡的青山上

到处野菊飘香

我们也曾历尽苦辛

到处奔波流浪

我们也曾终日逍遥

荡桨在清波上

但如今却劳燕分飞

远隔大海重洋

让我们紧紧挽起手

情谊永不相忘

举杯痛饮齐声颂扬

友谊地久天长

（邓映易译配，《友谊地久天长》）

翻译难点聚焦

1. 译曲如何传递出原曲的情感？

2. 译曲如何成功实现风格移植？

3. 译曲如何重现原曲韵律之美？

名译赏析

原作简介

《答案就在风中飘》（"Blowin' in the Wind"）是美国歌手鲍勃·迪伦（Bob Dylan）的代表作。这是他的一首抗议歌曲，反映了越战时期的美国社会，因迎合了当时的社会思潮而迅速风靡全世界，这首歌也在电影《阿甘正传》中出现过。从歌词里可以看出他对传统观念上的"男子汉"表示质疑，希望人们可以用和平的方式去解决争端，而不是采取激烈对抗的手段让那些无辜的人丧生于硝烟战火之中。本首歌的歌词还在 2016 年为鲍勃·迪伦赢得了诺贝尔文学奖。

原文

How many roads must a man walk down

Before you call him a man

How many seas must a white dove sail

Before she sleeps in the sand

How many times must the cannon balls fly

Before they're forever banned

The answer, my friend, is blowin' in the wind

The answer is blowin' in the wind

（Bob Dylan, "Blowin' in the Wind"）

译文

译文一

问：一个人要走多少道

才能有人的称号

问：小白鸽要飞多少海

才能在沙里睡觉

问：大炮还要轰多少回

才能彻底销毁掉

答案自己找，它在风中飘

答案它就在风中飘

（薛范译配，《答案就在风中飘》）

译文二

男人要经历多少磨难

才算真正男子汉

白鸽要飞越几重海洋

方能安歇于海滩

嘿　大炮要发出多少枚炮弹

战争才一去不返

答案啊，朋友，在风中飘荡

答案啊在风中飘荡

（覃军译配，《答案在风中飘荡》）

赏析思路点拨

歌曲《答案就在风中飘》（"Blowin' in the Wind"）的两个译本分别由薛范和覃军所作，两种版本均可配曲入唱。

歌曲翻译主要分为两步，先翻译再配曲。因为要实现配曲入唱，不仅要求歌词押韵，还要求一个音节对应一个字，所以译者还需要对初步翻译好的版本再进行调整。

薛译本选择了一韵到底，韵脚是十三豪韵"ao"韵，而覃译本选择了十四寒韵"an"韵。两种选择均可，但覃译本的"an"韵与原曲的韵脚 /æ/ 发音相似，更加巧妙。薛译本在每句前都写了一个"问"字，笔者认为歌曲主要为入耳作品而非入眼作品，问句与陈述句可以根据语音语调辨别出来，故"问"字有些多余。整首歌覃译本主要采用了直译的手法，薛译本为了使译词与原曲在音节数和节奏上相符，采取了增译的手法。如，薛范将"a white dove"译成了"小白鸽"，增加了形容词"小"，最后一句，增加了"自己找"。此外，从含义与风格上看，原曲作者鲍勃·迪伦不仅是一名歌手，还是一名诗人，他所创作的歌词也体现出了他诗人的风格。歌词的第一句出现了两个"man"，薛范将其都翻译成了"人"，而覃军对这两个"man"有不同的理解。第一个"man"他译为"男人"，即指广义上所有的男性；而第二个"man"，他译为"真正男子汉"，指的是经历过风霜后磨炼而成的坚强的男人。对于第二句中的"sleep"和第三句的"forever banned"，薛范将其分别译为"睡觉"和"彻底销毁掉"，而覃军将其译为"安歇"与"一去不返"，显得更有诗意。

课后思考

1. 歌曲翻译如何再现原曲韵律？两个译本均采用"一韵到底"的原则，歌曲翻译是否一定要"一韵到底"？

2. 歌曲翻译如何保证译曲的可唱性？

3. 两种译本的不同之处体现在哪些方面？

延伸阅读

 原文

Edelweiss, edelweiss

Every morning you greet me

Small and white

Clean and bright

You look happy to meet me

Blossom of snow may you bloom and grow

Bloom and grow forever

Edelweiss, edelweiss

Bless my homeland forever

（Oscar Hammerstein II, "Edelweiss"）

译文

雪绒花，雪绒花

清晨迎接我开放

小而白

洁而亮

向我快乐地摇晃

白雪般的花儿愿你芬芳

永远开花生长

雪绒花，雪绒花

永远祝福我家乡

（薛范译配，《雪绒花》）

原文

Dashing through the snow

In a one-horse open sleigh

Over the fields we go

Laughing all the way

Bells on bobtail ring

Making spirits bright

What fun it is to ride and sing

A sleighing song tonight!

Jingle bells! Jingle bells! Jingle all the way

Oh, what fun it is to ride in a one-horse open sleigh

（James Lord Pierpont, "Jingle, Bells"）

译文

冲破大风雪

我们坐在雪橇上

快奔驰过田野

我们欢笑又歌唱

马儿铃声响叮当

令人心情多欢畅

我们今晚滑雪多快乐

把滑雪歌儿唱

叮叮当，叮叮当，铃儿响叮当

今晚滑雪多快乐我们坐在雪橇上

（邓映易译配，《铃儿响叮当》）

原文

Let it go, let it go

Can't hold it back anymore

Let it go, let it go

Turn away and slam the door

The snow glows white on the mountain tonight

Not a footprint to be seen

A kingdom of isolation

And it looks like I'm the Queen

The wind is howling like this swirling storm inside

Couldn't keep it in, heaven knows I've tried

Don't let them in, don't let them see

Be the good girl you always have to be

Conceal, don't feel, don't let them know

Well, now they know

Let it go, let it go

Can't hold it back anymore

Let it go, let it go

Turn away and slam the door

And here I stand, and here I stay

Let it go, let it go

The cold never bother me anyway

（Robert Lopez & Kristen Anderson-Lopez,"Let it go"）

译文

随它吧，随它吧

回头已没有办法

随它吧，随它吧

一转身不再牵挂

白雪发亮铺满我的过往

没有脚印的地方

孤立国度很荒凉

我是这里的女皇

漫天飞霜像心里的风暴一样

只有天知道我受过的伤

不让别人进来看见

做我自己就像我的从前

躲在现实梦境之间

不被发现

随它吧，随它吧

回头已没有办法

随它吧，随它吧

一转身不再牵挂

悬崖上让我留下

随它吧，随它吧

反正冰天雪地我也不怕

（陈少琪译配，《随它吧》）

第二节

经典汉语歌曲英译

习近平总书记在中央政治局第三十次集体学习时强调："要更好推动中华文化走出去，以文载道、以文传声、以文化人，向世界阐释推介更多具有中国特色、体现中国精神、蕴藏中国智慧的优秀文化。"歌曲作为文化软实力的一部分也应随着其他文化一起"走出去"，将中文歌曲译介到国外有助于促进中国文化在海外的交流与传播。乾隆年间，《茉莉花》（"Jasmine Flower"）就成为最早被译介到国外的中国民歌（乔建中，2002：102）。后来《玫瑰玫瑰我爱你》（"Rose, Rose I Love You"）、《月亮代表我的心》（"The Moon Represents My Heart"）、《康定情歌》（"A Love Song of Kangding"）、《青花瓷》（"Laurence Larson"）、《童话》（"Fairytale Story"）等经典歌曲也相继走出国门。歌曲译配这个行业也加入了许多新鲜血液，如湖北民族大学覃军、新西兰歌手罗艺恒、华裔歌手陈以桐、英语教师杨家成、上海外国语大学的 MelodyC2E 团队等。在信息时代，多模态的媒体手段更利于译配歌曲的传播，歌曲翻译工作者应该遵循歌曲译配的"五项全能原则"[1]，加强歌曲译配实践，将歌曲译配这种"二度创作"

1　彼得·洛（Peter Low）的歌曲翻译"五项全能原则"包括可唱性（singability）、词意（sense）、自然性（naturalness）、节奏（rhythm）和韵脚（rhyme）。

的艺术做到入乎其内、出乎其外，让更多的中国歌曲在异域文化中传承文明，传递艺术感染力，用歌曲传播中国声音，讲好中国故事（覃军，2020：128）。本节讨论的是经典汉语歌曲的英译，可为读者学习歌曲翻译提供一定的批评与鉴赏角度。

课前准备

 翻译热身

男：喝你一口茶呀
　　问你一句话，
　　你的那个爹妈（噻）
　　在家不在家

女：你喝茶就喝茶呀
　　那来这多话
　　我的那个爹妈（噻）
　　已经八十八

男：喝你二口茶呀
　　问你二句话
　　你的那个哥嫂（噻）
　　在家不在家

女：你喝茶就喝茶呀
　　那来这多话，
　　我的那个哥嫂（噻）
　　已经分了家
　　…………

男：喝你六口茶呀

　　问你六句话，

　　眼前这个妹子（噻）

　　今年有多大

女：你喝茶就喝茶呀

　　那来这多话，

　　眼前这个妹子（噻）

　　今年一十八

　　呦耶呦耶吃呦呦耶，

　　眼前这个妹子（噻）

　　今年一十八（耶）

（湖北恩施民歌，《六口茶》）

参考译文

Man: The first sip of your tea

brings a question to me

How are your dearest parents

And now where are they?

Woman: Just enjoy your tea

and try to save your words

My dear father and mother

are all in eighties.

Man: The second sip of your tea

brings a question to me

How is your dearest brother

And now where is he?

Woman: Just enjoy your tea

and try to save your words

My dear elder brother is

living on his own.

……

M: The sixth sip of your tea

brings a question to me

How old is the pretty girl

Who's in front of me?

W: Just enjoy your tea

and try to save your words

The girl who's in front of you

is in her eighteen.

Yo-yea-o——yo-yea-o-o-yea

The girl who's in front of you

is in her eighteen.

（覃军译配，"Six Sips of Tea"）

 翻译难点聚焦

1. 译者是如何处理翻译中的文化缺失这一现象的？

2. 译曲是否准确传递出了男女的心思和情感？

3. 为了保证歌曲的可唱性，译者采用了哪些翻译策略？

名译赏析

原作简介

《我和我的祖国》由张藜填词，秦咏诚作曲，经李谷一演唱后，广为流传。2019年，随着同名电影的上映，该歌曲经歌手王菲翻唱，再度回响于大街小巷。此曲也入选中宣部评出的"庆祝中华人民共和国成立70周年优秀歌曲100首"。填词人没有选择华丽的辞藻，而是用最朴实真挚的文字，利用"大海""浪花""母亲""孩子"等形象比喻，再结合优美动听的旋律，表达了对祖国的热爱。由于意境美，旋律美，情感真挚，这首歌成为脍炙人口、家喻户晓的名曲名歌。

原文

我和我的祖国

一刻也不能分割

无论我走到哪里

都流出一首赞歌

我歌唱每一座高山

我歌唱每一条河

袅袅炊烟小小村落

路上一道辙

我最亲爱的祖国

我永远紧依着你的心窝

你用你那母亲的脉搏

和我诉说

我的祖国和我

像海和浪花一朵

浪是那海的赤子

海是那浪的依托

每当大海在微笑

我就是笑的旋涡

我分担着海的忧愁

分享海的欢乐

我最亲爱的祖国

你是大海永不干涸

永远给我碧浪清波

心中的歌

（张藜，《我和我的祖国》）

译文

译文一

My home country and I

will never asunder go.

Wherever I roam and go,

there always streams a song yo.

I sing for mountains high and low.

I croon for rivers that flow.

Wisps of smoke grow;

small vills we know.

A trail's seen aglow.

Oh, my dearest home country,

I cuddle up to your warm heart for aye.

The pulse you as a mother bestow

touches me slow.

My home country's to me

as a sea's to a billow.

Waves are the sons of the sea.

The sea is where billows glow.

Whenever the sea's smiles show,

I am her whirlpool below.

I am sharing the sea's sorrow,

enjoying all her glee.

Oh, my dearest home country,

You are the sea, ne'er dry you grow.

For good you throw

blue waves I go

to sing solo.

la…la…

For good you throw

blue waves I go

to sing solo.

（许景城译配，"My Home Country and I"）

译文二

My motherland and I,

apart we will never go

No matter where I am, there

flows a song, a song to flow

I sing of a mountain high and,

I sing of a river blue

A curl of smoke

over the vill,

a trail down below

My dearest motherland o,

forever your warm heart I fast cling to

With your mother's pulse you feel,

you tell me so

My motherland and I,

like the sea and waves to blow

Waves are the sea's sons and,

the sea is where waves throw

Whenever the sea smiles,

I am the whirlpool smiling through

I share all with the sea

and share all her weal and woe

My dearest motherland o,

you're the sea, dry you never go

It's always a song for me to sing,

sing waves blue lala

It's always a song for me to sing,

sing waves blue

（赵彦春译配，"My Motherland and I"）

译文三

China catches my heart

No one can break us apart

No matter where I travel

You are what I'm singing for

I'm singing of your high mountains

Sing of your land and rocks

Sing of hometown, the big or small

Sing of them once more

Oh China how I love you

When I nestle in your arms feeling blue

You share with me the stories before

Make me cheerful

My motherland and me

Are the spindrift and the sea

I am your dear spindrift

You are the sea that hugs me

Whenever you get to smile

You raise me up, make me high

I share all your sorrows and joys

Share seashells on the shore

La... la... la... la... la... la... la...

You're the mother we all adore

We all adore

（覃军译配，"My Motherland and Me"）

赏析思路点拨

经典歌曲会受到众多译者的青睐，本书选择了许景城、赵彦春、覃军的译本。首先，歌曲翻译与文学翻译的差别就在于歌曲翻译要配曲入唱，这就要求单词的重音落到音乐的强拍上。三个译本中，覃军的译本与节奏更加相符，更具演唱性。其次，对于歌曲的曲名，三名译者采取了不同的译法。覃军和赵彦春均将"祖国"译为"motherland"，而许景城将其译为"home country"。根据《牛津高阶英汉双解词典》，"motherland"一词的含义为"the country that you were born in and that you feel a strong emotional connection with"，更加符合"祖国"一词所要表达的感情，而"home country"缺乏此感情色彩。再论赵译和覃译的区别，覃译本歌名中的"me"，严格来说，不符合语法，却在口语中经常使用，如2008年北京奥运会主题曲《我和你》的英文译名为"You and Me"。覃军将歌名译为"My Motherland and Me"不仅更加地道，而且还使用了头韵的修辞手法，赋予了歌名音韵美。最后，从含义上看，覃译因更注重歌曲的可唱性，对有些歌词进行了意译甚至改写。例如对于"路上一道辙"的翻译，许译为"a trail's seen aglow"，赵译为"a trail down below"，而覃译为"sing of them once more"。前两个译本选择忠于意思，而覃译选择忠于韵律。但覃译对"我分担着海的忧愁"一句的翻译欠妥，因为"make me high"含义不符。从整首歌曲来看，许译形式上更加对等，但许译在用词上过于书面化，如"asunder""bestow"等；覃译用词更加简单自然，更适合传唱；赵译准确地传递了原文的意思与意境，但在歌曲的可唱性上稍逊一筹。

课后思考

1. 为传播具有中华民族特色的音乐，中文歌曲的英译是否可以异化为主，以归化为辅？

2. 对歌曲翻译来说，忠实性和可唱性哪个原则为首要原则？

3. 影响歌曲翻译的因素除译者外还有哪些？演唱者是否是影响因素之一？

延伸阅读

原文

跑马溜溜的山上

一朵溜溜的云哟

端端溜溜地照在

康定溜溜的城哟

月亮——弯——弯

康定溜溜的城哟

李家溜溜的大姐

人才溜溜的好

张家溜溜的大哥

看上溜溜的她哟

月亮——弯——弯

看上溜溜的她哟

一来溜溜地看上

人才溜溜的好哟

二来溜溜地看上

会当溜溜的家哟

月亮——弯——弯

会当溜溜的家哟

世间溜溜的女子

任我溜溜地爱哟

世间溜溜的男子

任你溜溜地求哟

月亮——弯——弯

任你溜溜地求哟

（吴文秀、江定仙，《康定情歌》）

译文

Horses run on the mountain

Clouds over there can be seen

Gently they are floating

Over the town of Kangding

The moon… hanging

Over the town of Kangding

The Lees have a good lady

Charming, graceful and shapely

A young man of her neighbour

Has fallen in love with her

The moon … shining

Over the town of Kangding

She can be a good girlfriend

And a wife that prominent

She is not only pretty

And runs well her family

The moon… hanging

Over the town of Kangding

Of all girls in the whole town

To him she's the only one

Of all men in the whole world

He is the one that loves her

The moon… shining

Over the town of Kangding

（覃军译配，"A Love Song of Kangding"）

 原文

忘了有多久

再没听到你

对我说你最爱的故事

我想了很久

我开始慌了

是不是我又做错了什么

你哭着对我说

童话里都是骗人的

我不可能是你的王子

也许你不会懂

从你说爱我以后

我的天空星星都亮了

我愿变成童话里

你爱的那个天使

张开双手

变成翅膀守护你

你要相信

相信我们会像童话故事里

幸福和快乐是结局

（光良，《童话》）

译文

Don't know how long

It's been a while since

You told me your favorite story

It's been on my mind

Driving me crazy

Am I the reason that you're crying now

I see the tears in your eyes

They tell me you don't believe

That I can't be your prince charming

Maybe you can't understand

But when you say you love me

My life was changed and I wish you could see

I'm willing to be the one

And the angel that you love

With open arms,

I will always be there

You must believe

That you and me will end up happily living

In our own, fairytale story

（陈以桐译配，"Fairy Tales"）

第六章

诗歌翻译

诗歌是诗人用高度凝练、生动形象、富有节奏和韵律的语言来抒发自己思想感情的一种文学艺术。在古代，诗和歌本为一体，不能合乐的为诗，能合乐的即为歌。我国的诗歌具有悠久的历史，从《诗经》《楚辞》《汉乐府诗》《魏晋南北朝民歌》到唐诗、宋词、元曲、明清诗歌再到现代诗、新诗，每一个阶段都留下了宝贵的文化遗产。诗歌的内容丰富，形式多变，根据内容，可以将其分为抒情诗、送别诗、山水田园诗、叙事诗、边塞诗、怀古诗等；根据其音韵格律和结构形式又可以分为格律诗、自由诗、散文诗、韵脚诗和现代诗。我国现代诗人何其芳曾说："诗是一种最集中地反映社会生活的文学样式，它饱含着丰富的想象和感情，常常以直接抒情的方式来表现，而且在精炼与和谐的程度上，特别是在节奏的鲜明上，它的语言有别于散文的语言。"（何其芳，1956：27）这个定义说明诗歌具有高度的概括性、丰富的形象性、强烈的抒情性以及独特的音乐性。

在研究诗歌翻译之前，可以先讨论一个问题——诗，可译不可译？19世纪英国诗人雪莱（Percy Shelley）曾说："译诗是徒劳无益的，把一个诗人的创作从一种语言译成另一种语言，犹如把一朵紫罗兰投入坩埚，企图由此探索它的色泽和香味的构造原理"（转引自薛范，2002：32）。美国诗人罗伯特·弗罗斯特（Robert Frost）也曾说，诗就是"通过翻译而失去的东西"（转引自薛范，2002：32）。当然认为诗可译者，也不乏其人，其中比较具有代表性的就是获得我国首次设立的彩虹翻译终身成就奖的江枫。他认为："诗，在一般情况下都是可译的。世界上的大多数读者都是通过译本了解不同语言不同民族的诗作的。如果不可译，不同语言不同民族的读者和作者便会无法沟通。诗之所以可译，是因为它是世界文化活动的一部分，各民族之间尽可以千差万别，但是同为人类则各不相同的文化活动也总会有共同之处，这也就成了可译的基础。"（许钧，2001：113）因为诗在形式上以行而不是以一个句子为单位，且分行主要是根据其节奏而非意思，这就给译者造成了极大的困难，诗歌翻译常常因只保得住内容而抛弃形式，或者因追求形式而改变了内容。

基于诗歌翻译的特点，诗歌翻译的批评与赏析一般主要关注以下几个方面。第一，关注诗歌意象的移植。意象是诗歌的灵魂，作为诗歌情感的载体，意象的作用在于借景抒情、托物言志。诗人将自己主观的情感寄托于客观事物，将抽象的感受寄托于具体物象或事象。例如在中国古诗词中，"梅花"是常见的一个意象，寓意贞洁、不屈不挠，"杨柳"寓意离别、依依不舍；而在英诗中，"dove"（鸽子）象征着和平，"rose"（玫瑰）象征着美丽。所以译者在翻译诗歌的时候，需要重点关注诗歌中意象的移植与意境的创造。第二，关注诗歌音韵和形式的再现。诗歌的音韵美在于其声调和谐、节奏分明、气韵流畅，形式美在于其分拆诗行、整齐对仗、语言色彩。译者应该秉持"以诗译诗"的原则，除译出诗歌的意境外，还应尽量译出原诗的神韵与形美。第三，关注诗歌文化的转换。诗词蕴含了一个国家丰富的文化底蕴，由于各民族的生活环境、风俗习惯、价值取向、思维模式各不相同，译者在翻译诗词中的特有文化时，需要采取合适的翻译策略来促进各民族之间的交流，传播本民族文化。

本章主要关注诗歌翻译，为丰富诗歌翻译鉴赏的内容，设置中国古代诗词英译、中国现代诗歌英译以及英美诗歌汉译三个小节，提出了诗歌翻译中的主要问题，提供多种译本供读者批评鉴赏。

第一节

中国古代诗词英译

中国是诗词的国度，唐诗的气势磅礴、洒脱飘逸，宋词的清新不俗、豪迈奔放，元曲的曲折煽情、雅俗共赏，均让人回味无穷，拍案叫绝。古诗词的艺术魅力也引得国内外众多优秀学者将其译成英文。1984 年美国出版伯顿·沃森（Burton Watson）翻译的《哥伦比亚中国诗选》（*The Columbia Book of Chinese Poetry*），书中说道："西方读者越来越认识到中国传统诗歌的重要意义和魅力"（转引自许渊冲，2003：80）。在国内诗歌翻译界比较有影响力的当属许渊冲，他提出了"三美"论——"意美""音美""形美"。他指出："译诗要和原诗一样能感动读者的心，这是意美；要和原诗一样有悦耳的韵律，这是音美；还要尽可能保持原诗的形式（如长短、对仗等），这是形美。"（许渊冲，2003：85）除此之外，国内还出现了自由体译者杨宪益、戴乃迭夫妇，散文体译者翁显良，格律体译者徐忠杰等杰出译者。如果说中国译者对中国古诗词的理解略胜一筹，那么外国译者在地道英语的使用上更有优势。在国外也涌现了一批优秀的译者，如格律体的译者翟理思（H. A. Giles）和约翰·特纳（John Turner）、自由体的译者亚瑟·伟雷（Arthur Waley），以及伯顿·沃森。每个译者都有着自己的翻译风格，本节中我们主要探讨中国古代诗歌的英译，下文提供了经典古诗词的翻译供读者讨论交流。

课前准备

翻译热身

床前明月光，
疑是地上霜。
举头望明月，
低头思故乡。

（李白，《静夜思》）

参考译文

Before my bed a pool of light—

O can it be frost on the ground?

Looking up, I find the moon bright;

Bowing, in homesickness I'm drowned.

（许渊冲译，"Thoughts on a Tranquil Night"）

翻译难点聚焦

1. 译文是如何移植原诗中的"床""明月""霜"等意象的？
2. 译文是如何保留原诗的朦胧之美的？
3. 译文是如何再现原诗的音韵美和形式美的？

名译赏析

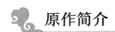 原作简介

《水调歌头·明月几时有》是宋代文学家苏轼的作品。苏轼在月明之夜，不禁想起七年未见的胞弟，思念尤甚，他将人世间的离合悲欢与宇宙人生哲学相联系，将仕途的失意挥洒一方，与清影为伴，在月下起舞。全词意境豪放而阔大，情怀豁达而乐观，对明月的向往之情，对胞兄的思念之情，对人间的眷念之情在词人清雄旷达的风格和行云流水的语言中，体现得淋漓尽致。该作品成为中秋词中的绝唱。

原文

明月几时有？把酒问青天。

不知天上宫阙，今夕是何年？

我欲乘风归去，又恐琼楼玉宇，高处不胜寒。

起舞弄清影，何似在人间？

转朱阁，低绮户，照无眠。

不应有恨，何事长向别时圆？

人有悲欢离合，月有阴晴圆缺，此事古难全。

但愿人长久，千里共婵娟。

（苏轼，《水调歌头·明月几时有》）

译文

译文一

Bright moon, when was your birth?

Wine cup in hand, I ask the deep blue sky;

Not knowing what year it is tonight

In those celestial palaces on high.

I long to fly back on the wind,

Yet dread those crystal towers, those courts of jade,

Freezing to death among those icy heights!

Instead I rise to dance with my pale shadow;

Better off, after all, in the world of men.

Rounding the red pavilion,

Stooping to look through gauze windows,

She shines on the sleepless.

The moon should know no sadness;

Why, then, is she always full when dear ones are parted?

For men, the grief of parting, joy of reunion,

Just as the moon wanes and waxes, is bright or dim;

Always some flaw — and so it has been since of old.

My one wish for you, then, is long life

And a share in this loveliness far, far away!

（杨宪益、戴乃迭译，"To the Tune of Shui Diao Ge Tou"）

译文二

How long will the full moon appear?

Wine cup in hand, I ask the sky.

I do not know what time of year

It would be tonight in the palace on high.

Riding the wind, there I would fly,

Yet I'm afraid the crystalline palace would be

Too high and cold for me.

I rise and dance, with my shadow I play.

On high as on earth, would it be as gay?

The moon goes round the mansions red

Through gauze-draped window soft to shed

Her light upon the sleepless bed.

Against man she should have no spite.

Why, then, when people part, is she oft full and bright?

Men have sorrow and joy; they part or meet again;

The moon is bright or dim and she may wax or wane.

There has been nothing perfect since the olden days.

So let us wish that man

Will live long as he can!

Though miles apart, we'll share the beauty she displays.

（许渊冲译，"Tune：Prelude to Water Melody"）

译文三

"When did this glorious moon begin to be?"

Cup in hand, I asked of the azure sky:

And wondered in the palaces of the air

What calendar this night do they go by.

Yes, I would wish to mount the winds and wander there

At home; but dread those onyx towers and halls of jade

Set so immeasurably cold and high.

To tread a measure, to sport with fleshless shade,

How alien to our frail mortality!

Her light round scarlet pavilion, 'neath broidered screen, down streams

On me that sleepless lie.

Ah, vain indeed is my complaining:

But why must she beam at the full on those that sundered sigh?

As men have their weal and woe, their parting and meeting, it seems

The moon has her dark and light, her phases of fullness and waning.

Never is seen perfection things that die.

Yet would I crave one solitary boon:

Long be we linked with light of the fair moon

Over large leagues of distance, thou and I.

（John Turner译，"To the Tune of 'Barcarole Prelude'"）

译文四

How rare the moon, so round and clear!

With cup in hand I ask of the blue sky,

"I do not know in the celestial sphere

What name this festive night goes by?"

I want to fly home, riding the air,

But fear the ethereal cold up there,

The jade and crystal mansions are so high!

Dancing to my shadow,

I feel no longer the mortal tie.

She rounds the vermilion tower,

Stoops to silk-pad doors,

Shines on those who sleepless lie.

Why does she, bearing us no grudge,

Shine upon our parting, reunion deny?

But rare is perfect happiness ——

The moon does wax, the moon does wane,

And so men meet and say goodbye.

I only pray our life be long,

And our souls together heavenward fly!

（林语堂译，"Mid-Autumn Festival, to the Tune of Shuitiaoket'ou"）

赏析思路点拨

　　《水调歌头·明月几时有》这首词历来备受推崇，众多优秀译者都将其译成了英文，传播海外。本节选取的是杨宪益和戴乃迭、许渊冲、约翰·特纳（John Turner）、林语堂的译本。

　　意象是诗词的灵魂，本首词中也出现了许多意象——"明月""青天""琼楼玉宇""天上宫阙"等，不同的译者对这些意象有不同的解读。如，"明月"的翻译，杨宪益夫妇译为"bright moon"，许译为"full moon"，特纳译为"glorious moon"，林译为"moon"。笔者认为，此诗为中秋佳节之作，中秋应当是满月之时，四个版本中，只有许译很好地传递了"明月"这一意象。特纳用了"glorious"一词，"glorious"有"令人愉快的，美好的"之意，不符合词人在中秋之时还与胞弟分离的忧愁之情。紧接着对于"青天"的解读，杨宪益夫妇和林语堂均译为"blue sky"，许译为"sky"，特纳译为"azure sky"。考虑到词人是在夜晚创作的这首词，夜晚看不见天空的颜色，所以许渊冲没有添加任何形容词，只用一个"sky"来翻译，十分灵活。

双关是诗词中常见的修辞手法，双关可使语言表达更加含蓄、幽默。本首词中也含有双关，如"乘风归去"。乘风归去，归何处去？一语双关。一是词人想飞到天上，向往自由；二是词人想回到朝廷，为君效力。四个译本中，林语堂与特纳将"乘风归去"译成了"归家"，而许渊冲和杨宪益夫妇都使用了模糊的翻译手法，没有明确地指出归去哪儿，既保留了原词的双关，也给读者留下了更多想象的空间。许译对于"照无眠"的译法也有异曲同工之妙。无眠，谁无眠？许译并未给出答案，而是用"无眠之床"（sleepless bed）代替"无眠之人"，更加传神地传递了这一意境。

全文的最后"但愿人长久，千里共婵娟"情感上升至顶峰，是整首词的精髓。林语堂对此句使用了创造性译法，打破了原文的限制，更加巧妙地传递了词人的豁达与乐观。

最后，在诗歌翻译的形美方面，特纳的译本与原词字数相差较大，林语堂的译本与原词差异最小。例如，"转朱阁，低绮户，照无眠"的翻译，林语堂对应用了三个动词"round"，"stoop"和"shine"，不仅保留了原词语句较短的特点，又与原文的"转""低""照"形成了整齐的对应。而许渊冲对此句的翻译体现出了诗词的音韵美，"red""shed""bed"，接连三押，韵味十足。

课后思考

1.诗歌翻译中，要不要重现原诗的意象，如何重现原诗的意象？

2. 译者应该采用什么技巧来再现原诗的音韵美，如每行诗用多少音节或音步?

3. 四个译本的不同之处体现在哪些方面?

原文

寻寻觅觅，冷冷清清，凄凄惨惨戚戚。乍暖还寒时候，最难将息。三杯两盏淡酒，怎敌他、晚来风急! 雁过也，正伤心，却是旧时相识。

满地黄花堆积，憔悴损，如今有谁堪摘? 守着窗儿，独自怎生得黑! 梧桐更兼细雨，到黄昏、点点滴滴。这次第，怎一个愁字了得!

（李清照，《声声慢·寻寻觅觅》）

译文

So dim, so dark,

So dense, so dull,

So damp, so dank,

So dead!

The weather, now warm, now cold,

Makes it harder

Than even to forget

How can a few cups of thin wine

Bring warmth against

The chilly winds of sunset?

I recognize the geese flying overhead:

My old friends,

Bring not the old memories back!

Let fallen flowers lie where they fall.

To what purpose

And for whom should I decorate?

By the window shut,

Guarding it alone,

To see the sky has turned so black!

And the drizzle on the kola nut

Keeps on droning:

Pit-a-pat, pit-a-pat!

Is this the kind of mood and moment

To be expresses

By one word "sad"?

（林语堂译，"Forlorn"）

 原文

枯藤老树昏鸦，小桥流水人家，古道西风瘦马。夕阳西下，断肠人在天涯。

（马致远，《天净沙·秋思》）

译文

Crows hovering over rugged old trees wreathed with rotten vine — the day is about done. Yonder is a tiny bridge over a sparkling stream, and on the far bank, a pretty little village. But the traveler has to go on down this ancient road, the west wind moaning, his bony horse groaning, trudging towards the sinking sun, farther and farther away from home.

（翁显良译，"Autumn"）

第二节

中国现代诗歌英译

　　改革开放以来，随着我国综合国力的提高，中国文学走出去的浪潮已势不可挡。中国古典文学因其博大精深、内涵深厚吸引了不少外国读者，中国现代文学也因其新颖独特、形式多变获得了越来越多的关注。诗歌是文学史上的一颗恒星，超越了民族和国界。我国的白话诗最早始于 1917 年胡适在《新青年》上发表的《白话诗八首》。胡适主张新诗应该创立自由、不拘格律的文体。之后又相继涌现出刘半农、郭沫若、闻一多、徐志摩、戴望舒、艾青、何其芳、臧克家、卞之琳等卓越诗人。而对白话诗的译介可以追溯到 1935 年创办的《天下月刊》。1936 年第一本英译诗集《现代中国诗选》（*Modern Chinese Poetry*）出版，之后由罗伯特·白英（Robert Payne）编写的《当代中国诗选》（*Contemporary Chinese Poetry*）、许芥昱编写的《二十世纪中国诗》（*Twentieth Century Chinese Poetry*）、奚密（Michelle Yeh）编写的《中国现代诗选集》（*Anthology of Modern Chinese Poetry*）、戴乃迭翻译的《闻一多诗文选》、辜正坤翻译的《毛泽东诗词：英汉对照韵译》等也相继问世，为中国文学走出去做出了巨大贡献（李德凤、鄢佳，2013：26）。

　　本节我们主要讨论中国现代诗歌英译。一方面，读者可以在比较中感受古诗词与现代诗歌的差别；另一方面，读者可以更加深入地学习诗歌翻译。

课前准备

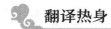 **翻译热身**

小时候，
乡愁是一枚小小的邮票，
我在这头，
母亲在那头。

长大后，
乡愁是一张窄窄的船票，
我在这头，
新娘在那头。

后来啊，
乡愁是一方矮矮的坟墓，
我在外头，
母亲在里头。

而现在，
乡愁是一湾浅浅的海峡，
我在这头，
大陆在那头。

（余光中，《乡愁》）

参考译文

When I was young,

Nostalgia was a tiny, tiny stamp,

Me on this side,

Mother on the other side.

When I grew up,

Nostalgia was a narrow boat ticket,

Me on this side,

Bride on the other side.

But later on,

Nostalgia was a lowly grave,

Me on the outside,

Mother on the inside.

And at present,

Nostalgia becomes a shallow strait,

Me on this side,

Mainland on the other side.

（余光中译，"Nostalgia"）

翻译难点聚焦

1. 译文对"乡愁""坟墓""海峡"等词的翻译是否准确，可否分别译成"homesick""tomb""channel"？

2. 译文是否移植了原诗的音韵美，重现了原诗的修辞手法？

3. 译文是否传递了原诗的思乡之情？

名译赏析

原作简介

《再别康桥》是中国现代诗人徐志摩的诗作，是新月派诗歌的代表作。此诗以离别康桥时的感情起伏为线索，抒发了对康桥依依惜别的深情。全诗语言轻盈柔和，形式精巧圆熟。诗人用虚实相间的手法，描绘了一幅幅流动的画面，构成了一个个美妙的意境，细致入微地将诗人对康桥的爱恋，对往昔生活的怀念，对眼前的无可奈何的离愁，表现得真挚、浓郁、隽永，是徐志摩诗歌中的绝唱。

原文

轻轻的我走了，
正如我轻轻的来；
我轻轻的招手，
作别西天的云彩。

那河畔的金柳，
是夕阳中的新娘；
波光里的艳影，

在我的心头荡漾。
软泥上的青荇，
油油的在水底招摇；
在康河的柔波里，
我甘心做一条水草！

那榆荫下的一潭，
不是清泉，是天上虹；
揉碎在浮藻间，
沉淀着彩虹似的梦。

寻梦？撑一支长篙，
向青草更青处漫溯；
满载一船星辉，
在星辉斑斓里放歌。

但我不能放歌，
悄悄是别离的笙箫；
夏虫也为我沉默，
沉默是今晚的康桥！

悄悄的我走了，
正如我悄悄的来；
我挥一挥衣袖，
不带走一片云彩。

（徐志摩，《再别康桥》）

译文

译文一

Silently I go,

As silently I came.

Silently I wave my hand

And bid farewell to the western clouds.

The golden willows on the river bank

Are brides beneath the setting sun:

Their flaming shadows in the wave's light

Move softly on my heart.

Green weed in soft clay,

Greenly tossing beneath the water:

In the soft waves of Cam

I am content to be a weed.

The pool under the elms' shadow

Is not a clear spring, but a rainbow

Shattered among pondweeds,

Falling at last into rainbow dreams.

Who seeks dreams? Poling a long pole,

Roving through places greener than green grass,

A boat fully loaded with starlight

Sings beneath splendid stars.

Now I cannot sing aloud,

And silent are the farewell flutes:

Even the insects are silent for me

On this silent Cambridge night.

Silently I go,

As silently I came.

I wave my sleeves,

Carrying away no silk of clouds.

（袁可嘉译，"Farewell to Cambridge"）

译文二

Softly I am leaving,

As I softly came;

I wave my hand in gentle farewell

To the clouds in the western sky.

The golden willow on the riverbank

Is a bride in the sunset;

Her luminous reflection in the ripples

Is swaying in my heart.

Plants in the soft mud

Wave in the current;

I'd rather be a water reed

In the gentle river of Cam.

The pool in the elm shade

Is not clear but iridescent;

Wrinkled by the swaying algae,

It settles into a rainbowlike dream.

In search of a dream? With a long pole,

Sail toward where the grass grows greener;

In a skiff loaded with starlight,

Sing among the shining stars.

But I cannot sing tonight;

Silence is the tune of farewell.

Summer insects are quiet for me, too;

Silent is Cambridge tonight.

Quietly I am leaving,

As I quietly came;

I raise my sleeve and wave,

Without taking away a whiff of cloud.

（Michelle Yeh译，"Second Farewell to Cambridge"）

译文三

Quietly I am leaving

Just as quietly I came;

Quietly I wave a farewell

To the western sky aflame.

The golden willow on the riverbank,

A bride in the setting sun;

Her colorful reflection

Ripples through my heart.

The green plants on the river bed,

So lush and so gracefully swaying

In the gentle current of the Cam

I'd be happy to remain a waterweed.

The pool under an elm's shade

Is not a creek, but a rainbow in the sky

Crushed among the floating green,

Settling into a colorful dream.

In search of a dream? You pole a tiny boat

Toward where the green is even more green

To collect a load of stars, as songs

Rise in the gleaming stellar light.

But tonight my voice fails me;

Silence is the best tune of farewell;

Even crickets are still for me,

And still is Cambridge tonight.

Silently I am going

As silently I came;

I shake my sleeves,

Not to bring away a patch of cloud.

（许芥昱译，"Second Farewell to Cambridge"）

赏析思路点拨

本首诗的题目为《再别康桥》，袁译为"Farewell to Cambridge"，奚密和许芥昱均译为"Second Farewell to Cambridge"。袁译"Farewell to Cambridge"意思为"康桥再见"，与原文"再别康桥"有区别，没有把题目中的"再"译出来。原诗中出现了许多唯美意象，这些巧妙的意象使得整首诗具有了色彩美与动态美，而三位译者对其中一些意象的翻译也出现了差异。如"青荇"，袁译为"green weed"，奚译为"plants"，许译为"green plants"。许译和奚译用"植物"（plants）这个总称代替了这一具体的意象，意象之美有所损失。青荇是一种多年生草本植物，浮在水面，根生在水底，所以青荇实际上也是一种水草，因此，袁译更准确地传达出了这一意象。接下来，对于"柔波"一词，袁译为"soft waves"，奚译为"gentle river"，许译为"gentle current"。作者用了"柔"来形容康河，而"waves"指的是大海的波涛，即海浪，给人一种汹涌的感觉，不符合作者想表达的优美柔和的康河形象。笔者认为，"ripple"一词可能更符合意境，试联想，风一吹，康河就会泛起涟漪，温柔恬静。最后从诗歌的整体结构与修辞上看，首尾呼应是本诗的一大特点，作者在开头和结尾均使用了"云"这一意象，三个译本所使用的句子结构基本与原文相符。但对两个副词"轻轻"和"悄悄"的翻译，三个译本有所差别。袁译均用了"silently"，许译用了"quietly"和"silently"，而奚译用了三个不同的词，从"softly"到"gentle"再到"quietly"，展现了这一过程的变化，从脚步轻柔，再到沉默，最后无声离去。此外，原诗基本保持隔行押韵，但三个译本未能做到如此整齐。原诗的标点在三个译本中也有所改变，如原诗有两处使用了感叹号，体现出作者对康桥的深深眷恋，而三个译本均未保留这一标点。

课后思考

1. 标点符号在诗歌翻译中是否重要？诗歌翻译是否必须保留原诗标点？

2. 有时候诗歌的作者与译者是同一人（如余光中的《乡愁》），即为"自译"，那么"自译"有何优势？

3. 三个译本在闻一多先生提出的诗学"三美"即"音乐美、绘画美、建筑美"上有何不同？

延伸阅读

 原文

北国风光，千里冰封，万里雪飘。望长城内外，惟余莽莽；大河上下，顿失滔滔。山舞银蛇，原驰蜡象，欲与天公试比高。须晴日，看红装素裹，分外妖娆。

江山如此多娇，引无数英雄竞折腰。惜秦皇汉武，略输文采；唐宗宋祖，稍逊风骚。一代天骄，成吉思汗，只识弯弓射大雕。俱往矣，数风流人物，还看今朝。

（毛泽东，《沁园春·雪》）

译文

What a scene is in the north found!

A thousand li of the earth is ice-clad aground,

Ten thousand li of the sky is snow-bound.

Behold! At both sides of the Great Wall

An expanse of whiteness conquers all;

In the Yellow River, up and down,

The surging waves are gone!

Like silver snakes the mountains dance,

Like wax elephants the highlands bounce,

All try to be higher than heaven even once!

Come, when the day is fine and bright,

How you'll be enamoured of the beautiful sight,

To view the land adorned in red and white.

With so much beauty is the land endowed,

So many heroes thus in homage bowed.

The first king of Qin and seventh king of Han,

Neither was a true literary man;

The first king of Song and the second king of Tang,

Neither was noted for poetry or song.

Even the Proud Son of Heaven, for a time,

Called Genghis Khan, in his prime,

Knowing only shooting eagle, over his tent with a bow so bent.

Alas, all no longer remain!

For truly great men!

One should look within this age's ken.

（辜正坤译，"Snow to the Tune of Spring Beaming in Garden"）

原文

假如我是一只鸟，

我也应该用嘶哑的喉咙歌唱：

这被暴风雨所打击着的土地，

这永远汹涌着我们的悲愤的河流，

这无止息地吹刮着的激怒的风，

和那来自林间的无比温柔的黎明……

——然后我死了，

连羽毛也腐烂在土地里面。

为什么我的眼里常含泪水？

因为我对这土地爱得深沉……

（艾青，《我爱这土地》）

译文

If I were a bird,

I would sing with my hoarse voice

Of this land buffeted by storms,

Of this river turbulent with our grief,

Of these angry winds ceaselessly blowing,

And of the dawn, infinitely gentle over the woods…

— Then I would die

And even my feathers would rot in the soil.

Why are my eyes always brimming with tears?

Because I love this land so deeply…

（欧阳桢、彭文兰、玛丽莱·金译，"I Love This Land"）

第三节

英美诗歌汉译

文学没有国界，在推出我国优秀文化的同时，我国也在译介西方优秀文学作品，其中自然也涉及英美诗歌的翻译。我国译介西方诗歌已有较长的历史了，进入我国的第一首汉译英诗是由一位西方来华传教士译介的英国诗人弥尔顿（John Milton）的十四行诗"On His Blindness"（《论失明》）（沈弘、郭晖，2005：44）。后来江枫的《雪莱诗选》、卞之琳的《英国诗选》、屠岸的《莎士比亚十四行诗一百首》等陆续出版。对于诗歌翻译，卞之琳等前辈提出了"以顿代步"的翻译策略，认为"以顿为节奏单位既符合我国古典诗歌和民歌的传统，又适应现代口语的特点。我们的方块字是单音字，我们的语言却不是单音语言。我们平常说话以两个字、三个字连着说为最多，而不是一个字一个字分开说的，因此在现代口语中，顿的节奏也很明显"（转引自罗新璋，1984：665）。对于英诗的汉译，逐渐形成不同的流派。本节我们主要讨论英美诗歌的汉译，下文提供了几首英美诗歌的原文和译本供读者学习、鉴赏。

课前准备

翻译热身

Two roads diverged in a yellow wood,

And sorry I could not travel both

And be one traveler, long I stood

And looked down one as far as I could

To where it bent in the undergrowth;

Then took the other, as just as fair,

And having perhaps the better claim,

Because it was grassy and wanted wear;

Though as for that the passing there

Had worn them really about the same,

And both that morning equally lay

In leaves no step had trodden black.

Oh, I marked the first for another day!

Yet knowing how way leads on to way,

I doubted if I should ever come back.

I shall be telling this with a sigh

Somewhere ages and ages hence:

Two roads diverged in a wood, and I—

I took the one less traveled by,

And that has made all the difference.

(Robert Frost, "The Road Not Taken")

参考译文

黄色的树林里分出两条路，

可惜我不能同时去涉足，

我在那路口久久伫立，

我向着一条路极目望去，

直到它消失在丛林深处。

但我却选了另外一条路，
它荒草萋萋，十分幽寂，
显得更诱人，更美丽；
虽然在这条小路上，
很少留下旅人的足迹。

那天清晨落叶满地，
两条路都未经脚印污染。
啊，留下一条路等改日再见！
但我知道路径绵延无尽头，
恐怕我难以再回返。

也许多少年后在某个地方，
我将轻声叹息将往事回顾：
一片树林里分出两条路——
而我选择了人迹更少的一条，
从此决定了我一生的道路。

（顾子欣译，《未选择的路》）

翻译难点聚焦

1. 译文是否传达出了"road""traveler"等意象的象征意义？

2. 译文没有按照原文的形式，而是选择自由体来译，这样处理有什么好处？

3. 原诗的第四节运用了反讽的手法，拓宽了诗歌的阐释空间，相比之下，译文是否丰富了主题意象的内涵？

名译赏析

原作简介

　　十四行诗是欧洲一种格律严谨的抒情诗体，而莎士比亚的十四行诗采用了四行和一副对句的结构。在其创作的所有十四行诗里，第十八首（Sonnet 18）是莎翁的经典之作，也是莎翁最广为流传的诗歌之一。全诗用新颖巧妙的比喻、丰富恰当的修饰使人物形象富有活力。一方面诗人赞美了"你"的美貌，另一方面诗人又歌颂了诗歌艺术的不朽。他化抽象概念为具体形象，用理性去思考和感受这个物质世界，凸显了那个时代背景下的人文主义精神。

原文

　　Shall I compare thee to a summer's day?

　　Thou art more lovely and more temperate:

　　Rough winds do shake the darling buds of May,

　　And summer's lease hath all too short a date:

　　Sometime too hot the eye of heaven shines,

　　And often is his gold complexion dimm'd;

　　And every fair from fair sometimes declines,

　　By chance or nature's changing course untrimm'd.

　　But thy eternal summer shall not fade,

　　Nor lose possession of that fair thou owest;

　　Nor shall Death brag thou wander'st in his shade,

　　When in eternal lines to time thou grow'st.

　　So long as men can breathe or eyes can see,

So long lives this, and this gives life to thee.

（Willian Shakespeare, "Sonnet 18"）

译文

译文一

我是否可以把你比喻成夏天？

虽然你比夏天更可爱更温和：

狂风会使五月娇蕾红消香断，

夏天拥有的时日也转瞬即过；

有时天空之巨眼目光太炽热，

它金灿灿的面色也常被遮暗；

而千芳万艳都终将凋零飘落，

被时运天道之更替剥尽红颜；

但你永恒的夏天将没有止尽，

你所拥有的美貌也不会消失，

死神终难夸口你游荡于死荫，

当你在不朽的诗中永葆盛时：

只要有人类生存，或人有眼睛，

我的诗就会流传并赋予你生命。

（曹明伦译，《莎士比亚十四行诗·第18首》）

译文二

我能否把你比作夏季的一天？

你可是更加可爱，更加温婉；

狂风会吹落五月的娇花嫩瓣，

夏季出租的日期又未免太短：

有时候苍天的巨眼照得太灼热，

173

他金光闪耀的圣颜也会被遮暗；

每一样美呀，总会失去美而凋落，

被时机或者自然的代谢所摧残；

但是你永久的夏天决不会凋枯，

你永远不会丧失你美的形象：

死神夸不着你在他影子里踯躅，

你将在不朽的诗中与时间同长。

只要人类在呼吸，眼睛看得见，

我这诗就活着，使你的生命绵延。

（屠岸译，《莎士比亚十四行诗·第18首》）

译文三

我可能把你和夏天相比拟？

你比夏天更可爱更温和：

狂风会把五月的花苞吹落地，

夏天也嫌太短促，匆匆而过：

有时太阳照得太热，

常常又遮暗他的金色的脸；

美的事物总不免要凋落，

偶然的，或是随自然变化而流转。

但是你的永恒之夏不会褪色，

你不会失去你的俊美的仪容；

死神不能夸说你在他的阴影里面走着，

如果你在这不朽的诗句里获得了永生；

只要人们能呼吸，眼睛能看东西，

此诗就会不朽，使你永久生存下去。

（梁实秋译，《莎士比亚十四行诗·第18首》）

赏析思路点拨

诗歌讲究形式与格律，三个译本中，曹译每行十二个字，最为工整，而梁译选择了散文体。本首诗歌中也出现了很多意象，如"summer""rough winds""buds of May""the eye of heaven"，三位译者对其中的一些意象有着不同的解读。如"the eye of heaven"，梁译为"太阳"，丢了暗喻，过于平实，原文意象有所损失。屠译为"苍天的巨眼"，曹译为"天空之巨眼"，译出了诗味，保留了原诗形象。从语言上论，曹译措辞优美，诗意满满，如"红消香断""转瞬即过""凋零飘落""流传"；梁译忠实平和，通俗易懂；而屠译多为直译，颇具现代汉语气息，如"每一样美啊""夸不着""未免太短""出租"。最后从修辞上讲，原诗使用了丰富的修辞手法，如"his gold complexion"使用了拟人的修辞手法，三个译本都保留了此修辞手法，但梁译"金色的脸"使得诗意有所流失。"When in eternal lines to time thou grow'st"一句用了提喻的修辞手法，用"诗行"代替了整个"诗篇"，曹明伦与屠岸均译为"诗"，只有梁实秋译成了"诗句"，保留了提喻的修辞手法。

课后思考

1. 诗歌翻译如何实现"神似"与"形似"？

2. 诗是否需要诗人来译？

3. 诗歌翻译如何处理好理解、表达与读者的三维关系？

延伸阅读

原文

I said, "I have shut my heart,

As one shuts an open door,

That Love may starve therein

And trouble me no more."

But over the roofs there came

The wet new wind of May,

And a tune blew up from the curb

Where the street-pianos play.

My room was white with the sun

And Love cried out in me,

"I am strong, I will break your heart

Unless you set me free."

（Sara Teasdale, "Over the Roofs"）

 译文

我说"我把心收起，

像人家把门关了

叫'爱情'生生的饿死，

也许不再和我为难了。"

但是五月的湿风，

时时从屋顶上吹来；

还有那街心的琴调

一阵阵地飞来。

一屋里都是太阳光，

这时候"爱情"有点醉了，

他说，"我是关不住的，

我要把你的心打碎了！"

（胡适译，《关不住了》）

 原文

When we two parted

In silence and tears,

Half broken-hearted

To sever for years,

Pale grew thy cheek and cold,

Colder thy kiss;

Truly that hour foretold

Sorrow to this.

The dew of the morning

Sunk chill on my brow —

It felt like the warning

Of what I feel now.

Thy vows are all broken,

And light is thy fame;

I hear thy name spoken,

And share in its shame.

They name thee before me,

A knell to mine ear;

A shudder comes o'er me —

Why wert thou so dear?

They know not I knew thee,

Who knew thee too well:—

Long, long shall I rue thee,

Too deeply to tell.

In secret we met —

In silence I grieve,

That thy heart could forget,

Thy spirit deceive.

If I should meet thee

After long years,

How should I greet thee? —

With silence and tears.

（George Gordon Byron, "When We Two Parted" ）

译文

想当年我们俩分手，

也沉默也流泪，

要分开好几个年头

想起来心就碎；

苍白，冰冷，你的脸，

更冷是嘴唇；
当时像真是预言
今天的悲痛。

早晨的寒露在飘落，
冷彻了眉头——
仿佛是预先警告我
今天的感受。
你抛了所有的信誓，
声名也断送：
听人家讲你的名字，
我也就脸红。

人家当我面讲你
我听来像丧钟——
为什么我从前想象你
值得我这么疼？
谁知道我本来认识你，
认识得太相熟：——
我今后会长久惋惜你，
沉痛到说不出！

你我在秘密中见面——
我如今就默哀：
你怎好忍心来欺骗，
把什么都忘怀！

多年后万一在陌路
偶尔再相会，
我跟你该怎样招呼？——
用沉默，用眼泪。

（卞之琳译，《想当年我们俩分手》）

第七章

影视翻译

影视从狭义上来讲就是电影以及电视节目。从广义上来看，影视包括了各种以视觉为载体的传播媒体。随着全球化的深入，越来越多的国外影视作品进入中国，丰富了中国观众的娱乐生活，传播了不同的文化。与此同时，中国的影视作品也逐渐在海外占有一席之地。国内外影视作品的有效传播，首先要克服的就是语言文化上的障碍。字幕及其翻译便成为影视作品"引进来"和"走出去"的关键。

影视作品的翻译实际上并非仅仅是对成片字幕的翻译，对于一部国际团队合作或者多国合拍面向全球发行的影片，翻译需要从创意开始，贯穿电影剧本创作、融资、制作、宣传、发行的全过程。但是，本书所关注的是文学翻译的层面，即要回归文本。那么，从影片的成片来看，文学翻译文本也不仅仅包括字幕，还包括片名、片头字幕、对白字幕、片尾字幕。从文学赏析和批评的角度出发，我们在本章将目光聚焦对白字幕，赏析和批评其翻译。

影视作品的对白字幕具有一定的特点。首先，字幕虽然以文字呈现，但其具有口语性。其次，字幕具有一定的传播性。一些流行的表达、特别的说法、俏皮话、方言等都会通过字幕的呈现进一步巩固其声音上的传播性。再次，字幕具有一定的服务性。字幕和画面相互配合，构建意义。因此，字幕的翻译不仅仅停留于文本层面，还要考虑画面、声音甚至每一帧的停留时间。

对白字幕翻译不仅要符合字幕本身的特点，更要符合影视行业的相关规范，例如：中文不能有标点符号，而英文必须要有完整的标点符号，所以断行、断句处理要得当；在翻译字幕时尊重目标观众的语言习惯和文化差异，不得直白翻译；在制作字幕时要选用简洁明了、便于识辨的外文字体。

本章关注中外影视翻译，为了丰富影视翻译的欣赏和批评内容，设置了经典英剧的汉译和国产剧的英译两节内容。前者聚焦针对角色身份和地位不同的人物对白如何译，为何如此译；后者关注在中外文化差异、时代差异较大的情况下如何译，为何如此译。同时也鼓励欣赏者和批评者从画面、声音、受众习惯、观影习惯等方面进一步探讨对白字幕的翻译，更鼓励他们在探讨与思考之后，付诸实践，自己亲自去翻译对白字幕。

第一节

经典英剧的汉译

近年来英剧成为海外观众的新宠，英剧最大的特点就是短小精悍，以三集到六集为主，类似于单本剧、电视电影、迷你剧这些电视类型。从体裁来看，英剧主要有改编剧、时代剧和现代剧三种形式。其中，改编剧严谨，时代剧庄重，现代剧则有丰富的个性甚至较为尖锐。

《唐顿庄园》属于时代剧，华丽复古、从容大气。人物的言谈、举止、服装、造型都还原了历史面貌。该剧表现了变革中的英国和冲突中的英国。冲突表现在由财产继承权引发的冲突以及新旧思想的冲突，变革表现在工业革命和第一次世界大战引发的变革。

在这样的冲突下，剧中人物，无论是贵族还是平民，无论是主人还是仆人，他们的对白集中表现了冲突这一时代主题。同时，随着剧情的发展，这些人物的对白还有可能出现一些话语上的变化，反映出新旧思想的碰撞。由于"变革"这一时代主题，剧中人物的文化身份可能会发生一定的变化，而身份的变化也会引起话语的变化。通过对字幕译本的阅读、欣赏和批评，读者不仅可以在语言的层面进一步认识对白字幕翻译的策略和技巧，更能从时代主题、文化身份等层面探索为何如此译，进而拓宽翻译研究的思路和视野。

课前准备

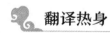 翻译热身

Chauffeur	Here we are, ma'am, Crawley House.
Mathew	For good or ill.
	I still don't see why I couldn't just refuse it.
Mrs. Crawley	There's no mechanism for you to do so.
	You will be an earl. You will inherit the estate.
	Of course, you can throw it away when you have it.
	That's up to you.
Molesley	Can I help?
	I'm Molesley, sir,
	your butler and valet.
Mathew	Mr Molesley, I'm afraid...
Mrs. Crawley	May I introduce ourselves?
	I am Mrs. Crawley
	and this is my son, Mr. Matthew Crawley.
Molesley	I'll just give Mr. Taylor a hand with the cases.
Mathew	I can...
Mrs. Crawley	Thank you, Molesley.
Mathew	I won't let them change me.
Mrs. Crawley	Why would they want to?

Mathew	Mother, Lord Grantham has made the unwelcome discovery
	that his heir is a middle-class lawyer
	and the son of a middle-class doctor.
Mrs. Crawley	Upper middle class.
Mathew	He wants to limit the damage
	by turning me into one of his own kind.
Mrs. Crawley	When you met him in London, you liked him.
Cora Grantham	I simply do not understand why we are rushing into this.
Lord Grantham	Mathew Crawley is my heir.
Cora Grantham	Patrick was your heir, he never lived here.
Lord Grantham	Patrick was in and out of this house since the day he was born.
	You saw how many of the village turned out for the service.
Cora Grantham	But nothing's settled yet.
Lord Grantham	It is settled, my dearest one, whether you like it or not.
Cora Grantham	I wouldn't say that.
	Not while your mother breathes air.

参考译文

司机	我们到了　夫人　卡劳利公馆
马修	好歹来了
	我还是不明白　为什么我不能直接推辞

克劳利夫人	你无法这么做
	你将成为伯爵　并继承庄园
	当然　继承之后你想败家弃位也行
	这都取决于你
马修	有事吗
莫斯利	我是莫斯利　先生
	您的管家兼贴身侍从
马修	莫斯利先生　恐怕
克劳利夫人	我谨自我介绍一下
	我是克劳利夫人
	这是我儿子　马修·克劳利先生
莫斯利	我先去帮泰勒先生搬行李
马修	我能
克劳利夫人	谢谢你　莫斯利
马修	我不会让他们改变我的
克劳利夫人	为什么他们会改变你
马修	妈妈　格兰瑟姆伯爵不幸发现
	他的继承人是一名中产阶级律师
	是一名中产阶级的医生的儿子
克劳利夫人	是中上阶级
马修	为了补偏救弊
	他定会把我改造成他的同类
克劳利夫人	你在伦敦见他时　还挺喜欢他的

格兰瑟姆伯爵夫人	我只是不知道为何如此匆忙
格兰瑟姆伯爵	马修·克劳利是我的继承人
格兰瑟姆伯爵夫人	帕特里克也是 他可从没在这里住过
格兰瑟姆伯爵	帕特里克从小就在这宅子里进进出出
	你也看到了 追思会那天村里来了多少人
格兰瑟姆伯爵夫人	一切尚未确定
格兰瑟姆伯爵	板上钉钉 亲爱的 不管你喜不喜欢
格兰瑟姆伯爵夫人	我看不见得
	老夫人只要尚有余息 绝不会善罢甘休

 翻译难点聚焦

1. 对白如何体现出不同角色的身份？

2. 如何在译文中传递贵族对白的尖酸刻薄之感？

3. 克劳利夫人在儿子马修说 "that his heir is a middle-class lawyer and the son of a middle-class doctor" 之后，补充了一句 "Upper middle class"。译为 "是中上阶级" 能够表现出其背后的深意吗？

名译赏析

 原作简介

《唐顿庄园》（*Downton Abbey*），是嘉年华电影公司为英国独立电视台（ITV）制作的一部时代迷你剧，创作人及主笔是演员兼作家朱利安·费罗斯（Julian Fellowes）。该剧时间设定在 20 世纪初，故事发生在英国君主乔治五世（George

Ⅴ）在位时约克郡一个虚构的庄园——"唐顿庄园"。唐顿庄园是本姓克劳利的世袭贵族格兰瑟姆伯爵夫妇的祖传府邸。这部剧便围绕着他们的家族和仆人们的生活展开。整个系列描写了多个现实中的历史事件。第一季第一集的故事时间设定于 1912 年 4 月，以泰坦尼克号沉没事故为引子。第二季的故事开场是第一次世界大战爆发后的 1916 年索姆河战役，其后还有 1918 年流感大流行。第三季的历史背景为爱尔兰独立战争导致形成爱尔兰自由邦。还有第四季的茶壶山丑闻案、1923 年英国大选及阿姆利则惨案，第五季的啤酒馆政变。第六季也是最终季描写了两次世界大战期间工人阶级的崛起，并暗示了英国贵族无可避免的衰落。

 ## 原文与译文

		（译文一）	（译文二）
Mrs. Crawley	Oh, Ellen.	艾伦	艾伦
	This is much better than I thought it would be.	这比我想象的好太多了	大大超出我预期啊
	You have done well.	你打点得真不错	打点得很不错
Ellen	Thank you, ma'am.	谢谢您 夫人	谢谢 夫人
Molesley	Would you like this in here, ma'am, or taken up to your room?	夫人 提包是放在这儿还是拿到您屋内	夫人 包放这儿还是拿上楼
Mrs. Crawley	In here, thank you.	放这儿吧 谢谢	这儿吧 谢谢
	So, are you the whole of our new household?	我们的新侍从就你一个人吗	我们新添的帮手就是你了

Molesley	There's a local girl, ma'am, Beth.	还有一位本地姑娘 夫人 名叫贝丝	还有贝丝 附近的姑娘
	She's to double under-housemaid and kitchen-maid.	她是杂物兼厨房女仆	杂役女仆 兼厨房帮佣
Mathew	This is ridiculous.	太荒谬了	搞什么搞
Mrs. Crawley	Thank you very much, Molesley.	非常感谢 莫斯利	非常感谢 莫斯利
	Might we have some tea?	能给我们上点茶吗	能上点茶吗
Molesley	Very good, ma'am.	当然 夫人	好的 夫人
Mathew	Well, he can go right now.	他现在就可以走了	他可以立马走人了
Mrs. Crawley	Why?	为什么	为什么
Mathew	Because we do not need a butler or a valet, if it comes to that.	因为我们不需要什么管家或是贴身侍从 若非如此的话	什么管家 贴身侍从 我们根本不需要
	We've always managed perfectly well with a cook and a maid,	我们向来只有一名厨子和一位女仆 不也过得很好	厨子女仆各一名 不也一直够用吗
	and they cannot expect us to alter our...	他们不能指望我们 改变自我	他们总不能当我们

Mrs. Crawley	What they expect, Mathew,	马修 他们指望的	他们当我们是粗俗的暴发户
	is that we won't know how to behave.	是我们不知道如何举止得体	
	So if you don't mind,	所以如果你不介意	千万别行差踏错落人口实
	I would rather not confirm their expectations.	我宁愿不要让他们的期望得逞	
Mathew	I have to be myself, Mother.	我得做我自己 妈妈	我得做我自己 母亲
	I'll be no use to anyone if I can't be myself.	否则我将一无是处	否则我一无是处
	And before they or you get any ideas,	在你或是他们擅作主张之前 我有言在先	我可有言在先
	I will choose my own wife.	婚姻大事 我要自己做主	婚姻大事我自己做主
Mrs. Crawley	What on earth do you mean?	你这话到底是什么意思	这话什么意思
Mathew	Well, they're clearly going to push one of the daughters at me.	显而易见 他们定要把一位女儿强嫁给我	他们肯定要强塞哪个女儿给我
	They'll have fixed on that when they heard I was a bachelor.	要是听说我还单身 他们就会确定婚事	一听说我单身就打好如意算盘了

Molesley	Lady Mary Crawley.	玛丽·卡劳利小姐到	玛丽·克劳利小姐到
Lady Marry	I do hope I'm not interrupting.	希望我没打扰到你们	没打扰你们吧
Mrs. Crawley	Lady Mary...	玛丽小姐	玛丽小姐
Lady Marry	Cousin Mary, please.	叫玛丽表亲就好	别见外 叫我玛丽吧
	Mama has sent me down to welcome you	妈妈命我来欢迎你们	妈妈命我邀你们
	and to ask you to dine with us tonight.	并邀请你们与我们共进晚餐	今晚共餐 接风洗尘
	Unless you're too tired.	除非你们舟车劳顿	若是旅途不太劳顿
Mrs. Crawley	We would be delighted.	我们乐意前往	我们很乐意
Lady Marry	Good. Come at 8:00.	那好 今晚八点见	那就好 今晚八点
Mrs. Crawley	Won't you stay and have some tea?	你不留下喝杯茶吗	要留下喝点茶吗？
Lady Marry	Oh, no, you're far too busy.	不了 你们这么忙	不了 你们太忙了
	And I wouldn't want to push in.	我又怎敢"强"留	我也不想强人所难
	Lynch, I think we'll go back by the South Lodge.	林奇 咱们从南屋那边回去吧	林奇 从南舍那条路回吧
Lynch	Very good, my lady.	是 小姐	遵命 小姐

Mathew	Lady Mary, I hope you didn't misunderstand me.	玛丽小姐 我希望你别误会	玛丽小姐 希望你别误会
	I was only joking.	我只是在开玩笑	我只是开玩笑
Lady Marry	Of course. And I agree.	当然 我也赞同	当然了 我也赞同
	The whole thing is a complete joke.	这整件事就是个天大的笑话	整件事就是个天大的笑话
Thomas	So what do you think we'll make of them?	你说他们会是什么样的人	你说他们是怎样的人
O'Brien	I shouldn't think much. She hasn't even got a lady's maid.	好不到哪去 她连贴身女仆都没有	没什么好说的 她连贴身女仆都没
Maid	It's not a capital offence.	又不是什么大忌	又不是罪大恶极
Bates	She's got a maid, her name's Ellen.	她有个女仆 名叫艾伦	她有女仆 叫艾伦
	She came a day earlier.	她提前一天到的	早一天到的
O'Brien	She's not a lady's maid.	她又不是贴身女仆	又不是贴身女仆
	She's just a housemaid that fastens hooks and buttons when she has to.	就是个持家女仆 招之即来 缝缝补补	就是个打杂的 随便使唤 缝缝补补罢了
	There's more to it than that, you know.	贴身女仆可比这讲究多了	当贴身女仆门道可多了
Mrs. Patmore	Daisy!	黛西	黛西

Anna	We'll want some very precise reporting when dinner's over.	晚饭后你再跟我们细说	晚餐后 你倒是详细说说
William	Are we to treat him as the heir?	我们要当他是继承人来服侍吗	要当他是继承人吗
O'Brien	Are we heck as like.	当他是就怪了	你倒是试试
	A doctor's son from Manchester?	就曼彻斯特一个医生的儿子	曼城一医生的儿子
	He'll be lucky if he gets a civil word out of me.	我要是给他好脸色就算他走运了	我要对他有好气 算他走运
Anna	We're all lucky if we get a civil word out of you.	你给我们谁好脸色 我们都感觉挺幸运的	你要有好气 大家都走运
Carson	Gwen, parcel for you. Came by the evening post.	格温 你的邮包晚班邮差送来的	歌薇 你的包裹晚班邮件一起的
	Thank you, Mr. Carson.	谢谢您 卡森管家	谢谢 卡森管家
William	Have you seen them yet, Mr. Carson?	您见过他们了吗卡森管家	您见过他们了吗卡森管家
Carson	By "them" I assume you mean the new family,	我想你说的是新来的那家	想必你指新来的那家
	in which case, no.	还没见过	还没见过
	I have that pleasure to look forward to this evening.	我有幸期待今晚得以一见	期待今晚有幸一见

Mrs. Patmore	Daisy, did you hear me call or have you gone selectively deaf?	黛西 你是没听见还是选择性耳聋	黛西 你故意当我耳旁风啊
Daisy	No, Mrs. Patmore.	没有 帕特莫太太	没有 帕特莫尔太太
Mrs. Patmore	Then might I remind you we are preparing dinner for your future employer.	那我是不是该提醒你 今晚我们可是为你未来主子准备晚宴	我可提醒你啊 今晚招待的可是你未来主子
	And if it goes wrong, I'll be telling them why.	如果出了差错 我可不会替你背黑锅	要有半点差错 仔细你的皮
Lady Marry	Why are they here at all when you're going to undo it?	你不是要撤销吗 怎么他们还是来了	不是要反对限定继承吗 还叫他们来
Cora Grantham	Your father's not convinced it can be undone.	你父亲不确定能够撤销	你父亲觉得希望不大
Lady Marry	But you'll still try.	但你还会争取	可你们还会争取
Cora Grantham	Granny and I are willing to try.	奶奶和我都会的	我和奶奶都会
Lady Marry	And Papa is not?	可爸爸不会	而爸爸不会
Cora Grantham	We'll bring him round, you'll see.	我们会说服他的	一定会说服他的
	We're trying to find a lawyer who'll take in on.	我们正打算找律师负责此事	在找律师处理此事

	So what are they like?	他们是什么样的人	他们人怎么样
Lady Marry	She's nice enough, but he's... very full of himself.	她人挺好的 但他 很是妄自尊大	她母亲还挺和善可他 却很自命不凡
Cora Grantham	Why do you say that?	何出此言	为什么这么说
Lady Marry	Just an impression.	印象而已	印象如此
	Let's go down and you can decide for yourself.	咱们下楼吧 您自可论断	下楼吧 你好眼见为实
Lord Grantham	Hello again.	又见面了	又见面了
	It's a pleasure to meet you at last, Mrs. Crawley.	很高兴终于见到你了 卡劳利夫人	很高兴终于见面了 克劳利太太
Mrs. Crawley	We're delighted to be here, aren't we, Mathew?	我们很荣幸光临贵府 对吧 马修	很荣幸登门拜访 是吧 马修
Mathew	Delighted.	很荣幸	没错
Cora Grantham	Welcome to Downton.	欢迎来到唐顿	欢迎来唐顿做客
Mrs. Crawley	Thank you. You've been so kind.	谢谢 您真是太好了	感谢您盛情相邀
Mathew	What a reception committee.	好隆重的迎接队伍	好大的迎宾阵仗

Mrs. Crawley	Yes, thank you.	是啊　谢谢	是啊　谢谢
Lord Grantham	This is Carson. We'd all be lost without him.	这位是卡森　万事打点都少不了他	这是卡森　我们不可或缺的管家
Lord Grantham	Mama, may I present Mathew Crawley and Mrs. Crawley.	妈妈　请允许我介绍马修和卡劳利夫人	妈妈　容我介绍马修和克劳利太太
	My mother, Lady Grantham.	我母亲　格兰瑟姆伯爵夫人	我母亲　格兰瑟姆伯爵夫人
Mrs. Crawley	What should we call each other?	你我该如何互相称呼	你我该如何相称
The Dowager	Well, we could always start with Mrs. Crawley and Lady Grantham.	可以叫卡劳利太太和格兰瑟姆伯爵夫人	叫"克劳利太太""格兰瑟姆夫人"总没错
Cora Grantham	Come into the drawing room	来客厅吧	来客厅
	and we can make all the proper introductions.	我们可以彼此正式介绍	——正式介绍吧
Lord Grantham	Do you think you'll enjoy village life?	不知两位乡村生活是否过得习惯	乡村生活不知是否合意
	It'll be very quiet after life in the city.	过惯了城市生活会觉得闲适很多吧	比起城市　要波澜不惊得多
The Dowager	Even Manchester.	即使跟曼彻斯特比	即便跟曼城比

Mrs. Crawley	I'm sure I'll find something to keep me busy.	我总会找到些事情做的	我肯定能找到事做
Cora Grantham	You might like the hospital.	也许医院合您的意	你可以考虑下医院
Mrs. Crawley	What sort of hospital is it? How many beds?	哪种医院 规模如何	怎样的医院 多少床位的
The Dowager	Well, it isn't really a hospital.	那儿可称不上是医院	算不上什么医院
Lord Grantham	Don't let Dr. Clarkson hear you.	别让克拉克森医生听见您这么说	别让克拉克森医生听到
	He thinks it's second only to St. Thomas'.	他认为那里仅次于圣托马斯医院	他认为就仅次于圣托马斯医院
Cora Grantham	It's a college hospital, of course, but quite well equipped.	虽说是所学校附属医院 可设备相当齐全	就是个诊疗所 但设施齐备
Mrs. Crawley	Who pays for it?	资金从哪里筹集	谁出资的
The Dowager	Oh, good, let's talk about money.	这可好 终于要提钱了	这下好了 餐桌上谈钱了
Lord Grantham	My father gave the building and an endowment to run it.	我父亲提供了场所并出资运营	家父捐赠的楼和运作基金
	In a way, he set up his own memorial.	他其实是给自己树碑立传	以此纪念他的丰功伟绩
Mrs. Crawley	But how splendid.	这种方式可谓高尚	但功德无量啊

Lord Grantham	And Mr Lloyd George's new insurance measures will help. ★★★	洛依德·乔治先生的保险新政也会有所帮助 （洛依德·乔治时为财政大臣后任首相）	还受益于财政大臣新推的国民保险法
The Dowager	Please don't speak that man's name. We are about to eat.	千万别提那人影响食欲	别提那人行吗我们还想吃饭
Thomas	I will hold it steady and you can help yourself, sir.	我会托住盘子您可随便取用先生	我托着盘　您来选　先生
Mathew	Yes, I know. Thank you.	当然　我知道谢谢	这我明白　谢谢
Lady Marry	You'll soon get used to the way things are done here.	你很快会习惯这里的生活方式	入乡随俗　你会习惯的
Mathew	If you mean that I'm accustomed to a very different life from this, then that is true.	如果你想说这与我平日生活 有天壤之别 诚然如此	这和我从前的生活方式 的确相去甚远
Sybil	What will you do with your time?	你打算如何消磨时光	那你平时要做什么

Mathew	I've got a job in Ripon, and I've said I'll start tomorrow.	我在里彭找了工作 明天就开始上班	我在里彭找到了工作 说好明天开始
Lord Grantham	A job?	你找了工作	工作
Mathew	In a partnership. You might have heard of it.	一家合伙人制律所 你们也许听过	哈维卡特律师事务所 也许你们听说过
	Harvell and Carter.	哈维－卡特事务所	
	They need someone who understands industrial law, I'm glad to say.	他们正需要一个懂工业法的人	他们正好缺懂劳工法的人
	Although I'm afraid most of it will be wills and conveyancing.	虽然恐怕大部分业务 还是遗产分配和产权转让	恐怕还是遗产分配 产权转让居多
Lord Grantham	You do know I mean to involve you in the running of the estate?	你该知道我打算让你参与管理庄园吧	我还想让你帮着打理家产呢
Mathew	Oh, don't worry. There are plenty of hours in the day.	不用担心 空闲时间很多	别担心 时间有的是
	And of course I'll have the weekend.	当然 还有周末	而且还有周末
Lord Grantham	We'll discuss this later, we mustn't bore the ladies.	迟些再谈吧 别让女士们觉得乏味	一会儿再谈 别让女士们乏味

The Dowager	What is a weekend?	什么是周末	什么 什么是周末
Daisy	Why shouldn't he be a lawyer?	当律师有什么不好	为啥他不能是律师
O'Brien	Gentlemen don't work, silly.	绅士不会去工作 傻丫头	绅士可不工作 傻瓜
	Not real gentlemen.	他不是真正的绅士	真正的绅士
Anna	Don't listen to her, Daisy.	别听她的 黛西	别听她的 黛西
Mrs. Patmore	No! Listen to me, and take those kidneys up to the server	还是听我的吧 快把那盘腰花端过去	该听我的把腰子送去备餐室
	before I knock you down and serve your brains as fritters!	要不我只能把你敲晕了用脑仁做煎饼	不然把你大卸八块 拿来下料
Daisy	Yes, Mrs. Patmore.	是的 帕特莫太太	这就去 帕特莫尔太太
Anna	Wonder what that Mr. Molesley makes of them.	不知莫斯利先生对他们怎么看	不知莫斯利管家做何感想
Thomas	Poor old Molesley.	可怜的老莫斯利	可怜的老家伙上了贼船了
	I pity the man who's taken that job.	得到这苦差事真让人同情	

Bates	Then why did you apply for it?	那你当初为什么申请	你不也求职了
Thomas	I felt it might help me to get away from you, Mr. Bates.	为了避开你 贝茨先生	一山容不下二虎啊 贝茨先生
Mrs. Crawley	I'm so interested to see the hospital.	我对那所医院很有兴趣	我很有兴趣看下医院
The Dowager	Ooh. Well, you would be, with your late husband a doctor.	可不是嘛 您先生以前就是位医生	那可不 你丈夫生前不就是医生嘛
Mrs. Crawley	Not just my husband.	不只我丈夫	不光是他
	My father and brother, too.	我的父亲和哥哥也是	还有我父亲和兄长
	And I trained as a nurse during the war.	大战时我也当过护士	我战时亦受过医护特训
The Dowager	Oh, fancy.	真厉害	了不得
Mrs. Crawley	I'd love to be involved in some way.	我非常愿意参与其中	我很想尽一份绵力
The Dowager	Well, you could always help with the bring-and-buy sale next month.	下个月的义卖会你倒是能帮上些忙	下月的义卖你总有用武之地
	That would be most appreciated.	我们会非常感激的	届时将感激不尽
Thomas	She's a match for the old lady,	她跟老太太真是棋逢对手	可不是 老太太棋逢对手了

	she wasn't going to give in.	她不会轻易让步的	人家可倔得很
Carson	What old lady are you referring to, Thomas?	你说的是哪位老太太 托马斯	你说哪个老太太 托马斯
	You cannot mean her ladyship, the Dowager Countess.	不会是老伯爵夫人吧	不可能是说老夫人吧
	Not if you wish to remain in this house.	如果你还打算在这里干下去	除非你想卷铺盖走人
Thomas	No, Mr. Carson.	不是 卡森先生	不想 卡森管家

 赏析思路点拨

影视作品的对白与人物的性格有着直接的联系。《唐顿庄园》中 Lady Marry 作为大小姐，气质高贵，仪态优雅，性格当中透着固执和强硬，她不会轻易改变自己的想法。从整部剧中其语言特色来看，她冷漠无情、尖酸刻薄，但是其与市井妇人有着极大的区别，她善于玩文字游戏，将"毒舌"转换成俏皮话。

Lady Marry 与 Mathew 初见时，恰巧听见了 Mathew 与母亲的对话："they're clearly going to push one of the daughters at me." Mathew 不愿接受自己是庄园继承人这一既定的事实，表现出对庄园及庄园相关事务的抵触。考察两个译文，译文一将"push"译为"强嫁"，译文二译为"强塞"。考虑到电影的对白口语性强，"强嫁"未免有点书本气，而"强塞"则更加口语化。不过，Mathew 的身份是中产阶级，虽然他不是贵族，但是他也受到过良好的教育。那么他的言行举止是否与"强塞"这样的话语搭配，这是读者需要进一步思考的问题。身份与语言的关系是读者在赏析译文时应该时刻考虑的问题。

  Lady Marry 在回绝 Crawley 一家留其喝茶的邀请时说："I wouldn't want to push in."这既起到了回绝的作用，更在一定程度上暗示，你们刚才的对话，我可是听见了，而且暗含着你们这种出身怎能配上我之意。虽然表面上轻描淡写，但是实际上火药味十足，显示出了这位唐顿庄园大小姐所使用的话术，体现了她的机智和性格。

  在《唐顿庄园》这部历史剧中，人物的身份、社会地位、特定时期的习俗等都影响和制约着对白的翻译。读者不妨顺着这一思路，梳理出相关人物的对白，考察人物的身份，回到当时的历史语境，从阶层、话语、语言政策、说话习惯等方面去探索，分析译文是否符合人物的身份。

课后思考

1. 对白字幕翻译如何在有限的空间内表现人物的性格与身份？
2. 在对白字幕翻译中，增加注释有何作用？如何自然地将注释融入画面中？
3. 如何在文字里体现出人物的特定语气？

延伸阅读

Daisy	I'll do it.	我来缝吧
	And cheer up, we've all had a smack from Mr. Carson.	别在意 谁没挨过卡森先生骂呢
Anna	You'll be the butler yourself one day,	总有一天你会成为管家
	then you'll do the smacking.	到时候你就可以去教训别人了
William	I could never be like him.	我可不会像他那样
	I bet he comes from a line	我打赌他家

	of butlers that goes back to the Conqueror.	祖祖辈辈都是给人做管家的
Bates	He learned his business	这是他从业多年的积累
	and so will you.	你早晚也会学到的
	Even Mr. Carson wasn't born standing to attention.	卡森先生也非生来就是谨言慎行
Thomas	I hope not for his mother's sake.	否则可够他母亲受的
William	This was at the back door.	这封信从后门送进来的
Carson	Thank you, William.	谢谢　威廉
Dr. Clarkson	It's kind of you to take an interest.	您对医疗事业真是有心了
Mrs. Crawley	I'm afraid it's a case of the warhorse and the drum.	这就像战马闻鼓声那种兴奋
	You know my late husband was a doctor.	您要知道先夫也是医生
Dr. Clarkson	I do. I'm familiar with Dr. Crawley's	卡劳利医生在
	work on the symptoms of infection in children.	儿童传染病症方面的著作我曾反复拜读
Mrs. Crawley	Oh. Even I studied nursing during the South African War.	英布战争中我本人也学过护理
	★★★	（英布战争 1899—1902）
Dr. Clarkson	Really?	真的
	Very distressing. Young farmer, John Drake.	真让人痛心　年轻的农夫约翰·德雷克

	A tenant of Lord Grantham's. He came in today.	伯爵的佃户 今天来就诊的
	It's dropsy, I'm afraid.	恐怕是积水
Mrs. Crawley	May I see him?	能让我看看吗
Dr. Clarkson	Yeah. By all means.	当然 请便
Mrs. Crawley	Is the dropsy of the liver or the heart?	是肝脏还是心脏
Dr. Clarkson	Everything points to the heart.	从各种症状来看是心脏
	All right, Mr. Drake, you're in safe hands now.	别担心 德雷克先生 你会没事的
Mrs. Crawley	What will happen to his wife?	他妻子该怎么办
Dr. Clarkson	She may try to keep the farm on.	她大概会努力让农场维持下去
	Grantham is not a harsh landlord, but her children are young.	伯爵对佃户向来宽厚 可毕竟她家孩子还小
Mrs. Crawley	What can I do to help?	我能帮上忙吗
	If I'm to live in this village, I must have an occupation.	如果我要在这儿住下 总得有些事做
	Please. Let me be useful.	请让我尽点力吧
Molesley	He chooses his clothes himself.	他亲自挑选衣服
	He puts them out at night and hangs the ones he's worn.	晚上取出来摆好 穿过的就挂在这儿
	I get to take the linen down to the laundry.	我负责把衣物送洗

	But that's about all.	差不多就这一件事
Bates	That's all?	就这样
Molesley	"I'll do this", he says,	"我自己来" 他总是说
	"I'll take the other". "I'll tie that".	"我要拿另一件" "我来系那个"
	And I'm just stood there like a chump watching a man get dressed.	而我就像个笨蛋一样站在那儿 看着他自己穿戴
	To be honest, Mr. Bates, I don't see the point of it.	老实说 贝茨先生 我不懂这有何意义
Lord Grantham	I thought you didn't like him.	我看您不大喜欢他
The Dowager	Well, so what?	那又怎样
	I have plenty of friends I don't like.	我不喜欢的人多了可还得逢场作戏
Lord Gramtham	Would you want Mary to marry one of them?	但您没打算让玛丽嫁给他们
The Dowager	Why do you always have	为什么每次
	to pretend to be nicer than the rest of us?	你都要装好人
Lord Gratham	Perhaps I am.	也许我本就如此
The Dowager	Then pity your wife,	那就可怜可怜你妻子吧
	whose fortune must go to this odd young man,	她的财产都得扔给这个古怪的年轻人

	who talks about "weekends" and "jobs".	说着什么周末什么工作的
	If Mary were to marry him then all would be resolved.	如果玛丽嫁给他一切问题迎刃而解
Anna	What've you got there?	看什么呢
Maid	Nothing.	没什么
Anna	What kind of nothing?	没什么是什么
	You haven't got an admirer?	不会是有人向你表白吧
Maid	I might have. Why shouldn't I?	也许有呢 我就不能有吗
	Don't tell Mrs. Hughes	可别让休斯太太听见
	or she'll bring the vicar round to have you exorcised.	否则她得找牧师给你驱鬼
Maid	How are we supposed to find husbands	她不让我们见男人
	if we're never allowed to see any men?	那还怎么找丈夫
Anna	Perhaps she thinks the stork brings them.	等喜鹊搭桥送来呗
	Lady Mary's in for a surprise.	玛丽小姐要大吃一惊了
	Thomas was in the library	托马斯说 他在图书馆里
	when old Violet came in from the garden.	听见老巫婆从花园进来
	Seems they want to fix her up with Mr. Crawley.	说要帮她和卡劳利先生牵线呢

Maid	Well, it makes sense. She was going to marry Mr. Patrick.	这说得通 她原本就要嫁给帕特里克少爷的
Anna	Would she have, though,	时候到了
	when it came to it? That's the question.	她真的会嫁给他吗 这才是问题所在
Mrs. Crawley	There you are, dear.	孩子 你可回来了
	I was hoping you'd be home in time.	我就怕你错过
	In time for what?	错过什么
	I've been paid the compliment of a visit.	有贵客上门拜访
Mathew	Hello.	两位好
Cora Grantham	Good afternoon, cousin Mathew.	马修表亲 下午好
The Dowager	Afternoon.	好
Cora Grantham	We were just saying how charming this room is now.	我们正说呢 这房间现在真漂亮
The Dowager	It always seemed rather dark	是啊 我婆婆生前住时
	when my mother-in-law lived here.	这儿总乌糟糟的
	But then she made everything rather dark.	不过话说回来 她能让所有事物都乌糟糟的
Molesley	Sir.	先生请用
Mathew	No, thank you.	不了 谢谢
Molesley	A cup of tea, sir?	喝茶吗 先生

Mathew	It's all right. I'll help myself.	没事 我自己来
The Dowager	So, Molesley, how do you find being home again?	莫斯利 重回故地 感觉怎样
	Your father must be glad you're back.	你父亲很为你高兴吧
Molesley	He is, Your Ladyship.	是的 夫人
The Dowager	Might I give you this cup?	帮我拿着吧
	I'm afraid we must be going.	我们得告辞了
	Thank you.	谢谢
Cora Grantham	You'll think about it?	考虑一下吧
Carson	I thought no one was here.	没想到这有人
Anna	Can I help, Mr. Carson?	要我帮忙吗 卡森先生
Carson	No. No, thank you, Anna.	不了 谢谢你 安娜
Mrs. Crawley	May I?	我听一下
Dr. Clarkson	I must compliment you, Mrs. Crawley.	我必须要称赞你 卡劳利夫人
	When you made your offer,	刚才您自荐时
	I thought you might be a "great lady nurse"	我以为您是要来装装样子
	and faint at the sight of blood.	见血就要晕了
	But I see you're made of sterner stuff.	没想到您训练有素
Mrs. Crawley	It's definitely the heart.	肯定是心包积水

	It's almost too quiet to hear at all.	心跳无力　基本听不到
Dr. Clarkson	I'm afraid so.	恐怕是的
Mrs. Crawley	I've been thinking about the treatments that are available.	我在琢磨可行疗法
	Considerable success have been achieved over the last few years	过去几年里许多医生成功地通过用针筒
	by draining the pericardial sac of the excess fluid	抽出心包积水并注入肾上腺素的方法
	and administering adrenaline.	治愈了病人
Dr. Clarkson	Mrs. Crawley, I appreciate your thoroughness.	卡劳利夫人　感谢您的周全考虑
Mrs. Crawley	But you're unwilling to try it?	但你不愿尝试吗
Dr. Clarkson	Injection of adrenaline is a comparatively new procedure.	注射肾上腺素的疗法是比较新的医疗手段
Mrs. Crawley	It's a while ago now,	尽管有一段时间了
	but I saw my husband do it. I know how.	但我观摩过我丈夫医治过现在还记得
Dr. Clarkson	Please, Mrs. Crawley, don't force me to be uncivil.	卡劳利夫人　请不要让我为难
	We would be setting an impossible precedent	一旦有此先例
	when every villager could demand the latest fad in treatment	村民佃户们一有点头疼脑热

	for each new cut and graze.	就都跑来要新疗法了
Mrs. Crawley	I would remind you that	恕我直言
	we're not talking of a cut or a graze,	这可不是头疼脑热
	but the loss of a man's life and the ruin of his family.	病人一旦不治　这个家就毁了
Dr. Clarkson	Of course. But I beg you to see that it is not reasonable.	您说得没错　但这实在不可行
O'Brien	I'm sorry but I have standards.	我可是有原则的
Anna	I've just seen something ever so odd.	今天有件怪事
O'Brien	And if anyone thinks I'm going to pull my forelock and curtsy	不是谁都受得起我伺候的
	to this Mr. Nobody from Nowhere...	尤其是这位不速之客
Cora Grantham	O'Brien!	奥布瑞恩
	Were you discussing Mr. Crawley?	你说的是卡劳利先生吗
O'Brien	Yes, my lady.	是的　夫人
Cora Grantham	Is it your place to do so?	这话轮得到你说吗
O'Brien	I've got my opinions, my lady, same as anybody.	我跟别人一样　有自己的见解　夫人
Mrs. Hughes	Can I help, Your Ladyship?	有事吩咐吗　夫人

Cora Grantham	This is the button we're missing from my new evening coat.	这是我新晚礼服掉的扣子
	I found it lying on the gravel.	我在碎石路上找到的
	But I was shocked at the talk I heard as I came in.	可进来时我听到些话　很震惊
	Mr. Crawley is His Lordship's cousin and heir.	卡劳利是老爷的表亲　也是继承人
	You will therefore, please,	因此　请你要
	accord him the respect he's entitled to.	给予他应有的尊重
O'Brien	But you don't like him yourself, my lady.	但夫人您也看不上他
	You never wanted him to...	您没想让他
Cora Grantham	You're sailing perilously close to the wind, O'Brien.	你真是太过分了　奥布瑞恩
	If we're to be friends, you will not speak in that way again	如果我们要继续做朋友　你就别乱嚼舌根子
	about the Crawleys or any member of Lord Grantham's family.	少议论他们母子和其他家族成员
	Now I'm going up to rest. Wake me at the dressing gown.	我上楼休息了　更衣时叫醒我

国产剧的英译

　　2012 年，电视剧《甄嬛传》热映，成为国产电视剧的传奇，其收视率排名全国第一。该剧的热度从中国大陆蔓延到了中国香港、台湾地区以及东南亚。在此影响力的推动下，两年后，美国公司购买了《甄嬛传》播放权并重新进行了剪辑，将 76 集的长剧精剪为 6 集、每集 90 分钟的英文版电视电影，在美国收费视频网站 Netflix 播出，但是其收视率并不理想。

　　分析这一跨文化传播案例，我们不难看出，在存在"时间差""语言差"的文化的交流中，诸多因素影响着国产剧的"走出去"，其中一个重要因素就是字幕的翻译。

　　本节聚焦电视剧《甄嬛传》的对白字幕翻译。该剧的时代背景为清朝雍正年间，主要讲述了女主角甄嬛选秀入宫，在皇后、华妃等几方势力夹击与宫闱斗争中，从不谙世事的闺阁少女成长为善于权谋的圣母皇太后的故事。《甄嬛传》所蕴含的文化、所使用的语言，迥异于西方电视剧。而通过字幕翻译，我们可以在东西方观众之间架起一座沟通的桥梁。赏析现有字幕译本，梳理其中所使用的策略，发掘其中所存在的问题，再结合影视翻译的行业规则、受众的预期等诸多因素，我们便可以总结出规律，形成对字幕翻译的正确认识，从而指导翻译实践。

课前准备

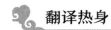 翻译热身

第 0 幕

旁白：公元一七二二年，清康熙皇帝驾崩，川陕总督年羹尧和步军统领隆科多在皇位继承人大战中为四阿哥胤禛登基立下汗马功劳，被雍正视作社稷重臣，一时权倾朝野，成为新政权的核心人物。

太监：跪！一叩首！再叩首！三叩首！兴！

苏培盛：奉天承运，皇帝诏曰：隆科多真圣祖皇帝忠臣，朕之功臣，国家良臣，袭一等公，授吏部尚书并兼管理藩院。川陕总督年羹尧授二等公，凡调遣军兵、动用粮饷之处，着边防办饷大臣及川陕云南督抚提镇等，俱照年大将军办理，钦此。

百官：谢主隆恩！

第 1 幕

官员甲：咱们皇上可真是器重年将军和隆科多大人。

官员乙：隆科多大人，恭喜恭喜啊！您可是国家的大功臣啊！

官员丙：年大将军，皇上对你可是垂青有加呀！

官员丁：年大人，您可是皇上的股肱之臣哪！

苏培盛：年大将军请留步。大将军——

年羹尧：苏公公，有何指教？

苏培盛：不敢。皇上惦记大将军您的臂伤，特让奴才将这秘制的金创药膏交给大人，叫您使用。

年羹尧：臣年羹尧恭谢皇上圣恩！敢问苏公公，小妹今日在宫中可好啊？

苏培盛：华妃娘娘凤仪万千、宠冠六宫啊，大将军您放心好了。

年羹尧：那就有劳苏公公了。

苏培盛：应该的。

 **参考译文**[1]

In the year 1722, Emperor Kangxi of the Qing Dynasty passed away. General Nian Gengyao and General Long Keduo played a crucial role in Emperor Yongzheng's accession to the throne. Emperor Yongzheng, 45, was the Fourth Prince named Yin Zhen. He held the two generals in high esteem, which won them unrivaled political powers.

All kneel!

All bow!

Second time!

Third time!

All rise!

(Long Keduo)

By the Grace of Heaven, His Majesty awards Long Keduo the First-Order Honor for his loyal service to the prior Emperor and His Majesty.

Zhang Tingyu [he's not happy]

Long Keduo is appointed as Minister of Personnel, and Director of Ethnic and Territorial Affairs.

His Majesty awards Nian Gengyao the Second-Order Honor.

1　译文为影片英文字幕，因此对话前未加讲话人。上页原文为了让读者作为阅读译文的参照，采用了剧本形式，加上了说话人。

He will be in charge of military affairs

(Zhen Yuandao)

He will be in charge of military affairs

(Guaerjia Emin)

and the appointment of frontier officials.

This is His Majesty's edict.

I thank His Majesty.

His Majesty does think highly of General Nian.

Congratulations, General Long!

We are grateful for your exceptional contribution to our country.

Congratulations, General Nian!

His Majesty truly appreciates your service.

Sir, you certainly are His Majesty's right-hand man.

General Nian!

Greetings, General Nian!

How can I help you, Mr. Su?

His Majesty is concerned with your arm injury.

He instructed me to send you the

specially-made ointment for the wound.

I HUMBLY thank His Majesty for the heavenly grace.

May I ask how my sister is doing in the palace?

No one is comparable with your sister, Consort Fleur.

There's nothing to worry about her.

Thanks for taking care of her.

My pleasure.

翻译难点聚焦

1. 中国古代的官职如何翻译？

2. 历史剧中，礼仪性话语采用怎样的策略进行翻译？

3. 姓氏采用音译和意译在字幕翻译中会有何不同的效果？

名译赏析

 原作简介

电视剧《甄嬛传》围绕一位出身官宦人家的汉军旗女子甄嬛展开，她聪明伶俐，美貌与智慧并存。她自小的梦想是"愿得一心人，白首不相离"，并没有入宫为妃的打算。不想入宫的她，却意外留在宫中，初入宫就吸引皇帝的目光，但受到几乎全后宫的嫉妒和暗算。在几次受宠与失宠之际，她看透了后宫的真面目。从不谙世事的善良女子成长为善于权谋的深宫妇人，借由才智自无数次失势中翻身，终究登峰造极，成为至高无上的皇太后，同时体验到深宫中的冰冷孤寂。

 原文与译文

苏培盛	皇上　敬事房的人来了	Your Majesty, an official from Attendance Services is here.
徐进良	请皇上翻牌子　皇上　您这半个月都没进后宫了　要是今天再不翻牌子　那太后一定会怪罪奴才的　皇上	Your Majesty, please select one. Your Majesty has not been visiting any consorts for the past two weeks. Her Majesty the Empress Dowager is going to blame my negligence. Your Majesty, please!

皇帝	哪来那么多话	She'll just blame you for talking too much.
小厦子	皇上 太后来了	Her Majesty the Empress Dowager is here.
皇帝	快 请太后进来	Show her in quickly.
小厦子	嗻	Yes.
苏培盛	太后万安	Peace to Your Majesty.
皇帝	给皇额娘请安	Greetings, Mother.
太后	天热 我叫御膳房做了绿豆百合粥 哀家吃着不错 知道你还没睡 给你送一碗过来	The Imperial Kitchen made me sweet mung bean soup with lily roots. It calms me down on such a hot night. I brought you some, figuring you must be awake.
皇帝	多谢皇额娘	Thank you so much.
竹息	皇上 这是隆科多大人打扬州给太后新弄来的酱菜 说是比三必居的爽口	General Long got the pickles for Her Majesty from the south. It is more refreshing than what we have here in Beijing.
徐进良	来来来	Here we go.
苏培盛	也别苦着张脸了 左不过天天都是这样子	Don't be upset. We'll get used to it.
徐进良	皇上登基都已经大半年了 可是这每个月进后宫的日子 掰着指头都数得清楚	It's been over 6 months since his coronation. But you can count on one hand the times he slept in the harem.

苏培盛	唉 这敬事房的差事一闲 太后难免会责问 这倒难为你两头为难了	I understand your frustration of displeasing both His Majesty and Her Majesty.
徐进良	哎呀 多亏有苏公公体谅 还望在皇上面前多多提醒才是 后宫那些小主们 盼皇上就像久旱盼甘霖呢	Thank you for your understanding. I would be most grateful if you could often remind His Majesty that his concubines miss him like desserts miss the rain.
苏培盛	哎呀 哪有不劝的 只是皇上这两天哪 忙于朝政 连睡觉都只睡两三个时辰 咱们做奴才的想劝也张不了口啊	I would like to oblige, but His Majesty has been so busy lately that he could only sleep for 4-6 hours.I had no chance to mention the concubines.
皇帝	皇额娘要是嫌天热 儿子可以让他们拿些冰 放在额娘的宫中	Mother, if you are bothered by the heat, I will have ice sent to your palace.
太后	人老了 倒也不怕热 叫人放心不下的是皇帝你 早晚忙着朝政的事 自己的身子要有数	My aging body is not as sensitive to the heat.You should care more about your health. Work cannot be finished in one day.
皇帝	儿子知道	I understand.
太后	你这么忙着 可有关心三阿哥的功课	Did you take some time to look into the Third Prince's schoolwork?
皇帝	前两天还查了他的功课 字是练得不错 学问上长进不大	I did. He was coming along with his calligraphy, but not so much with the books.

太后	先帝有你们二十四个儿子 皇帝就不如先帝了	Your three sons cannot compare to the prior Emperor's 24 smart princes.
皇帝	儿膝下福薄 只有三个皇子 让皇额娘挂心了	I understand your concern. I am not as blessed as Father.
太后	也不怪你 先帝嫔妃多 自然子嗣多 你后宫才那么几个人 皇后 端妃 齐妃 她们年纪都不小了 想要延绵子嗣也难	It's not your fault. He had more children because he had more concubines. Your harem is almost empty. The Empress, Consort Honnête, and Consort Astuce, they are not getting any younger.
皇帝	儿子不是不为子嗣的事着想	I understand.
太后	皇家最要紧的是要开枝散叶 绵延子嗣 才能江山万年 代代有人 为此才要三年一选秀 充实后宫	It is the Imperial Family's priority to have children in plenty, so that we can pass the throne through generations. That is why we have a Concubine Selection every three years.
皇帝	皇额娘教训的是	Of course.
太后	那么 选秀的事就定了	So, we will have a Selection.
太后	一切听皇额娘安排	Yes, I accept your arrangement.
太后	哀家老了 还能安排什么呀 让内务府挑个好日子 一轮一轮挑下来 挑到出色的给你为嫔为妃 哀家就等着含饴弄孙了	I am too old to arrange for you. The Imperial Household Department will set the dates for a few rounds of selection. I will just happily wait for more grandchildren.

皇帝	皇后事多　华妃协理六宫　选秀的事宜就让华妃去操办吧	I will let Consort Fleur take charge of the Selection, not to put more burden on the Empress.
太后	华妃能干　漂亮　你宠了她这么多年了　选个新人进来也好　平分春色总胜于一枝独秀	Consort Fleur is more than just a pretty face. You have loved her exclusively for years, and now it's better that you have someone to balance with her.
皇帝	是　皇额娘　儿子还有一件事	Sure. But there's something I'd like to change.
太后	什么	What is it?
皇帝	既然选秀　儿子想这一次也就够了　如果真的三年一次　也太铺张了　另外　儿一直觉得应该满汉一家　所以这次想多从汉军旗里选几个秀女	One Selection is enough for me. It is costly to do it every three years. I see Han people [the dominant ethnic group] as family to us Manchus. I'd like more concubines from the Han Banners. [Banner is a military establishment in 8 ranks]
太后	这些都是小节　无妨　皇帝愿意选新人就好　只是也别冷落了旧人　朝政再要紧　后宫还得常去　还有皇后　再怎么说也是中宫啊	I'm fine with that. I'm glad you are having new concubines. But do not make the old ones feel neglected. You should often visit them no matter how much work you have. Especially the Empress, she is the pillar of your harem.
皇帝	儿子知道	I'll remember that.

赏析思路点拨

电视剧《甄嬛传》中的中国传统文化、清代宫廷故事为翻译带来了一定的挑战。面对这样的文本，译者往往会通过注解的方式进行传译。不过，对于文学作品来说，"厚译"有其局限性。影视字幕尤其如此，影视剧中每一帧字幕的字符数有严格的限制，字符如果过多，会极大地影响观感。

不过，影视作品并非仅由文本构成，在文本之外，还有声音、画面等。当然，译者不能通过画外音的方式就某些陌生的概念向观众进行解释，但译者可以利用银幕来加以补充说明。

例如，剧中出现"敬事房""翻牌子"等概念，由于字幕字符数的限制，译者将其处理为"Attendance Service"。西方观众无法仅从这一短语了解敬事房的作用，也许还会产生误解。此时译者有必要用简略的语言，说明敬事房的作用在于管理和记录皇帝与后妃的房事。但是，这一信息不能出现在字幕中，因为这会超越字符数的限制。

译者可以在敬事房总领内监徐进良出现在画面中时简略叙述他的职责，侧面突出敬事房的作用。所以，在影视剧对白翻译中，如果遇到需要注解的地方，译者尽可从画面中寻找合适的时机和空间，进行一种"亡羊补牢"式的解释，从而既不破坏字幕翻译规范，也不会让观众对某些概念一头雾水，甚至产生误解。

另外，我们也注意到，《甄嬛传》字幕译者将诸多隐喻的喻体进行了消解。例如，"平分春色总胜于一枝独秀"被译为"now it's better that you have someone to balance with her"。这句话传递出了原文的意思，但是此句话出自太后之口，从其身份的角度考量，其语言定然很"雅"，译者如何在此既体现出太后用语的"雅"，又保留原语的隐喻便成了一个不小的挑战。

课后思考

1. 影视作品中每行字幕的字数有一定限制，翻译字幕时，应如何应对这种限制？

2. 如何利用图像手段来突破字幕字数限制？

延伸阅读

皇后	这个时候要妹妹来　打扰妹妹午睡了	Thanks for coming at this time. I hope I did not interrupt your afternoon nap.
华妃	臣妾哪有娘娘这么清闲有福啊　不知娘娘召臣妾来有何要事	Your Majesty does always have the time to nap. I am not as fortunate.
皇后	选秀就快到最后一轮殿选了　妹妹准备得怎样了	I was just wondering if everything is ready for the final round of the Selection.
华妃	娘娘放心　午后黄规全回话了　说已经妥当　反正皇上有旨　库银空虚　一切都要以节俭为主　臣妾手里虽说变不出银子　但总要顾得皇上的体面　这个中滋味岂是旁人能知道的呀	There is nothing you should worry about. Huang Guiquan had everything ready by noon. His Majesty is on a tight budget to select concubines. But I must not make him lose face. Who could understand the difficulty of my job?
皇后	真的有劳妹妹了　哦对了　本宫叫人做了一些新的点心　请妹妹尝个鲜	I must thank you for your hard work. I hope you will like the new pastries I ordered for you.
剪秋	绘春	Spring. [Another maid of the Empress]

皇后	妹妹自己选　自己喜欢吃什么就拿吧　怕是妹妹也吃腻了吧　剪秋啊　把那碟牡丹卷给华妃	Please help yourself. Or would you like a recommendation? Autumn, bring forward the peony rolls.
剪秋	是	★★★
华妃	颂芝	Song Zhi. 　[Consort Fleur's maid]
颂芝	是	Thank you, Your Majesty.
	皇后娘娘赎罪　皇后娘娘赎罪　奴婢不是故意的	I am terribly sorry, Your Majesty. I didn't mean to.
华妃	真不懂规矩　好好的把娘娘的心意都给砸了　还不快向娘娘请罪	What is wrong with you? It is not your first day in the Palace. You must beg for Her Majesty's forgiveness.
颂芝	皇后娘娘恕罪　皇后娘娘恕罪	I do beg your pardon, Your Majesty.
华妃	你是本宫的家生奴才　竟这般不懂规矩　本宫也不便教你了　若是皇后不饶恕你　本宫也不会轻放了你	I did expect more from you as my dowry maid. If Her Majesty does not forgive you, I shall not let you off easy.
皇后	妹妹　只是小事　不用动这么大的气呀	It's all right, Shilan. Nothing to be angry about.
华妃	她本是粗笨　不机灵　幸得娘娘体恤　臣妾回去一定会好好教导她的	Thank you for your magnanimity to my clumsy maid. She will be better trained next time.

皇后	颂芝原是妹妹的陪嫁丫鬟 身份不同一些 怎能让她这样端茶倒水的 你若觉得颂芝不好 也不必生气 对吧 福子	A dowry maid is different from the other servants. Song Zhi must be inexperienced with menial jobs. There is no need to be mad at her, is there? Fuzi.
福子	皇后娘娘金安 华妃娘娘金安	Peace to Your Majesty. Peace to Your Highness.
皇后	内务府新挑来的丫头 叫福子 本宫看她机灵，便拨给你使唤吧。	Fuzi was recently sent to my palace by the Household Department. She's a competent maid. I'll let you have her.
华妃	颂芝虽粗笨 但是翊坤宫还不缺宫女 还是皇后自己留着用吧	Song Zhi is good enough, and my palace is well staffed. Your Majesty should keep Fuzi.
皇后	早听说翊坤宫的宫女做事利索 是该让福子她们这些小丫头学学了 有妹妹调教着 帮着颂芝做些粗活 也能叫她们学得乖一些	Your palace is staffed with the best servants. I hope Fuzi will have the chance to learn from them. She can also do menial jobs for Song Zhi.
华妃 颂芝	臣妾先告退了 还不快走 是	I have to go now. Move!
皇后	也不知道这届秀女选得怎么样了 后宫是该好好添几个新人 为皇上延绵子嗣了	I hope everything is fine with the Selection. His Majesty does need new concubines for the family.
颂芝	去去去 凭你也配走在娘娘身边 去 后边去	Stay away! Don't you know your place? Stay out of Her Highness's sight.

甄嬛	信女虽不比男子可以建功立业　也不愿轻易辜负了自己　若要嫁人　一定要嫁于这世间上最好的男儿　和他结成连理　白首到老　但求菩萨保佑　让信女被撂牌子　不得入选进宫	Dear Buddha, although I am unable to choose my own husband, I wish to marry the best man in this world. I hope we will end up old and gray together. Dear Buddha, I wish not to be selected as a concubine. I wish not to be selected as a concubine.
浣碧	都说这儿的菩萨最灵验　小姐的心思一定能如愿	This is a wish fulfilling temple. My Lady, your wish will come true.
流朱	小姐　别的秀女都在求中选　唯有咱们小姐想被撂牌子　菩萨一定记得真真儿的	My Lady, every other girl is wishing to be selected while you want the opposite. The Buddha will always remember you.
甄嬛	嘘　都说许愿说破是不灵的	Shh! A wish will not come true if you tell it.
浣碧	今天是什么日子　怎么温大人也来求菩萨	Look! It's Mr. Wen! Is he here to make a wish?
流朱	这个温太医啊　也是古怪　谁不知太医不得皇命不能为皇族以外的人请脉诊病　他倒好　十天半月便往咱们府里跑	Mr. Wen has been strange lately. Imperial doctors cannot pay home visits without the Emperor's permission. But he's been a frequenter of our residence.
甄嬛	你们俩话太多了　我该和温太医要一剂药　好好治治你们	Stop it! I'll ask Mr. Wen for a prescription for gossiping.
甄嬛 温实初	实初哥哥 嬛妹妹　刚刚我去府上请脉　听甄伯母说你来这里进香了	Hi, Shichu! Hi, Huan'er [Huan->Huan'er like Max -> Maxie].

甄嬛 温实初	出来走走 也是散心 嬛妹妹 你就不要再瞒我了 我知道为了殿选之事 你已经烦恼多日了	Your mother told me you came to the temple. I was just taking a walk. You don't have to hide from me. I knew you were worried about the Final Selection lately.
甄嬛	嬛儿是尽人事以听天命	I did my best, and Buddha will do the rest.
温实初	嬛妹妹 家父在世的时候常说，一片冰心在玉壶 他让我把此壶交予我们温家未来的 其实这也是我一直以来的心意 你若接受的话 就不用再去宫中殿选了	Huan'er, this heirloom jade teapot is a symbol of pure love. My father would like me to give it to my future...I have always wanted to marry you. You don't have to attend the Selection if you're married.
甄嬛	顺治爷在世的时候就定下定例 所有未经选看的秀女断不可私下结亲 实初哥哥想一时救急 也不必拿出这么贵重的东西来 嬛儿受不起	The prior emperor's demanded that qualified girls for the Selection should not be arranged into marriage. Thank you for trying to help, but the jade teapot is too valuable for me. Sorry, I cannot accept it.
温实初	嬛妹妹 我虽是一介御医 俸禄微薄 可是我保证会一生一世对你好 疼爱你 保护你 永远事事以你为重 本来每半月一次到府上去请脉 能够偶尔见一次妹妹的笑靥 已经心满意足了 可谁知 而且我也知道 妹妹心里是不愿意去殿选的	Huan'er, I know I am just an undistinguished doctor. But I promise to love and cherish you all my life. I will put you before anything else. I am satisfied just to see you whenever I pay visits to your parents. But you were unexpectedly selected, and you are not willing ...

甄嬛	实初哥哥这么说 就枉顾我们一直以来的兄妹情谊了 嬛儿没有哥哥 一直把你当作自己的亲哥哥一样看待 自然相信哥哥会待妹妹好的 自然了 以后有了嫂子 你也会对嫂子更好	Shichu, I'm sorry that I do not feel the same about you. I always see you as my elder brother. And you treated me like your own sister. I believe you will marry the girl you really love.
温实初	实初虽然唐突了妹妹 却是真心实意地希望妹妹不要去应选 这不仅仅是因为我心里一直把妹妹当成 其实更是因为甄伯父曾经救过家父的性命	I'm sorry for the sudden proposal. But I really wanted to spare you from being selected. Not only for my feelings about you, but also for my gratitude to your father, who saved my father's life.
流朱、浣碧	啊 说什么哪	Why is it taking so long?
甄嬛	我们两家是世交 昔年恩义 不过是父亲随手之劳 不必挂怀	Our fathers have long been friends. It was our pleasure to help. Think nothing of it.
温实初	可是我父亲当年被诬 起因也是因为后宫争斗 不能独善其身 一介御医尚且如此 何况妹妹如果被选中的话 会身在其中啊	My father was incriminated because of the rivalries in the harem. Even an imperial doctor can fall victim to the competitive harem, let alone a concubine inside it.
甄嬛	实初哥哥的话我都明白 只是我不去应选 迟早也是玉娆 家中无子 女儿还能不孝吗	I understand your concern. But even if I avoid the Selection, my younger sister will have to go the next time. My parents only have two daughters, and I don't want to put my sister through the Selection.

侍女	真是太好看了	She's gorgeous!
沈母	走几步让我看看	Let me look at you, Meizhuang. Walk around.
姨娘甲	很好　我们大小姐走得极好	My Lady, Miss Shen walks with grace.
姨娘乙	腰肢儿更软些　皇上会喜欢	His Majesty will like her slender waist.
沈母	说句话听听	Now, talk.
眉庄	臣女沈眉庄参见皇上太后　愿皇上太后万福金安	May peace and grace be with Your Majesty. My name is Shen Meizhuang.
姨娘甲	不错　很合规矩	Good. Well mannered.
沈母	若是皇上问你读过什么书呢	What if His Majesty asks about your education?
眉庄	诗经　孟子　左传	I learned Poetry, Confucianism, and History.
沈母	错了　皇上今天是选秀女　充实他自己的后宫　繁衍子嗣　不是考状元　问学问的	Wrong. His Majesty is selecting concubines to have children with. Not scholars.
姨娘甲	女子无才便是德	"The lack of talent is the virtue in a woman."
眉庄	是　女儿明白了	Thanks, I understand.

太监甲 黄规全	公公您来了 都过来都过来　奉华妃娘娘的旨意　这体元殿离殿选的日子还有十日　务必要打扫得一尘不染　又干净又亮堂　若是出了半点差错　你们可是知道娘娘的　小心你们的脑袋	Greetings, Mr. Huang. Come together you all. Consort Fleur sent me to inspect your work as the Final Selection will be held here in ten days. The hall must be presented in pristine condition. Otherwise, you would offend Her Highness at the expense of your lives.
众太监 黄规全 众太监	公公放心 都干活去吧 是	Yes, Mr. Huang. Now get back to work!
剪秋 皇后 剪秋	娘娘先用膳吧 再等一会吧 皇上已经有十多天没来用晚膳了　听说华妃宫里已经去请过了　估计皇上今晚在华妃那儿用膳　您要是再等　就饿着了	Please eat, Your Majesty. Just one more moment. It's been over ten days since His Majesty came for dinner. Consort Fleur has sent someone to wait for His Majesty. He is likely to have dinner with her tonight. Your Majesty should eat if you are hungry.
皇后	再过几天就是殿选了　皇上今天一定会来	It's almost the day for the Final Selection. I am certain His Majesty will come today.

张廷玉	皇上对年大将军等爱臣的宠信优渥 可但凡人臣大多数是 成功易 守功难	Your Majesty, Nian Gengyao is a successful general, but a success is easier made than kept.
皇帝	你是提醒朕提防有些人倚功造过 兴风作浪吗	Do you view his new-found fame with caution?
张廷玉	皇上明察 微臣大概过虑了 微臣告退	Only Your Majesty can be the judge. I hope I am overthinking. I shall take my leave.
苏培盛	皇上您的茶凉了吧 奴才替您换一杯	Your Majesty, the tea is cold. Let me change it for you.
皇帝	不用了	No, thank you.
苏培盛	翊坤宫的周宁海在外头候着 华妃娘娘请皇上移步翊坤宫用膳	Mr. Zhou from Consort Fleur's palace is waiting for you outside. Her Highness wishes to have dinner with you.
皇帝	朕不过去了	I desire not to go.
苏培盛	那皇上的意思是	Er...Your Majesty prefers to ...
皇帝	朕去瞧瞧皇后	I will eat with the Empress.
苏培盛	嗻 摆驾景仁宫	His Majesty is leaving for Palace of Great Benevolence.
颂芝	娘娘 这菜都凉了 我再拿去热热吧	Your Highness, the food is cold. Should I reheat it now?
华妃	等皇上来了再热吧	Not until His Majesty arrives.
周宁海	禀娘娘 皇上今日在景仁宫用膳	Your Highness, His Majesty is going to eat at Palace of Great Benevolence.
华妃	知道了	All right then.

周宁海 华妃	娘娘　您别生气 哼　有什么好生气的　皇后终归是皇后　皇上陪她用顿膳是应该的　今儿又不是十五	Please don't be upset, Your Highness. About what? She's the Empress after all. She deserves a meal with His Majesty. I just thought that they only eat together on the 15th of each month.
皇帝 皇后 皇帝	皇后的手艺又精进了 皇上喜欢就好 如今你贵为皇后　后厨的事就让下人去做吧	This is delicious! Thanks, I made it myself. You are the Empress, you should let the servants cook.
皇后	臣妾虽为皇后　也是皇上的妻子　身为人妻　侍奉夫君　怎么会觉得累呢	I am your empress and your wife. It is a pleasure to cook for you.
皇帝 皇后	这汤炖得入味　剪秋 皇上　老祖宗的规矩　食不过三　这道鸭子汤虽然好　可已经是第三碗了　若再动筷　恐怕这菜十天半个月也上不了桌了	It is a fusion of flavors. Autumn. Your Majesty, our ancestors believed that a third helping is excess eating. If you are going to have the third serving, I'm afraid the soup will not be made again in a while.
皇帝	幸亏皇后提醒	Thank you for your reminder.
皇后	不偏爱　懂节制　方得长久	Healthy eating requires balance and self-restraint.
皇帝	饮食如此　人亦如此　你是想说这个吧	That not only holds true for food, but also for people. Is that what you wish to tell me?
皇后	皇上圣明　皇上喜欢这道菜　再尝些吧	You read my mind. Your Majesty likes eggplant. Have some more.

皇帝	食不言　寝不语	"Eat in silence, sleep in quietness."
皇后	今日新沏的茶极好　皇上尝尝	Would you like some tea?
皇帝	不了　朕去瞅瞅华妃	No, thank you. I need to go check out Consort Fleur.
皇后	恭送皇上	I bid you a good night.

第八章

网络小说与儿童文学翻译

网络小说的翻译

2014 年 12 月，美籍华人赖静平创办网站"Wuxiaworld"，开中国网络小说英译浪潮之先河（邵燕君、吉云飞、肖映萱，2018：120）。除"Wuxiaworld"外，国外的中国网络小说翻译网站还有 2015 年 1 月建立的"Gravity Tales"（引力传说）和同年 12 月建立的"Volare novels"（沃拉雷小说），它们与"Wuxiaworld"一道，并称为中国网文三大英译网站（欧阳友权，2021：116）。中国作家协会发布的《2020 中国网络文学蓝皮书》显示，截至 2020 年，中国网络文学海外传播作品 1 万余部，其中，实体书授权超 4000 部，上线翻译作品 3000 余部。网站订阅和阅读 APP 用户 1 亿多，覆盖世界大部分国家和地区。中国网络文学"出海"势头强劲，日益受到国外读者的欢迎。

网络小说与传统小说最大的不同就在于传播渠道。传统小说通过传统媒介如杂志、报纸发表，或以书籍形式出版发行，而网络小说主要经由网络发表传播。由于传播渠道的不同，传统小说的读者与作者的互动受时空限制较大，相比之下，网络小说一经发布，读者就可以在网站上发表评论，跨越时空，与其他读者和作者进行交流。网络小说和传统小说的创作主体也存在差异。有研究者认为，网络技术消除了传统体制下文学作品的"出场"焦虑，拆卸了文学创作、发表资质认证的门槛，谁都有权力上网写作并发布自己的作品，谁也无权阻止他人创作和发表，这就给了每一个文学爱好者在网上圆梦的机会，使得人人都可以当作家，形成了"全民写作"的新机制（欧阳友权，2018：6）。此外，网络小说和传统小说评价体系和内容质量存在差异。传统小说有着稳定的质量评价体系，无论是在杂志上发表还是以图书形式出版，都经过了严格审稿、反复打磨，质量相对较高。

而网络小说的开放特性使得写作和发表门槛较低，加之评价体系不完善，作品的质量参差不齐。

根据网络文学的特点，我们在翻译网络文学作品时应当注意以下几个方面：第一，选择翻译作品应当谨慎，应选取质量相对较好且对国外读者来说更有吸引力的作品。第二，网络文学翻译注重情节，讲求速度。"尽管文学作品吸引读者的原因不一而足，但钟情于情节是世界各国读者的共相，情节的丰富性和生动性是读者永恒的追求。"（姜智芹，2016：105）翻译网络文学作品应当注意语言简洁流畅，一气呵成，翻译时将重点放在情节上。此外，作者要跟进原作的进度，这一点和影视作品翻译比较类似。要讲究时效性，及时翻译作品的后续章节，以保持对读者的吸引力，不然网络小说众多，读者可能就将目光转移到下一本去了，或者因阅读间隔时间太长，忘记前面的情节。第三，翻译网络文学作品应注意特色词汇的翻译方法。比如武侠、玄幻小说中会涉及大量的武术或者魔法的招数的称谓，修仙小说中会涉及仙侠的特定称谓。根据中国作家协会发布的《中国网络文学蓝皮书（2018）》，阅文国际中最受欢迎的作品大多带有较多的中国元素，这些词汇如何翻译需要斟酌。许多特色词汇都是外国语境中缺失的，翻译时无法就地取材，但可以参考借鉴已经存在的翻译，也可以根据语境，以让目标语读者能理解为目的进行翻译。第四，网络小说归根到底是小说的一种，译文要符合小说文体的特点，符合原作风格，要注意再现人物形象。第四，对于篇幅较长的网络小说，要注意专有名词等全书保持一致，可以建立一个小型语料库。第五，网络小说的翻译是中国文化走出去的渠道之一，在翻译中应关注译文如何以目标语读者易于接受的方式展现中国文化与价值观。

本章以赖静平翻译的网络小说《盘龙》（小说作者笔名"我吃西红柿"，生平不详）为例展开分析。赖静平的笔名是"任我行"（RWX），取自金庸《笑傲江湖》中的任我行一角。他是华裔，3岁时和父母前往美国，做过多年的外交官。因为对中国网络文学的热爱，他辞去工作，开始从事网络文学翻译。由于有英语国家的教育背景以及外交官的工作经历，其英文功底较佳，译文通顺流畅，符合英语国家的用语习惯。本章对小说《盘龙》的部分段落和赖静平的翻译进行赏析，希望对网络文学译者有一定的启发。

课前准备

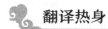 **翻译热身**

"你们都是普通人，不可能像那些大贵族一样有厉害的斗气密典修炼，想要出人头地，想要将来不被人瞧不起，你们就必须按照最古老、最简单、最基础的方法锻炼，锻炼身体、打熬力气，明白没有！"

（我吃西红柿，《盘龙》）

参考译文

"All of you are commoners. Unlike those noble families, you won't have access to any secret manuals teaching you how to cultivate battle *qi* [*dou qi*]. If you want to become someone of worth, if you wish to be respected, then all of you must use the most ancient, most simple, and most basic ways of improving yourselves—through exercising your bodies, and building up your strength! Am I clear?"

（I Eat Tomatoes，*Coiling Dragon*，translated by RWX）

翻译难点聚焦

1. 译文是怎样再现角色的价值观的？

2. 译文是如何再现原文中角色的形象的？

3. 原文中的短句，译文如何处理才能保持同样风格？

名译赏析

原作简介

《盘龙》讲述了一个少年意外得到盘龙戒指里的魔法导师的指导，通过自己的努力，一步一步走向成功的故事。书中展现了一个奇幻的武侠魔法世界，传达出中国传统的文化与价值观，深受外国读者的喜爱，是网络武侠小说的成功之作。

原文

"早晨，朝阳升起，万物生机勃勃。此刻正是吸收天地的精华，提高我们身体潜力的最好时候，老规矩，双腿分开与肩同宽，双膝微微弯曲，双手收于腰部位置，成'蕴气式'，做蕴气式的时候，要谨记'集中注意力，保持心中平静，呼吸要自然'。"希尔曼冷漠说道。

（我吃西红柿，《盘龙》）

译文

"When the sun rises in the morning, all things begin to thrive. This is the best time to absorb the natural energy from your surroundings and improve the conditioning of our bodies. Same rules as always—Legs spread apart, as wide as your shoulders! Both knees bent slightly, both hands pressed down at the waist. Assume the '*Qi* Building Stance'. When assuming this stance, remember—'Focus your concentration, maintain a calm mind, and breath naturally'." Hillman coldly instructed.

（I Eat Tomatoes, *Coiling Dragon*, translated by RWX）

赏析思路点拨

这部小说名为"盘龙"，赖静平将其译为"Coiling Dragon"。"dragon"在英语文化中是要被铲除的妖怪，是邪恶的，但在中国文化中，"龙"是尊贵的、吉祥的象征。"盘龙"戒指是主人公林雷的传家宝，里面是一路指导他的导师的魂，因此，此处的"龙"明显具有正面的含义。但是这里赖静平并没有做任何归化处理，而是直译。这客观上能起到在潜移默化中改变英语读者对"龙"这一意象的感受，逐渐引导读者理解"龙"在中国文化中的不同含义的作用。

原文中的"气"，赖译为"Qi"。《柯林斯词典》（在线版）[1]对"Qi"做了如下解释："(in Chinese medicine, martial arts, etc.) vital energy believed to circulate round the body in currents"。这里将"气"直译为"Qi"，并在全文贯穿使用，英语读者能够直观感受到"气"这一概念的所指，增进对"气"这一特殊词汇的理解。

原文

原本和蔼可亲的德林柯沃特，这个时候却有些生气不满了："林雷，我告诉你，各系魔法中，单论攻击力，各有千秋！"

"比如火系，禁忌魔法'天火燎原、地火焚城'，此招一出，一座巨大城池都会被焚烧得干干净净。比如水系，禁忌魔法'绝对零度'一出，数十万人口会瞬间被冻死。比如雷系，禁忌魔法'天雷灭世'一出，那千万道雷电狂劈，谁能幸存？比如风系，禁忌魔法'毁灭风暴'一出，那漫天漫地都是如同刀子一样的风暴，那结果……"

（我吃西红柿，《盘龙》）

---

1 https://www.collinsdictionary.com/dictionary/english/qi.

译文

The formerly amiable Grandpa Doehring suddenly turned angry as he grumbled, "Linley, let me tell you that when it comes to attack power, each elemental style has its strengths!"

"For example, the forbidden fire-style spell of 'Heavenly Fire Burning the Fields, Earthly Fire Burning the Cities' can burn an entire city to ashes, true. But the water-style has the forbidden spell of 'Absolute Zero', which when unleashed can freeze to death hundreds of thousands of people. Thunder-style's 'Heavenly Lightning of Absolute Destruction' can unleash tens of thousands of lightning bolts, which no one can survive. Wind-style's forbidden spell, 'Annihilating Tempest', can fill the entire sky with blade-like gusts of wind…"

（I Eat Tomatoes，*Coiling Dragon*，translated by RWX）

赏析思路点拨

从人名的翻译上讲，主人公"林雷"译为"Linley"，"德林柯沃特"译为"Doehring Cowart"，译名顺口，符合英语习惯，从读者来看也与原文较为符合。选段中盘龙戒指里的德林柯沃特爷爷开始向林雷介绍魔法威力，提到了不少魔法术语。比如，"天火燎原、地火焚城"，赖静平译为"Heavenly Fire Burning the Fields, Earthly Fire Burning the Cities"，"绝对零度"他译为"Absolute Zero"。这些魔法术语都是可以从上下文推断出其效果的，因此，译文直接保留了原文的表达。总的来说，网络小说译文的语言一般浅显易懂，魔法术语大多采用直译，这样的陌生化译法，能让国外读者耳目一新，突出魔法世界的奇特。

课后思考

1. 网络小说翻译如何重现原文的魔幻色彩？
2. 网络小说翻译如何实现语篇的流畅？
3. 网络小说中特色词汇的翻译是否完全再现了原文的含义？

延伸阅读

 原文

"这，这不就是……"林雷眼睛一下子瞪得滚圆。

这一刻，时间宛如静止！

连远处奥古斯塔口中射出的那一道透明流光，速度都似乎变得很慢很慢。

"对！就是这样！"

这么多年来，林雷一直追求着，想要让四种不同法则玄奥融合为一，可是，即使修炼到瓶颈，可最后一步让四种迥异的玄奥完美融合，林雷始终无法突破，无法越过那一个"槛"，而此刻感受到四种特殊能量完美的结合，对天地的影响……

就好像一个个苦苦追求着技艺的雕刻师，陡然看到某位雕刻宗师的作品，瞬间领悟了一般。

林雷此刻就是这样！

…………

青火，为水属性，水，柔和，包容万物。

玄武，为大地属性，大地，厚重。

白虎，为风属性，风，无形无影，聚散无常。

朱雀，为火属性，火，炽热疯狂，暴怒无常。

这"时空错乱"，其实也是"地火水风"的结合。

…………

陷入瓶颈，可能亿万年都无法突破，却也可能，几天就突破。这需要机遇，需要突然的灵光一闪。林雷上一次只是在旁观战，感受不深，加上当时四法则融合还未到最后地步，自然没什么感觉。

（我吃西红柿，《盘龙》）

译文

"This…isn't this…" Linley's eyes instantly turned round. In this moment, time itself stood still! Even that ray of translucent light which shot out of Augusta's mouth seemed to have suddenly become very, very slow.

"Right! That's exactly it!" All these years, Linley had always been in pursuit of completely fusing those four profound mysteries from different Laws into a complete whole. However, although he was able to train to the bottleneck, the final step of completely, perfectly fusing the four Laws was something Linley was still yet to be able to do; he wasn't able to overcome this threshold. But now, when sensing the unique, perfect fusion of those four types of energy, and how they manipulated the heavens…

It was as though a master sculptor who had bitterly toiled in pursuit of perfect suddenly saw the sculpture of a grandmaster sculptor, and instantly gained enlightenment. This was the current Linley!

The Azure Dragon was water-attribute. Water was soft and gentle, capable of encompassing and absorbing everything.

The Black Tortoise was earth-attribute. The earth was vast, heavy, and ponderous.

The White Tiger was wind-attribute. The wind was invisible and formless, appearing and disappearing without any pattern.

The Vermillion Bird was fire-attribute. Fire burned and blazed wildly, filled with violent fury which was unpredictable.

This "Spacetime Paradox" was actually the combination of earth, fire, water, and wind.

When one was stuck at a bottleneck, one might spend a trillion years without breaking through. But it was also possible that one would break through after a few days. This required luck; required a sudden flash of insight. Last time, Linley was just watching the battle, and so he hadn't sensed too deeply into the technique. In addition, last time, he hadn't reached this bottleneck in the fusion of the four Laws, and so naturally he hadn't gained any insights.

（I Eat Tomatoes，*Coiling Dragon*，translated by RWX）

第二节

儿童文学的翻译

儿童文学（literature for children），顾名思义，就是以少年儿童为目标读者创作的文学作品。一般来说，儿童文学适合3至17岁的读者，但事实上，很多儿童文学作品因其精彩的故事情节、优美的语言和深刻的教育意义，在成年人中也颇受欢迎。儿童文学强调趣味性，因此作者一般通过塑造性格鲜明的人物形象和跌宕起伏的故事情节来吸引读者，其目的还在于寓教于乐，让小读者从故事中得到启示、受到教育。总体而言，儿童文学的语言具有以下几个特点：第一，用词通俗易懂，句式简洁。儿童难以理解复杂的语言，故儿童文学的语言应清晰、简朴，并在此基础上表现语言的多样性。第二，语言生动，描述形象。生动且有趣的语言可以激发儿童的联想和想象，让其身临其境，进而对作品更加感兴趣。第三，儿童文学的语言应优美、动听、富有节奏感，诗歌、儿歌一类的文学作品还应该富有韵律、朗朗上口。第四，儿童文学的修辞应尽量贴近儿童的生活，让儿童更好地理解。

儿童文学的翻译应首先明确目标读者，也就是秉持儿童本位观，语言要简洁、形象、生动，可多使用儿童喜闻乐见的词语，使用拟声词、语气词、儿化音等，多使用简单句型，并尽量少使用抽象概念。除了语言方面，翻译中还要特别注意文化差异的处理，翻译过来的儿童文学可以让儿童了解他国的风土人情，拓展儿童的知识面，因此在翻译中如何保留原语作品的文化因素，又能让儿童容易理解，是译者需要注意的。

本节聚焦目前儿童文学市场上广受欢迎的读物——儿童绘本。儿童绘本（Picture Book），顾名思义，就是"图画书"，这类书以图片为主，图片旁附有少量的文字。儿童绘本在儿童教育方面起着积极的作用，它不仅启迪儿童的智慧，还能通过图片使其受到艺术的熏陶，从而在思想感情、精神面貌、审美情操等方面给儿童以积极的影响。绘本是一种独特的图书形式，书中的文与图有紧密的内在关系，文字与图画共同参与叙事，产生意义。文字与图片没有孰轻孰重之分，而是一种平衡的关系，图文相互补充、相互衬托、相互拓展。在传统的儿童读物中，较常见的图文关系是文字为主，图片为辅。而在儿童绘本中，图文共同参与叙事，图画为主要的叙事手段，甚至在某些绘本中是唯一的叙事手段。但图片的叙事毕竟有局限之处，因此对于图片不能传达的信息，文字具有补充和拓展的作用。图文关系对于表现绘本的主题也发挥着重要的作用，因此，绘本区别于其他儿童文学读物的本质特征就是多模态的文本叙事。在翻译儿童绘本的过程中，译者如果能够意识到绘本中图文关系的重要性，在文字转换过程中照顾到图片的相关内容，甚至在必要的情况下重构图文关系，便能对绘本翻译的成功产生积极影响。

课前准备

翻译热身

Little Nutbrown Hare, who was going to bed, held on tight to Big Nutbrown Hare's very long ears.

He wanted to be sure that Big Nutbrown Hare was listening.

"Guess how much I love you," he said.

"Oh, I don't think I could guess that," said Big Nutbrown Hare.

"This much," said Little Nutbrown Hare, stretching out his arms as wide as they could go.

Big Nutbrown Hare had even longer arms. "But I love you this much," he said.

Hmm, that is a lot, thought Little Nutbrown Hare.

Then Little Nutbrown Hare had a good idea. He tumbled upside down and reached up the tree trunk with his feet.

"I love you all the way up to my toes," he said.

（Sam Mcbratney & Anita Jeram, *Guess How Much I Love You*）

参考译文

深棕色的小兔子要去睡觉了，它紧紧地抓住深棕色大兔子的长耳朵。

它想确认深棕色大兔子在听他说话。"猜猜我有多爱你？"它问。"哦，我不认为我能猜到。"深棕色大兔子回答。

"这么多，"深棕色小兔子一边说，一般尽力伸出它的两只手臂，伸到它能够到的最宽的程度。

棕色的大兔子有更长的手臂。"但是我爱你这么多。"它伸出手臂说道。嗯，真是多，深棕色小兔子想到。

然后，深棕色小兔子想到一个好主意。它倒立起来，用它的脚触碰到树干。"我爱你一路向上，直到我的脚趾到达的地方那么高！"它说。

（柿小桔译）

 翻译难点聚焦

儿童绘本中的图文关系有时是复杂的，某些绘本中，文字模态的叙事缺乏连贯性，靠图片填补叙事空白；在某些图片承担主要叙事任务的绘本中，文字可能概括几幅画面的内容。图片的叙事特点是无法体现时空的转换，无法体现角色行为的动态性，而文字的叙事特点是缺乏生动性和趣味性，两种模态的叙事特征决定了翻译中不能将文字和图像模态割裂开来，应该将两者结合，构建译本的意义。

名译赏析

 原作简介

美国著名的儿童绘本《好脏的哈利》（*Harry The Dirty Dog*）是吉恩·蔡恩（Gene Zion）与他的妻子玛格丽特·布罗伊·格雷厄姆（Margaret Bloy Graham）共同创作的一本图画书。蔡恩创作故事，格雷厄姆绘制插画。该绘本内容轻松幽默、简单易懂，自诞生以来广受欢迎，并入选纽约公共图书馆"每个人都应该知道的100种图画书"。《好脏的哈利》作为典型的儿童读物，语言简洁生动，图画恰当地配合文字，充分体现了多模态文本的优势与特色。

原文与译文

原文一

Harry was a white dog with black spots who liked everything, except…getting a bath. So one day when he heard the water running in the tub, he took the scrubbing brush…

（Gene Zion & Margaret Bloy Graham, *Harry the Dirty Dog*）

译文

哈利是一只有黑点的白狗，它什么都爱，就是不爱洗澡。有一天，哈利刚听到从浴室传来的放水声，就咬着刷子逃跑了……

（林真美译）

哈利是只有黑点的白狗。他什么都喜欢，就是不喜欢一件事——洗澡。有一天，他听到浴缸放水的声音，马上叼起刷子就跑下楼。

（任溶溶译）

原文二

…and buried it in the backyard. Then he ran away from home.

（Gene Zion & Margaret Bloy Graham, *Harry the Dirty Dog*）

译文

……它把刷子埋在后院，然后，溜到外头。

（林真美译）

……他把刷子埋在后院里。接着就跑了出去。

（任溶溶译）

原文三

He played where they were fixing the street and got very dirty.

（Gene Zion & Margaret Bloy Graham, *Harry the Dirty Dog*）

译文

它跑到修马路的地方玩，玩得一身都是泥巴。

（林真美译）

他到修路的地方去玩，把身上弄脏了。

（任溶溶译）

原文四

He played at the railroad and got even dirtier.

（Gene Zion & Margaret Bloy Graham, *Harry the Dirty Dog*）

译文

它跑到铁轨上的天桥玩，玩得一身都是煤烟。

（林真美译）

他又到铁路那里去玩，把身上弄得更脏。

（任溶溶译）

原文五

He played tag with other dogs and became dirtier still.

（Gene Zion & Margaret Bloy Graham, *Harry the Dirty Dog*）

译文

它和一群小狗玩捉迷藏，把自己弄得更脏了。

（林真美译）

他又跟许多狗玩捉迷藏，于是身上更脏了。

（任溶溶译）

原文六

He slid down a coal chute and got the dirtiest of all. In fact, he changed from a white dog with black spots to a black dog with white spots.

（Gene Zion & Margaret Bloy Graham, *Harry the Dirty Dog*）

译文

它在装煤炭的卡车上面溜滑梯，溜得身上一团黑。因为弄得太脏了，哈利从一只有黑点的白狗，变成了一只有白点的黑狗。

（林真美译）

他像滑滑梯那样从运煤车的传送带上滑下来，弄得身上脏得不能再脏。这下，他从一只有黑点的白狗变成了一只有白点的黑狗。

（任溶溶译）

原文七

Although there were many other things to do, Harry began to wonder if his family thought that he had really run away.

He felt tired and hungry too, so without stopping on the way he ran back home.

（Gene Zion & Margaret Bloy Graham, *Harry the Dirty Dog*）

译文

哈利还想再玩，可是，让家里的人以为它离家出走，就糟了。又饿又累的哈利不再流连街头，它用跑的回家。

（林真美译）

虽然还有许多东西好玩，可哈利开始担心，家里人是不是以为他当真离家跑掉了。而且他累了，肚子也饿了。于是他赶紧往家跑。

（任溶溶译）

赏析思路点拨

从以上例子可以看出，林真美和任溶溶的译文都体现了图文重构。比如，在原文一中，末尾是省略号，没有说"ran away"，但根据语境和图片可以推断出，哈利就是不想洗澡，一听见浴室水声，就赶紧咬着刷子逃走了。因此，林真美增译了"逃跑了"，任溶溶译文增译了"跑下楼"。原文中的图文关系是图片延展、补充了文字的内容，而两个译本的图文关系则是图片直观展现了文字本身描绘的内容。

同时，这两个译本在图文重构的选择上又有所不同。比如原文四中，原文为"railroad"，任溶溶直接译为"铁路"，林真美译文增译了"天桥"。任溶溶选择和原文的图文关系保持一致，林真美则根据图片在文字上具体体现了哈利玩耍的地点，文字和图片相对应。再比如，"got very dirty" "got even dirtier" "became dirtier still"，林真美分别译为"玩得一身都是泥巴" "玩得一身都是煤烟" "把自己弄得更脏了"，任溶溶则译为"把身上弄脏了" "把身上弄得更脏" "于是身上更脏了"。相比之下，林真美的译法更符合儿童读物的特点，语言多变活泼，增强了趣味性。这三个短语的翻译，任溶溶保留了原文含义，而林真美则根据图片内容调整了措辞，用文字说明了图片所有内容，图文呈现平行关系。

从图文重构层面来看，两个译本都体现了原作的内涵，同时重构了部分图文关系。总的来说，相比之下，任溶溶倾向于保留原作的图文互补关系，而林真美更倾向于适当增译，用文字说明图片内容。

课后思考

1. 多模态文本中的多种模态是表意整体，这给翻译带来了怎样的挑战？

2. 多模态文本翻译中兼顾多种模态的同时如何保证叙事的流畅与完整？

3. 儿童绘本的翻译应充分考虑到读者群的特殊性，既然如此，是否应该让文字模态的叙事更充分？

延伸阅读

 原文

Chapter II MISTRESS MARY QUITE CONTRARY

Mary had liked to look at her mother from a distance and she had thought her very pretty, but as she knew very little of her she could scarcely have been expected to love her or to miss her very much when she was gone. She did not miss her at all, in fact, and as she was a self-absorbed child she gave her entire thought to herself, as she had always done. If she had been older she would no doubt have been very anxious at being left alone in the world, but she was very young, and as she had always been taken care of, she supposed she always would be. What she thought was that she would like to know if she was going to nice people, who would be polite to her and give her her own way as her Ayah and the other native servants had done.

She knew that she was not going to stay at the English clergyman's house where she was taken at first. She did not want to stay. The English clergyman was poor and he had five children nearly all the same age and they wore shabby clothes and were always quarreling and snatching toys from each other. Mary hated their untidy bungalow and was so disagreeable to them that after the first day or two nobody would play with her. By the second day they had given her a nickname which made her furious.

It was Basil who thought of it first. Basil was a little boy with impudent blue eyes and a turned-up nose, and Mary hated him. She was playing by herself under a tree, just as she had been playing the day the cholera broke out. She was making heaps of earth and paths for a garden and Basil came and stood near to watch her. Presently he got rather interested and suddenly made a suggestion.

"Why don't you put a heap of stones there and pretend it is a rockery?" he said. "There in the middle," and he leaned over her to point.

"Go away!" cried Mary. "I don't want boys. Go away!"

For a moment Basil looked angry, and then he began to tease. He was always teasing his sisters. He danced round and round her and made faces and sang and laughed.

"Mistress Mary, quite contrary,

How does your garden grow?

With silver bells, and cockle shells,

And marigolds all in a row."

He sang it until the other children heard and laughed, too; and the crosser Mary got, the more they sang "Mistress Mary, quite contrary"; and after that as long as she stayed with them they called her "Mistress Mary Quite Contrary" when they spoke of her to each other, and often when they spoke to her.

"You are going to be sent home," Basil said to her, "at the end of the week. And we're glad of it."

"I am glad of it, too," answered Mary. "Where is home?"

"She doesn't know where home is!" said Basil, with seven-year-old scorn.

"It's England, of course. Our grandmama lives there and our sister Mabel was sent to her last year. You are not going to your grandmama. You have none. You are going to your uncle. His name is Mr. Archibald Craven."

"I don't know anything about him," snapped Mary.

"I know you don't," Basil answered. "You don't know anything. Girls never do. I heard father and mother talking about him. He lives in a great, big, desolate old house in the country and no one goes near him. He's so cross he won't let them, and they wouldn't come if he would let them. He's a hunchback, and he's horrid." "I don't believe you," said Mary; and she turned her back and stuck her fingers in her ears, because she would not listen any more.

(Frances Hodgson Burnett, *The Secret Garden*)

译文

第二章　玛丽小姐倔乖乖

玛丽以前总爱从稍远处凝视她的母亲，认为母亲非常漂亮，不过因为对母亲不是很熟悉，所以实在是说不上对死去的母亲有多少的爱，是怎样的思念。事实上，她可以说一点儿都没有想念母亲，因为她是个自顾自的孩子，脑子里想的都是自己的事，她从小就是这样的。

倘若年纪再大上几岁呢，那她自然就会对孤零零地留在世界上非常担忧了。可是她还太小，又一直是由别人在照顾着，她总以为以后也必定会是这样的。她脑子里想的只是：自己要去的是不是好人家，是不是会对她很和蔼，让她想怎么做就怎么做，如同她自己的阿妈和其他土著佣人过去所做的那样。

她知道，自己是不会一直留在一开始送去的那位英国教士的家里的。她也不愿意留在那里。那位英国教士很穷，自己已有五个大小差不多的孩子，他们衣衫褴褛，总在吵吵闹闹，为争夺玩具而打来打去。玛丽讨厌这所不整洁的平房，跟这些人都合不来，来了没两天，就谁也不愿意跟她玩了。她来到的第二天他们就给她起了个外号，这就使她心里更窝火了。

首先想到这档子事的是巴兹尔。巴兹尔是个长了双放肆无顾忌的蓝眼睛和一只翘鼻子的小男孩，玛丽很讨厌他。玛丽在一棵树下独自玩耍，就像霍乱突然暴发的那天一样。她正在拢土、造路，打算弄成一个小花园，这时巴兹尔走过来站在边上看她怎么干。不一会儿，他产生了兴趣，突然提出一个建议。

"你干吗不在那儿堆一些石子，算是假山呢？"他说，"喏，就在中间这儿。"说着还弯腰到她头上来指点给她看。

"滚开！"玛丽喊道，"我不和男孩玩。给我滚开！"

有一会儿，巴兹尔像是很生气，但是接下去他变得调皮起来了。

他也总是这样作弄自己的姐妹的。他绕着玛丽跳圈子，一边做鬼脸，一边又唱又笑：

玛丽小姐倔乖乖，

花园真能造出来？

银铃铛、花贝壳，

金盏花儿插起来。

他一遍又一遍地唱着，直到别的孩子都听到了并且一个个都哈哈大笑，乐不可支。他们越是唱"玛丽小姐倔乖乖"，玛丽越是生气。从此以后，她住在他们家，他们提到她时总称她为"玛丽小姐倔乖乖"，还时不时当面这样叫她。

"你就要给送回家了，"巴兹尔对她说，"就在这个周末。我们都希望你快点走。"

"我还巴不得快点走呢，"玛丽反唇相讥，"不过家在哪儿呢？"

"她连自己家在哪儿都不知道！"巴兹尔说，还用了七岁儿童的嘲讽口气。"自然是在英国啦。我们家的奶奶就是住在英国，去年我大姐梅布尔也送到那里去了。你是不会去奶奶家的。你没有奶奶。你要被送到你姑父那里去。他是阿奇博尔德·克雷文先生。"

"这人我怎么连听都没听说过。"玛丽还要强词夺理。

"我就知道你不会知道。"巴兹尔回答道，"你什么都不知道。女孩就是傻。我是听我爸爸妈妈说起他的。他住在乡下一座又高又旧的空荡荡的大房子里，没有人跟他要好。他脾气太坏，不愿意见人，到后来他请人家来人家都不来了。他是个罗锅，可吓人了。"

"你的话我不信。"玛丽说。她转过身去，用两只手指塞住自己的耳朵，这样的话她再也不想听了。

（F. H. 伯内特，《秘密花园》，李文俊译）

参考文献

艾青，1982. 艾青诗选 [M]. 欧阳桢，彭文兰，金，译. 北京：外文出版社.

奥斯丁，2009. 理智与情感 [M]. 孙致礼，译. 南京：译林出版社.

奥斯丁，2010. 理智与情感 [M]. 武崇汉，译. 上海：上海译文出版社.

奥斯汀，2015. Pride and Prejudice[M]. 天津：天津人民出版社.

奥斯汀，2018. 傲慢与偏见 [M]. 王科一，译. 上海：上海译文出版社.

卞之琳，1996. 英国诗选 [M]. 北京：商务印书馆.

伯内特，2011. 秘密花园 [M]. 李文俊，译. 南京：译林出版社.

蔡恩，格雷厄姆，2012. 好脏的哈利 [M]. 任溶溶，译. 北京：新星出版社.

蔡清富，2009. 朱自清散文选集 [M]. 天津：百花文艺出版社.

曹明伦，2004. 散文体译文的音韵节奏 [J]. 中国翻译（4）：89-90.

曹明伦，2006. 论以忠实为取向的翻译标准——兼论严复的"信达雅"[J]. 中国
   翻译（4）：12-19.

陈红，2014. 英美文学精粹赏析 [M]. 北京：人民邮电出版社.

德莱塞，2003. 嘉莉妹妹 [M]. 潘庆舲，译. 北京：人民文学出版社.

邓映易，2001. 英文经典歌曲 101 首 [M]. 北京：人民音乐出版社.

杜红玲，2013. 漫谈英剧的兴起 [J]. 电影文学（16）：10-12.

高健，1985. 浅谈风格的可译性及其他——翻译英美散文的一点体会 [J]. 中国翻
   译（1）：19-22.

高健，2002. 英美散文名作一百篇 [M]. 北京：中国对外翻译出版公司.

辜正坤，1993. 毛泽东诗词：英汉对照韵译 [M]. 北京：北京大学出版社.

韩子满，2019. 翻译批评的惟文学思维 [J]. 上海翻译（5）：1-6+94.

何其芳，1956. 关于写诗和读诗 [M]. 北京：作家出版社.

胡凤华，2007. "歌曲译配"与"歌曲翻译"辨 [J]. 安徽大学学报（哲学社会科学版）（5）：96-100.

胡适，1998. 尝试集 [M]. 北京：人民文学出版社.

纪欧，葛雷汉，2009. 好脏的哈利 [M]. 林真美，译. 台北：远流出版社.

姜智芹，2016. 序跋在莫言作品海外传播中的作用 [J]. 外国语文（6）：102-107.

金庸，1981. 金庸作品集 [M]. 香港：明河社.

金庸，2008. 鹿鼎记：壹 [M]. 广州：广州出版社.

李德凤，鄢佳，2013. 中国现当代诗歌英译述评（1935—2011）[J]. 中国翻译（2）：26-38+127.

李建军，2016. 并世双星：汤显祖与莎士比亚 [M]. 南昌：二十一世纪出版社集团.

梁实秋，2002. 莎士比亚全集——十四行诗 [M]. 北京：中国广播电视出版社.

廖七一，2020. 翻译的界定与翻译批评 [J]. 中国外语（6）：77-82.

林语堂，2009. 古文小品译英 [M]. 北京：外语教学与研究出版社.

罗新璋，1984. 翻译论集 [M]. 北京：商务印书馆.

孟伟根，2012. 戏剧翻译研究 [M]. 杭州：浙江大学出版社.

明言，2014. 从《外国名歌200首》看人音社的"人民性"——为庆祝人民音乐出版社建社60周年而写 [J]. 人民音乐（12）：62-64.

欧阳友权，2019. 中国网络文学二十年 [M]. 南京：江苏凤凰文艺出版社.

欧阳友权，2021. 中国网络文学海外传播的形态、动力与屏障 [J]. 贵州师范大学学报（社会科学版）（6）：115-123.

乔建中，2002. 中国经典民歌鉴赏指南：上 [M]. 上海：上海音乐出版社.

乔萍，瞿淑蓉，宋洪玮，2011. 散文佳作108篇 [M]. 南京：译林出版社.

萨克雷，1957. 名利场 [M]. 杨必，译. 北京：人民文学出版社.

莎士比亚，2008. 莎士比亚十四行诗集 [M]. 曹明伦，译. 保定：河北大学出版社.

莎士比亚，2015. 罗密欧与朱丽叶 [M]. 辜正坤，译. 北京：外语教学与研究出版社.

莎士比亚，2016. 莎士比亚悲剧集 [M]. 朱生豪，译. 北京：作家出版社.

邵燕君，吉云飞，肖映萱，2018. 媒介革命视野下的中国网络文学海外传播 [J].
    文艺理论与批评（2）：119–129.

沈弘，郭晖，2005. 最早的汉译英诗应是弥尔顿的《论失明》[J]. 国外文学（2）：
    44–53.

苏东坡，2012. 东坡诗文选（汉英对照）[M]. 林语堂，译. 合肥：安徽科技出版社.

覃军，2020. 中国歌曲"走出去"的"译"定之规——兼与刘瑞强先生及同行商榷 [J].
    中国文化研究（1）：118–128.

汤显祖，2000. 牡丹亭（英汉对照）[M]. 汪榕培，译. 上海：上海外语教育出版社.

汤显祖，2000. 牡丹亭（汉英对照）[M]. 汪榕培，译. 长沙：湖南人民出版社.

童兆升，卢志宏，2009. 散文语言的音乐美与翻译 [J]. 山东外语教学（1）：5.

屠岸，1992. 莎士比亚十四行诗一百首 [M]. 北京：中国对外翻译出版公司.

王宏印，2010. 文学翻译批评论稿 [M]. 2 版. 上海：上海外语教育出版社.

王克非，2021. 翻译研究拓展的基本取向 [J]. 外国语（2）：69–74.

王庆云，等，1998. 中国古代文学·诗歌卷 [M]. 北京：华语教学出版社.

文军，2004. 翻译：调查与研究 [M]. 北京：北京航空航天大学出版社.

翁显良，1985. 古诗英译 [M]. 北京：北京出版社.

吴承恩，2004. 西游记 [M]. 长沙：岳麓书社.

向云，2017. 英汉歌曲译配：理论与实践 [M]. 广州：世界图书出版广东有限公司.

肖维青，2010. 翻译批评模式研究 [M]. 上海：上海外语教育出版社.

谢天振，2014. 中国文学走出去：问题与实质 [J]. 中国比较文学（1）：1–10.

许钧，2006. 翻译论 [M]. 武汉：湖北教育出版社.

许钧，等，2001. 文学翻译的理论与实践：翻译对话录 [M]. 南京：译林出版社.

许渊冲，1987. 三谈"意美、音美、形美" [J]. 深圳大学学报（人文社会科学版）
    （2）：70–77.

许渊冲，2003. 文学与翻译 [M]. 北京：北京大学出版社.

许渊冲，2007. 唐诗三百首 [M]. 北京：中国对外翻译出版公司.

许渊冲，2010. 中诗英韵探胜 [M]. 北京：北京大学出版社.

薛范，2002. 歌曲翻译探索与实践 [M]. 武汉：湖北教育出版社.

杨晓荣，2018. 翻译批评导论 [M]. 上海：华东师范大学出版社.

余秋雨，2013. 中国戏剧史 [M]. 武汉：长江文艺出版社.

俞元桂，1988. 中国现代散文史 [M]. 济南：山东文艺出版社.

张培基，1999. 英译中国现代散文选 [M]. 上海：上海外语教育出版社.

赵秀明，赵张进，2010. 英美散文研究与翻译 [M]. 长春：吉林大学出版社.

朱丹，2014. 论英剧《唐顿庄园》之大时代主题 [J]. 文学教育（12）：114-115.

BASSNETT S. 1985.Ways though the Labyrinth: strategies and methods for translating theatre texts [C] // HERMANS T. The manipulation of literature. London: Croom Helm.

BURNETT F H, 2005. The secret garden[M]. New York: W.W. Norton & Company, Inc.

CHA L, 1997. The deer and the cauldron[M]. MINFORD J, trans & eds. Oxford: Oxford University Press.

HSU K-Y, 1963. Twentieth century Chinese poetry [M]. New York: Doubleday.

NIDA E A, 2001. Language and culture: contexts in translating [M]. Shanghai: Shanghai Foreign Language Education Press.

PAYNE R, 1947. Contemporary Chinese poetry [M]. London and New York: Routledge.

STEINER G, 2001. After Babel: aspects of language and translation [M]. Shanghai: Shanghai Foreign Language Education Press.

TANG X Z, 2002. The peony pavilion [M]. BIRCH C, trans. Bloomington and Indianapolis: Indiana University Press.

TEASDALE S, 1914. Over the roofs [J]. Poetry, 3(6): 200.

THAKERAY W M, 1998. Vanity fair [M]. Ware: Wordsworth Editions Ltd.

WU C E, 2000. Journey to the west : Volume 1 [M]. JENNER W J F, trans. Changsha: Hunan People's Publishing House.

WU C E, 2012. The journey to the west: Volume 1 [M]. Revised Edition. YU A C, trans. Chicago: The University of Chicago Press.

YEH M, 1992. Anthology of modern Chinese poetry [C]. New Haven: Yale University Press.

ZION G, GRAHAM M B, 1956. Harry the dirty dog [M]. New York: Harper Collins.